A Rather Cryptic
Crime

To Simon,
All the best for
The future,
Julie

J WILCOX

Grosvenor House
Publishing Limited

The right of J Wilcox to be identified as the author of this
work has been asserted in accordance with Section 78
of the Copyright, Designs and Patents Act 1988

The book cover is copyright to Jo Callan Downs

This book is published by
Grosvenor House Publishing Ltd
Link House
140 The Broadway, Tolworth, Surrey, KT6 7HT.
www.grosvenorhousepublishing.co.uk

This book is a work of fiction. Any resemblance to
people or events, past or present, is purely coincidental.

A CIP record for this book
is available from the British Library

ISBN 978-1-80381-835-1

For Dorothy who loved a murder mystery

Acknowledgements

Thank you to everyone who has helped to get my debut novel into print. To Jonathan and Lynne for reviewing the drafts, and giving encouragement, and for Lynne's invaluable culinary contributions (her cooking is every bit as good as Leslie's); to Christine for her very helpful feedback and practical suggestions; to Margaret for spurring me on; to Jo for the generous use of her beautiful artwork, and for her time and interest; to Jasmine for guiding me through the publication process, and to John, whose ideas were the inspiration behind the main characters.

Prologue

Of all the damn fool things to have a row about, a garden gnome had to be the most ridiculous. Thoroughly annoyed with himself, Leslie poured a cup of camomile tea, and pulled up the collar of his dressing gown against the cold. It was stupid to have been so bothered about the incident in the first place, and now wide awake with irritation, he was letting it deprive him of his bed on this bitter night. To add to his vexation, Bennett, having wreaked havoc, was now deep in blissful sleep.

Clutching the hot cup in his freezing hands, Leslie peered through the window into the night. The kitchen, his favourite room in the cottage, looked directly into the heart of the little Dartmoor village, with the imposing bulk of St Mary's Church at the centre. He switched off the light for a clearer view. A late frost glittered in the bright moonlight, silvering the thatched roofs of the Daffodil Tea Shop and the dozen or so pretty cottages and shops that made up Dartonleigh's village centre. The cobbled road was narrow, and circled the church like a moat, quaint and picturesque, endearingly unsuited to traffic.

Leslie flicked the light switch back on and huddled at the table to finish his drink. He turned over the aggravating events again in his mind, but with more resignation now. After all, hurling the nearest thing to hand from the bedroom window at a screeching fox, with no regard for the outcome, was just the sort of thing Bennett would do.

The problem wasn't really the smashed gnome or the soaking slipper: it was the principle of the thing. Had Bennett apologised then Leslie's wrath, always short-lived, would have vanished in an instant. But sorry was a word that seemed to be missing from Bennett's extensive vocabulary. Instead, he had simply muttered something about 'an ugly monstrosity' and returned to bed.

1

Leslie drained his cup and took a last look through the kitchen window at the peaceful and silent village. It was a wintery-looking scene, but this was deceptive given that Easter was nearly upon them. Indeed, in Leslie's neat front garden, the snowdrops had long finished flowering, and the daffodils and hyacinth spears were braving this cold night. He adored the village in all weathers and seasons, and he had never once regretted retiring to this tranquil backwater, where nothing more exciting than a baying fox or a broken gnome was ever likely to happen.

The church clock struck the hour, two o'clock, as Leslie made his way back to bed. Bennett's shabby slippers were too big for him, and he gripped the freezing banister for safety. At the top of the stairs he pulled back the landing curtain. It was a light night, but fortunately from this window he could not see the shattered remains of Alf the Angler, nor his own slipper floating in the garden pond. Vast constellations twinkled overhead and the bulky thatch of the village pub was silhouetted against the night sky, sparkling with frost and utterly enchanting. Even righteous indignation could not dispel the night's charms.

A single pair of headlamps could just be made out in the distance, flickering through the gaps in the hedge as a car made its way up Stag Lane. It must be that fool Clarissa on her way home so late. It was a wonder George put up with it; he must know what she was up to. Everyone else in the village did.

Leslie climbed into bed and, with renewed irritation, he turned over and purposely dragged most of the duvet over himself as a punishment for Bennett's interminable indifference. Bennett slept on unperturbed.

1

"What shall I do next, Mr Mountfield?"

Leslie viewed the devastation in his beloved garden, wrought by this boy in the short time his back was turned. He said, far more kindly than he felt, "I think that's all that needs doing for now, Jamie."

The boy looked disappointed. "I like working here," he said, taking the cup of coffee from the tray.

Leslie sat next to him on the garden bench and drank green tea to revive himself. He tried to be positive: the hedge would grow back eventually, and some of the trampled plants would survive. Spring was now well underway after all, and a pair of size ten boots would not triumph over Mother Nature for long in Leslie's well-stocked flowerbeds.

"I'm having a sort of gap year. Trying to save for uni, but it's impossible. There aren't any jobs round here. I went to stay with Dad, but that didn't work out." The boy looked troubled at the memory. "I came back to the village, thinking I'd get my job back at The Daffodil when it opened again for Easter. I worked there last summer – you probably remember? They told me they didn't need anyone, but now they've gone and taken on someone else." His voice was heavy with resentment, but Leslie didn't blame them if what he'd heard was true. Apparently, Jamie had been about as much use in a tea shop as he was in a garden and, after being corrected for the umpteenth time by the manageress, had vented his frustration on a customer. "It wasn't fair giving him the job," said Jamie indignantly. "He doesn't even come from round here."

To change the subject Leslie asked, "What are you hoping to do at university?"

"Art. My ma said I should try and get some work in that art shop in Temple Ducton, but there was nothing doing. You know the one I mean? It opened up last year."

"I've heard about it, but I don't go into Temple very often. Doesn't the chap run art classes there?"

It was there that the bored Clarissa had gone to occupy herself, and had started what was reported to be a rampant affair with the artist, half her age.

"I'm glad he didn't want me, actually," went on Jamie. "The guy's a right letch. Someone told me he's been with half the girls in town." His face flushed and he lowered his voice to a conspiratorial whisper. "They do it in the studio out the back of the shop."

The artist sounded loathsome, but Leslie had to suppress a smile at the coyness of Jamie's reaction. He was an odd boy, in many ways he was more like a pre-adolescent, and it was no wonder he'd had difficulty in getting work. The contrast with the good-looking, self-assured lad now working in The Daffodil Tea Shop couldn't have been greater. Leslie guessed that Jamie's animosity towards him extended beyond resentment about the job.

It was interesting, though, what Jamie had said about the artist. Clarissa was, presumably, unaware of her lover's promiscuous antics, and she certainly didn't endure the indignity of a backroom in the art shop. Her liaisons with him took place at The Imperial Hotel, where it was rumoured she always paid the bill. The hotel staff included several local people, providing a rich source of gossip for the village.

"I've heard them say Mrs Harrington-Thomas has been with him, but that can't be true," Jamie whispered incredulously.

Leslie looked at the boy; he was completely in earnest.

"I'm not doing any more work up at the Grange, though," he said vehemently. "I can't stand Mr Harrington-Thomas."

"Have you had some trouble, then?" enquired Leslie, rather surprised. If it had been an altercation with Clarissa he would have understood it, but not George.

Jamie muttered evasively, "Oh, nothing really," and sat clutching his coffee cup in a sullen silence.

Eventually the coffee and brooding were both finished. Against his better judgement, Leslie promised to find the boy some more odd jobs another day, and paid him far more than he deserved.

Putting the damaged hedge and flowerbeds from his mind, Leslie headed for the sanctuary of his greenhouse. He paused by the pond to adjust Arnold, Alf's replacement, bought in defiance of Bennett's objections. That was a month ago exactly. The date could not be forgotten; it was the weekend before Easter and, more notably, the day before the heart attack.

Leslie wondered how long it would be before Bennett's heart attack stopped preoccupying nearly every waking hour, consuming him with fear and guilt; fear that he would walk into the cottage and find Bennett collapsed over his work in the library; guilt that it was his rich cooking that had silently furred up Bennett's arteries. How else could a heart attack have happened to someone as lean and spare and impassive as Bennett? Had it been himself he could have understood it. He instinctively pulled his waistcoat down over his expanding midriff and sighed. Perhaps it was permissible for the belt to be let out a notch or two after retirement, even if one had retired very early. He reflected ruefully that Bennett hadn't put on an ounce and was still wearing the same clothes he'd worn when they had first met twenty years ago, in some cases literally. It was little wonder that the heart attack had been so unexpected.

Pottering about among the embryonic petunias and aubergines, Leslie tried to shake off his preoccupation with Bennett's mortality and thought instead about Clarissa and George. It was a wretched state of affairs. For Clarissa to be making a fool of herself like this would be bad enough at any time and Leslie always found infidelity shocking; but to betray a dying man was treachery.

* * *

Clarissa might have been gratified to know that not only had she occupied Leslie's thoughts that morning, but she was also the chief subject of conversation in the village shop. The opinions being passed there were not, however, flattering.

"Poor old George," sighed Janet, from behind the counter. "He was in here for his paper earlier and I didn't like the look of him at all. I don't know how long it must have taken him to walk back up the hill to the Grange. But he won't give up."

A short, red-haired lady put her basket on the counter. "I've heard he's only been given a few months," she said. She lowered her voice to a scandalised whisper. "How awful, and to have your wife cheat on you, too."

"The old boy's not what he was, Marian," laughed another customer, coarsely, "so she's gone elsewhere."

Leslie, who was making himself inconspicuous between the vegetable racks, winced. It was terrible to hear George being spoken of in this degrading way, but he had no intention of getting embroiled in the conversation. Marian and Vera were two of the most notorious scandal-mongers in the village, but on this occasion the talk of Clarissa's infamous behaviour did, unfortunately, seem to have its basis in truth.

In the five years since Clarissa had unexpectedly relieved George of his widowhood and his many years of solitude at Compton Grange, she had supplied the village with a steady stream of scurrilous tittle-tattle. No one, however, would have thought even Clarissa capable of carrying on a barely concealed affair when her poor husband had just been given his death sentence.

"It was a bad day he picked her for a dumman," said Irene, the shop assistant, and stomped into the stock room.

Leslie committed this oddity to memory; Bennett would enjoy it and might even know what it meant. Irene was one of the few inhabitants of the village who still uttered the occasional piece of dialect, but even then, it was with barely a trace of a West Country burr, which was rarely heard in the area. It was not just that Dartonleigh had become populated by affluent retirees from the Home Counties. Even among the native residents, the accent was unobtrusive; disappointing, of course, for holiday-makers hoping to hear "Oo arh" punctuating every conversation.

Vera picked through the newspaper racks and selected a glossy magazine. "I've seen it happen before," she said, sagely. "A forty-something divorcee marries for money. At the time it doesn't matter that he's ten or fifteen years older than her. Give it five years, though, and she's hooked up with an old man. He doesn't want a lover anymore; he needs a nurse. Do you remember George when he first came to the village?"

6

Marian sighed nostalgically. "I do indeed. Jet black hair, spine like a ram-rod, and fit as a butcher's dog."

"Now look at him," cut in Vera with contempt. "He's as deaf as a haddock and he can't even catch his breath."

"Some men don't age well," agreed Janet mildly.

"Well, I shouldn't think you would with a wife like Clarissa. She's been like it for years," said Vera. "Do you remember that carry-on with the director, when she took up amateur dramatics at Lymeford?"

"Yes, I do. I do indeed." Marian paid for her shopping, put her bag on the floor and perched on the stool by the counter. "They really shouldn't have cast her as Lady what's-her-name? Lady Windermere. She took the part far too literally."

Vera brought her basket to the counter. "And everyone knows she's been carrying on with the neighbour, that builder next door, though God knows what she sees in him. Anything in trousers, I suppose. And now she's turned her hand to cradle-snatching. The toy boy from Temple, every-one's calling him."

"I don't know how George puts up with it," said Marian.

"Perhaps he doesn't realise," sighed Janet. "Men can be awfully stupid. Maybe he really does believe she's doing art classes every evening. He may not know how late she comes in. By all accounts he does go to bed early these days."

"So does she," sniggered Vera. "Early, and often."

"She's lucky George hasn't divorced her," said Marian.

"George would never divorce her." Irene had reappeared from the stockroom. "He's a Catholic, isn't he."

"I'd forgotten that," Vera said. "Well, lucky for her. All she has to do is stick around for the will. By the sound of it, she won't have to wait much longer."

To Leslie's relief, the two ladies took their departure, no doubt to continue the assassination of Clarissa's character in the post office or the tea shop. At least it would save them from gossiping about him and Bennett, as he supposed they must do, since they slated everyone else in the village.

"Nice to see you, Leslie, love. How's Bennett getting on?" said Janet. "I hope we'll be seeing him out and about again soon."

Janet made small talk as Leslie sorted through the couscous, lentils and quinoa until he found a packet of risotto rice. It was easier to find a box of organic lentil burgers than a tin of baked beans on the shelves of the village shop, and on one memorable occasion Leslie had gone home with a jar of quails' eggs, mistaking them for pickled onions. Much as he loved the shop, and often enjoyed picking through the exotic goods, it could be rather tiresome when it was just a few basics that he needed. It was pointless, though, complaining to Janet who had little control over the stock. The shop was owned and managed as a co-operative by a small group of wealthy inhabitants who had rescued it when it was threatened with closure. They drove to the supermarket in Tiverley for their real shopping or had it delivered, but were determined that Dartonleigh should retain what they believed to be one of the quintessential features of a village. The shabby but functional general store had been renovated with the aid of some faded photographs. The outside now looked like a grocery shop from the nineteenth century and the inside resembled a Kensington delicatessen.

"Have you managed to persuade Bennett to get away for a bit of convalescence, yet?"

"He doesn't seem very keen," replied Leslie, making a gross understatement. "I'm still working on it, though."

"Good luck with that," said Janet as Leslie took his leave. "And tell Bennett I hope he's getting on."

Leslie stepped out of the shop into the golden sunshine of a glorious spring morning and turned towards his cottage. It looked especially lovely from here, in the lee of the church and framed against the backdrop of the distant moor, where just now a pair of buzzards wheeled high above, two tiny specks riding on the current. With its thatched roof and whitewashed, rose-clad exterior, Leslie thought the cottage utterly charming and, even after six years, he still hardly believed his luck in living there.

It was just the sort of day to set one's heart soaring, but Leslie felt his mood firmly earthbound. Janet was very kind, but she could have no idea of the effect of this preoccupation with Bennett's health, and every mention of it had the capacity to transport him back to the dreadful event, still painfully vivid. The awful shout in the night, so completely out of character; Bennett, breathless, waxen and sweating, clutching his chest; the terrible, terrible wait for an ambulance to make its slow journey along the narrow, winding lanes; the long and agonising night at the hospital, and the frightening days that followed.

These painful recollections were interrupted as Leslie heard a familiar voice calling his name. Turning, he saw Edgar advancing towards him. "How are you doing, Edgar?" said Leslie, regretting that he had lingered, for just at the moment he could have done with a more cheerful companion. He instantly felt guilty as the poor man looked even more overwrought than usual.

"Oh, I don't know. Not so good. You know how it is," Edgar gabbled. "I've just been to see George. Not for anything particular, of course, just to see him. Not for any reason, you know. He wasn't too bad. Under the circumstances, not too bad, you know."

"Do you fancy a coffee?" Leslie interrupted, steering the agitated man towards The Daffodil. If it was anyone else he would have suggested going back to the cottage, but Leslie knew from bitter experience that Edgar wasn't always easy to get rid of.

The tea shop was doing a lively trade as usual at this time of the year, but there was a free table in the corner. Half a dozen ladies from the Women's Institute were crowded round one of the tables and greeted them as they passed. Leslie overheard Brenda say, in what she must have thought was a whisper, "Edgar's aged, don't you think? He looks ten years older."

It was true. Edgar, who fortunately seemed oblivious to the comment, looked haggard.

They were served by Daniel, the usurper, the boy who had snatched the summer job Jamie had thought was his. Apparently, Daniel was taking a year out before starting a sports course at university, but it seemed a strange choice of gap year experience for an outgoing, athletic young man like him. Serving cream teas in Dartonleigh hardly compared to backpacking across Thailand or digging a well in Nepal.

Without prompting, Edgar launched into a long and tedious account of his troubles. His wife had died more than twenty years

9

ago, leaving him to raise his teenage son alone. Kenneth, or Kenny as he was known by everyone but Edgar, had not turned out well and had settled to nothing. The sad story of loneliness, struggle and failure would surely have elicited all Leslie's natural sympathies had he not heard it so many times, and had it not been such a tale of two victims. He had long since succumbed to compassion fatigue. Familiarity with the story meant that Leslie was able to give most of his attention to the other micro-dramas playing out in the tea shop. Daniel was unsuccessfully flirting with the young waitress. Why would that amiable girl be so very frosty to an attractive and personable, if rather cocky, young man?

Snatches of conversation came drifting from the WI's table. "No one's going to pay that for a trip," Brenda declared, and one of her companions struck something off on a sheet of paper.

A customer came in, looking anxiously round for a table. He was a young man, about twenty-four, Leslie thought, and he had all the paraphernalia of a walker: the boots, rucksack and walking poles. A couple with a small boy at the table next to Leslie and Edgar were just leaving and he hesitated nervously, as if unsure if he was permitted to sit there. Daniel came over, cleared the table and took his order. The young man huddled over his phone and when Daniel returned with his coffee, Leslie heard him ask if he knew of anywhere to stay in the village.

"It's no good asking me," laughed Daniel, "I'm new to the area myself. Let me get someone else."

A few minutes later the manageress appeared. "You're looking for somewhere to stay?" Annie asked.

"Yes. I thought I'd be able to find something when I got down here but I can't get a phone signal. I came past two or three places but they all had no vacancy signs up. I suppose I should have booked in advance."

"It does get pretty busy at this time of year," Annie said. "Have you tried The Woodman? It's the pub opposite and they have a couple of rooms upstairs. I've heard it's a bit basic but I don't suppose you'll mind that; it's usually walkers who stay there. If they can't take you, there are a couple of B&Bs at Stretton

Cross, which is about two miles from here. Otherwise I think you'll have to try out at Lymeford or Temple Ducton."

"Thank you very much," said the young man politely. "I'll try the pub. If not, is there a bus to… what was it called, Stretton Cross?"

"A bus?" smiled Annie. "I'm afraid not. They'd have a job getting a bus down that lane! It's only a couple of miles, surely you could walk it?" She was looking at his hiking gear. "But perhaps you've already had a long walk today?"

"No, not really," he replied rather sheepishly, and turned his attention to his coffee.

Facing the table where he was sitting, Leslie could not help but observe the young man while Edgar droned on. He looked uneasy, as though he had no business being there, and cast anxious glances over his shoulder.

Edgar was coming to the final part of his sorry saga. Having gone his own way for many years, Kenny had come back to live with Edgar a year ago and announced that he wanted to join his father in his firm. Edgar had yielded to Kenny's insistence that he should become a partner. The business was no longer going well.

Leslie sighed and signalled to Daniel for the bill. Poor Edgar. Kenny was a total waster; everyone knew that except his father. His gambling and drinking were notorious in the village. By Leslie's calculations Kenny must have been in his late thirties, forty perhaps, but Edgar spoke as though he was a teenager just making his way in the world. By the time Leslie managed to detach himself from Edgar outside The Daffodil, the young man who had been at the next table had finished and paid for his coffee, and hurried past them towards The Woodman. Leslie walked back to the cottage thoughtfully.

* * *

"He was a funny kind of a hiker," Leslie said to Bennett, later that afternoon. Talking and cooking were two of Leslie's chief passions, so whenever Bennett brought his newspaper into the kitchen while Leslie was preparing dinner, Leslie was at his most content.

He was relating the day's events to Bennett in minute detail, as was his custom. "He'd got all the right kit for a walker, but there was something wrong about him."

"You mean, apart from the fact that he's a hiker who needs to catch a bus for a two-mile country walk?" said Bennett, without looking up from his paper.

"Yes, apart from that," Leslie replied. "Even when he first came in, and when he was just sitting there in the tea shop – it was all wrong. I can't explain it. He was so.... That's it! He seemed so terribly self-conscious. He looked more like he'd accidentally gate-crashed a Girl Guides' meeting."

"Curious," Bennett remarked, reaching across to pinch a mushroom from the chopping board and earning a smack on the back of his hand from Leslie's wooden spoon.

The aroma of onions and garlic wafted up from the pan, and Leslie stirred a generous helping of white wine into the simmering risotto. Bennett sat at the table with his head in his newspaper and Leslie went on to relate all Edgar's woes.

"That man's a perfect fool," muttered Bennett, still engrossed in the paper. This seemed a harsh dismissal of Edgar and his problems but Bennett was probably right.

"Whatever he says, he must rue the day he brought Kenny into his business," commented Leslie. "I got the impression that it's pretty much on the rocks and that it started floundering when Kenny joined as a partner. Not that Edgar would ever blame Kenny for anything. He really can't see through him, can he?"

"Kenny's a complete oaf," declared Bennett as he continued reading.

A vision of Kenny and his vulgar habits intruded into Leslie's mind and he could not help but agree. "Poor old Edgar. I know he's a bit weak, but it's hard to know how he managed to produce quite such a repulsive son. Tragic, really."

Bennett had stopped reading now and was making some notes on a sheet of paper. Leslie added more stock to the pan and returned his thoughts to the morning's events. They were used to hikers in Dartonleigh, and they saw all sorts: groups, loners, the earnestly serious, the dangerously casual, and the strangely eccentric. With such a variety it was surprising that one young man could seem so out of place. Then Leslie's thoughts shifted to Daniel, and he wondered what he'd done to upset the waitress he was so obviously trying to impress, without success. Recalling the painful agonies of youth, Leslie sighed. Maybe middle-age wasn't so bad.

"Fake hair product smells unpleasant. Seven letters," Bennett said suddenly, looking up.

Leslie stirred the risotto thoughtfully and repeated the clue two or three times. "Can you give me any of the letters?"

"The second letter is H."

Leaving his cooking for a moment, Leslie took Bennett's pen and a fresh piece of paper from the table. He drew seven neat dashes, and placed the letter H on top of the second one. He repeated the clue again. "Got it!" he exclaimed in triumph. "Shampoo. It was 'hair product' that gave it away. There aren't too many hair products to choose from. It's a good clue, though."

Bennett grunted and returned to his notes. Leslie added more stock to the risotto; it could really do with a dollop of fresh cream but since the heart attack he'd tried to do without.

"What about this one?" said Bennett, and pushed a piece of paper across the table. Leslie turned the heat down under the pan, gave the risotto another stir, and took the paper. The clue was just one word, framed as a question: *Flower?* The answer had five letters, and Bennett had supplied the first and last letters, both R.

"R, blank, blank, blank, R," said Leslie pensively. He returned to the pan and swirled the rice around with his wooden spoon muttering, "Rose, no. Ribes... rubus, no. Definitely not rhododendron." After a while he shook his head. "You'll have to tell me," he said.

"River," said Bennett.

"River?" exclaimed Leslie in disbelief. "How come?"

Bennett took the paper back and wrote on it, *flow-er*.

Leslie picked up the piece of paper, screwed it into a ball and aimed it across the table at Bennett who had opened his newspaper again. The missile struck Bennett on the crown of the head, but he made no response and continued studiously to read.

The kitchen window looked directly into the village centre and Leslie could watch the comings and goings outside while he cooked. He glanced up and there outside the church, in front of a sign for the organ restoration fund, stood the young hiker. A very uncouth double-entendre occurred to Leslie as he read the church sign, and he was instantly dismayed that such a thought should come, unbidden, to his mind. To Bennett he simply remarked that the young man who he had been referring to earlier, was now standing outside in front of the church. "I think he must have found a room at The Woodman," he continued. "He doesn't have his rucksack or walking poles with him now."

Bennett put down the paper and came to the window. He took off his reading glasses and looked at him intently.

"I wonder who he is," said Leslie, "and what he's doing here."

2

It was nearly one o'clock in the morning, and Leslie lay listening to the regular sound of Bennett's breathing. Since the heart attack he had found it increasingly difficult to relinquish a sense of responsibility for Bennett's survival through the night, and surrender to sleep. The horror that he might wake and find Bennett dead beside him haunted him, and some nights he lay for hours, continuously waiting for the next breath.

Just then, he was distracted by a faint scuffling sound somewhere outside. There it was, once more, a little closer to the house. Foxes again; he would deal with them this time. He hadn't forgiven the foxes for that previous episode, and for the loss of his treasured gnome. He meant to get his revenge.

He rose cautiously from the bed and pulled on his dressing gown. Everything was silent now and the room was in pitch darkness. Leslie moved tentatively round the end of the bed, his eyes struggling to adjust to the lack of light.

Fumbling on the floor, he found a slipper, Bennett's this time, and crept silently onto the landing. It was a particularly dark night, and Leslie edged his way slowly and carefully down the stairs. He made his way towards the library, from where he would be able to get a good aim at his foe, without risk to Arnold. The cottage had that strange hollowness and unfamiliarity that comes with the night and, stupid though he knew it was, Leslie felt his throat tighten at every shadow and creak. He crept across the hall and went quietly into the library. Keeping all the lights off, he tip-toed noiselessly across the room and sidled up to the patio door. Sliding his hand behind the heavy brocade curtain, without a sound he lifted the latch. In one move, Leslie slid the door open, pulled the curtain back and stepped forward. He let out a terrified yell. He was face to face with a man.

For one horrifying moment, both men were motionless, staring into each other's eyes. Then the stranger turned and fled across the garden. As he went, there was a crack and the sound of shattering. At the same time, Bennett was hurtling downstairs and into the room with a speed and urgency Leslie didn't know he possessed. Bennett stopped abruptly and took in the situation. He looked at Leslie who was standing beside the half-open patio door in his silk dressing gown, brandishing a single slipper.

"Good evening, Dandini," he said. "Are you going out, or coming in?"

The sweet smell of the night air would have been pleasant on another occasion, but Bennett slid the patio door shut and snapped the lock home. Leslie, mobilised into life again, switched on the exterior light and peered out. The intruder had, of course, vanished, but Leslie exclaimed with renewed dismay: the shattered remains of Arnold could be seen beside the pond.

* * *

It was an hour later and Bennett and Leslie sat up in bed drinking brandy; Leslie, in order to steady his nerves, Bennett because it was always a good time for brandy.

"I've a good mind to make a complaint tomorrow," exclaimed Leslie. "Inferring that I was wasting police time, indeed."

"It may have been better if you hadn't mentioned the gnome," replied Bennett.

"That call handler, or whoever it was on the phone, misunderstood me on purpose."

"Perhaps your description of the prowler provoked them, too."

"I can't help it if he was medium height, medium build, ordinary-looking and youngish," protested Leslie. "He had his hood up; I could only see his face. What did they want me to say? That he had flame-red hair, a jagged scar on his cheek and walked with a limp?"

Bennett allowed himself a smile. "And you say it definitely wasn't that hiker staying at The Woodman, or one of the other young men around, the boy working at The Daffodil, or young Jamie?"

"Of course not. I'm absolutely certain it was no one I'd seen before."

The two men sat thoughtfully, both propped against their pillows on the wooden bed-head. Had the incident occurred earlier in the night, it might be surmised that the stranger was trying to take a shortcut from the pub, though odd to be so close to the cottage. It wouldn't be the first time a late-night drinker had vaulted over their wall in a misguided attempt to cut through the garden or, on one unpleasant occasion, to relieve himself in the shrubbery. The obvious conclusion was that Leslie had disturbed a potential burglar, but something seemed wrong with that explanation, not least the intruder's reaction. He had seemed petrified, more afraid even than Leslie had been. Hardly the reaction of a seasoned criminal. It was all very strange.

News of their nocturnal visitor spread quickly through the village the next morning. This was hardly surprising since, despite his disturbed night, Leslie paid an early visit to the village shop, the post office and The Daffodil to find out if anyone had been the victim of a crime or had seen the prowler, and to warn everyone to be on their guard. The news was received with gratifying interest, but it seemed that no one had seen a youngish, ordinary-looking man with a hood creeping about.

In the shop, Janet greeted the news with customary sympathy. "I can't believe it, Leslie, love," she said, patting his arm across the counter. "What a year you're having, what with Bennett's do and now this. I know not much seems to upset him, but he can do without anything that might cause a setback."

In The Daffodil, the response was much the same: fascinated interest, speculation, sympathy, but no information. As Leslie was making for the post office, he nearly collided with the young hiker who was engrossed in an Ordnance Survey map. After they had apologised to one another, Leslie asked if he needed any direction.

"I'm looking for this path," said the young man pointing uncertainly to the place where a dotted line joined Stag Lane before turning onto the moor. "I've just bought this map from the post office. I thought I'd be able to get the directions on my phone, but I can't seem to get a signal." As before, he was polite and well-spoken, and vaguely ill at ease.

"You need to take the footpath by the old pump and the war memorial," Leslie said indicating past his own cottage. "Then there's a stile that takes you up through a bit of woodland. Let me show you on the map." Leslie traced the path with his finger on the map and the young man watched attentively. "Are you making for anywhere in particular?" asked Leslie.

"Oh, I thought I might do a sort of circle and come back to the village." The young man's words were casual enough, but he fidgeted uneasily from foot to foot as he spoke.

"There's a really nice circular trail that goes that way," said Leslie kindly. Whoever he was, this young man was no walker and Leslie didn't want him straying off onto the moor. Leslie explained it as clearly as he could, and without reference to the map which he could see would be of little help. Leslie's kindness seemed almost more than the young man could bear and he hurried off in the direction Leslie had shown him.

* * *

Leslie and Bennett were having lunch by the French windows in the lounge. The glorious weather had continued and it was just the day for a walk. "I showed him the walk past Penley Farm and Gant's Boulder. It's only an hour or so and signposted for most of the way. I've seen some bad map readers in my time, but this boy couldn't even find his way out of the village. There's something the matter there, for sure," went on Leslie. "I nearly invited him in for lunch."

Bennett took another sandwich and said, "You'd have invited Hitler in for lunch if he'd looked out of sorts."

"Well," replied Leslie defensively, "perhaps he wouldn't have started a war if I had." Before this bizarre speculation had any opportunity to develop, the men were disturbed by a ring at the doorbell. Leslie was astonished to see two police officers in the porch. He had certainly not expected a visit for such a trivial incident, especially after the reception he had received when reporting it. The two officers looked very young, though Leslie knew this undoubtedly said more about his own age than theirs. One was tall, dark and lanky, the other short, ginger and stocky, a contrast that would probably have seemed comic if there had not been something rather scornful about the way the taller policeman was looking at them. He appeared to be in charge, and he moved his eyes between Leslie and Bennett as though making his mind up about something. It was subtle but Leslie felt his hackles rising. The officer introduced himself as PC Overton and his companion, who was PC Dunn.

"We had a phone call last night from a Mr Mountford, reporting damage to a garden gnome," he said, picking Bennett to direct the comment towards.

"It was me who telephoned," said Leslie, not bothering to correct his surname. "And I said no such thing. I reported a prowler in the garden."

PC Overton referred to his notes, affecting a faintly puzzled air. "You didn't report the breakage of a garden gnome?" he asked, his eyes flicking across to his colleague.

"I reported a prowler," said Leslie, irritated. "He broke the gnome, but that was incidental. Perhaps you'd better come inside." Leslie's usual sense of hospitality had deserted him and he took them no further than the hallway.

The officer took a few preliminary details from both the men before addressing Leslie again. "I see," he said with deliberate slowness. "There was someone in your garden last night who broke this incidental gnome?"

Leslie nodded but said nothing. The officer continued, "So, can you give me some more details about what he was doing?"

Bennett answered this time. "Fishing," he said.

"Fishing? The intruder was fishing?"

"Of course not," said Bennett. "The gnome was fishing. I thought you were interested in the gnome."

There was a very long pause. "Can you describe him?" said PC Overton at last, adding, "The man, that is, not the gnome."

"He was a young man," began Leslie, and hesitated, trying to think of something specific to describe him by.

"A young man?"

There was another very quick look exchanged between the two colleagues.

"And just what do you mean by—" Leslie began, but Bennett put his hand on Leslie's arm.

"Leave it, Les," he said quietly, and then to the policemen, "Thank you very much, officers, I don't think we wish to pursue this any further. Let me see you out."

Leslie was incandescent with rage when they were rid of the two officers, and vented his feelings with some rarely used expressions.

"I'd rather have the prowler in the house," was all Bennett had to say, and picking up the plate with his half eaten sandwich, he stomped off into the library to take refuge in his work.

Leslie felt too annoyed to settle to anything in the house and knew that it would be useless to try to engage Bennett in conversation. He decided to head for The Woodman next door. Although it was rather early in the day for a drink, he remembered that the pub hadn't yet been treated to the story of his nocturnal adventure.

As Leslie was unlatching his front gate, he caught site of the young hiker, evidently on his way back from his walk. Leslie was concerned to see that he was limping rather badly, so instead of turning right for the pub, Leslie walked casually towards him, trying not to look too purposeful. "Hello, again. Did you do the circular walk?" Leslie turned to walk back with him.

"Yes, thank you. It was lovely." The young man gave an unconvincing smile as he hobbled on.

"Are you all right? Have you turned your ankle?"

"No, it's blisters. Both feet, but the right one is the worst." He stopped and lifted one foot after the other behind him, wincing as he tried to pull the back of each boot away from his painful heels. "I'm going to see if the shop has some plasters," he went on, flinching as he put his foot back down to the ground.

"I've got plenty of plasters," said Leslie. "This is our cottage, here. Please do come in and we can sort your feet out properly. I'm Leslie, by the way."

"Robert," replied the young man hesitantly, but he shook the hand Leslie extended to him. He seemed uncertain about accepting Leslie's hospitality but it was obvious from the state of his feet that hobbling even the last few yards to the shop would be agony. "Perhaps I could just sit on your wall and put the plasters on here. I won't bother you any more than that." He sat down gratefully on the low wall in front of the cottage, but was immediately defeated by the agonising task of removing his boots. It took little persuasion after that for him to go inside, and moments later he found himself sitting on the sofa while Leslie eased the rigid boots over his badly skinned heels.

Leslie fussed about, happily bringing in first a towel for the floor, then a bowl of water for Robert's feet. Bennett chose that moment to walk in.

"You're rather late," he said. "Maundy Thursday was weeks ago."

Leslie glanced at Robert, ready to explain the allusion.

"I get it," Robert said, his smile genuine this time. "I went to a Church school." He lowered his feet gingerly into the bowl, grimacing as he did so, but after a moment or two he leaned back against the cushions on the settee and some of the anxious lines on his face disappeared. Leslie fetched a fresh pair of socks and some plasters and put them on the seat next to Robert. "This is really kind of you. I can't believe you're doing all this."

"Oh don't mind Leslie," said Bennett. "He would have made a good nurse."

Visions of cardiac monitors, alarms and ashen-faced patients rose up in Leslie's mind. "I don't think so," he said and retreated to the safety of the kitchen, reappearing shortly with a tray of coffees and a fruit cake. "I might make a passable waiter," he said.

"And a master baker," said Bennett, reaching for a slice of the cake.

"Did you make this?" asked Robert, taking the slice offered to him and trying it. "It's really good."

Leslie brushed off the compliment and turned the conversation to small talk about the pub and the village, while Robert, with his feet still soaking, finished his coffee and cake. "You have a beautiful house here," he said, "and I love the thatched roof."

"So do the birds and the mice," said Bennett.

"Take no notice of Bennett," said Leslie. "It is a lovely house; we're very fortunate. What brings you to Dartonleigh? Is it a holiday?"

He instantly regretted the questions as Robert retreated to his previously guarded state.

"I'm just staying for a few days," he answered evasively. "I'd heard it was a good place for walking."

"It's a delightful area," said Leslie neutrally. "I hope you enjoy your stay."

The spell was broken and, although scrupulously polite, Robert seemed anxious to finish his coffee, dry and plaster his feet, and be gone.

Robert's visit, and especially his hasty departure, left Leslie even more restless and preoccupied than before. Bennett returned steadfastly to his work and, after tidying up, Leslie remembered that he'd been making for the pub when he'd encountered Robert. With nothing better to do, he set off once more.

Leslie reached the gate as Daniel was crossing the road in front of the cottage from the direction of The Daffodil, and heading towards The Woodman. He was making rather unsteady progress across the cobbles, due to a tall stack of boxes he was carrying, which Leslie recognised to be the cake bases that the tea shop supplied for some of the desserts served in The Woodman's bistro.

"Can I give you a hand with those?" Leslie called after him. The lad couldn't see where he was going and the path to the pub was uneven.

"No, ta, I'm doing fine," he called back. His voice had more than a hint of arrogance and, although Leslie was generous enough to put it down to youth and ignorance, he didn't press his offer to help.

Daniel reached the pub door just as someone else was coming through the other way, in rather a hurry. Leslie could see the calamity before it happened but, despite shouting a desperate, "Watch out," was unable to prevent it. Boxes and cakes were everywhere. One sponge base rolled along the path on its edge like a wheel, for several feet, which was quite something given the roughness of the ground.

"What a moron. Haven't you got eyes in your head?" Daniel was furious.

"Oh, God, I'm sorry. I didn't mean—"

As Leslie approached to help, he could see that the stuttering wreck of a man, vainly collecting lumps of cake from the ground, was Robert. He seemed excessively upset by the incident. After firing off another insult, Daniel stomped into the pub with the few undamaged boxes, and Leslie guessed that gateaux would be off the menu tonight.

"Come back into the pub and I'll get you a drink," Leslie said to Robert, who was still stammering apologies to Daniel's retreating back.

"No, thank you. That's very kind but—" He seemed unable to complete the sentence and hurried off up the path, still hobbling slightly, without looking back.

As he watched Robert disappear round the corner, Leslie shook his head, bemused. It was odd behaviour from someone whose feet he'd just bathed and who was still wearing his socks, but some folk were hard to fathom, especially young people with their volatile moods.

Leslie turned back towards the pub. He never tired of the charm of the village, and The Woodman really was one of the jewels in its crown. It could quite literally be described as a picture-postcard of a pub, for a whole rack of cards featuring The Woodman with its neat thatch and gleaming whitewashed stone exterior, in all seasons of the year, were on sale in the village shop and the post office. At the front was a cottage garden, bright with spring flowers, and the wisteria growing over the thatched porch was just coming into flower. The interior was just as inviting with its wooden beams, granite walls and huge fireplaces. Not surprisingly, it did a lively trade all year.

Going inside, Leslie paused in the doorway of the snug. It was very crowded in there today; a party of visitors had pushed three tables together by the window and were having a noisy lunch. Then Leslie spotted Edgar alone in the corner, with a vacant chair. He was just wondering whether he could face another encounter with him when he saw Kenny stomping along the passageway from the lounge bar at the back of the pub, or more specifically from the gents, judging by the way he was adjusting his flies. Everything about Kenny was uncouth, and Leslie, abandoning Edgar to his son, passed on down to the rear of the pub.

The lounge bar was deserted by comparison. Daniel was at the bar counter in conversation with the landlady, presumably explaining himself. Only a couple of tables were taken, one of them by George.

"Can I join you, George?" said Leslie as he entered the room. "What can I get you?"

George did not answer immediately and, remembering George's deafness, Leslie went closer, ready to repeat the greeting. As he approached he was surprised at how unwell the man looked. His skin was ashen, and beads of perspiration covered his forehead. There was a look of deep anxiety, almost panic, on his face, and his hand, resting on the table, was shaking.

"Are you all right, old man?" said Leslie, full of concern. He leant towards George in an effort to be heard without attracting the attention of the room. "You don't look too well. Do you need a doctor?"

"No, no," said George, with great emphasis. "It's nothing like that."

"Well, can I get you something? A glass of water? A brandy?"

"A brandy would be good please, Leslie," he replied.

Leslie sat quietly as George drank the brandy. When he was looking a little steadier, Leslie said, leaning into his ear again, "I can fetch the car and drive you home, George. Or you could come across to our cottage. I could call the doctor from there if you're still feeling bad."

"No, please don't trouble yourself, there's no need. I'll be quite all right in a few minutes. Making a fool of myself like that – I'm sorry."

Seeing that George was embarrassed by the episode, Leslie made companionable small talk. He spoke of Bennett's progress, and how he hoped that George and Bennett would soon be back to their regular chess games. He related the story of their strange intruder in the night. Throughout, he was conscious that

George was paying little attention to anything he was telling him. Leslie had just paused for breath when George suddenly interrupted him.

"The thing is," he said, breathing heavily again, "I've just had a shock, a most terrible shock."

3

Leslie sat patiently while George composed himself.

"I'm not normally one to discuss my private affairs," he said at last, "and there aren't many people I would feel able to trust. But the thing is, there is a personal matter, something that I have told no one. Not even my wife. And today—"

Just at that moment, Edgar came blundering in. "Hello, George, hello, Leslie. Can I join you? Kenneth's gone and— Oh, I see you've got drinks; I'll just get myself one, then."

As Edgar went off to the bar, George shook his head. The moment had passed.

"Look, why don't you come back with me and see Bennett? You won't be interrupted there," said Leslie, hurriedly. "In any case, it would do Bennett good; he's hardly seen anyone since his heart attack."

"No, not now," said George, suddenly emphatic. "There's.... there's something I must do. I have to think this through."

"Are you certain? How about tomorrow, then? Come in for coffee in the morning," said Leslie. "It would do Bennett the world of good."

"Yes, I think perhaps I will, thank you," said George. Edgar was returning from the bar. "I might know something by then.... And I might need Bennett's advice. I'll knock when I've been in for my Sunday paper. That will give me the rest of the day to... to do what I have to do."

Leslie glowered at Edgar as he sat down, but Edgar was oblivious and launched into a long whining complaint about having to drive into Lymeford on business, despite it being the weekend. Leslie was overcome with impatience and irritation. George was looking better now, although he was lost in thought and clearly paying no attention to Edgar's drivel, so Leslie took his leave and went home.

Leslie usually tried to avoid interrupting Bennett when he was at work in the library, his reaction, like everything with Bennett, being hard to predict. At best, he would usually respond without looking up, and Leslie had once complained that he was more used to having a conversation with the top of Bennett's head than with his face. However, as he related this strange episode, Bennett put his pen down and gave him his full attention.

"That's not like George," he commented. "He's the last person to divulge his feelings."

Not quite the last person, thought Leslie, looking at Bennett, but out loud he said, "I wonder what it could have been. It's infuriating, not knowing. Trust Edgar to appear at that moment."

"That man's a damned fool."

"I know. Anyone could see we were having a private conversation."

Bennett turned his attention back to his work.

"Oh, well," continued Leslie, "we'll know what it's about soon enough. George always drives to the early mass at Sacred Heart in Lymeford, and then picks his paper up on the way home. He'll probably be here before we've had our breakfast. It's a shame he doesn't go to their main service still; we could have had a bit of a lie-in."

When Leslie and Bennett had first moved to Dartonleigh, George had been an active member of the Catholic Church which was in the neighbouring town. In recent years he had rescinded all his responsibilities and now only put in an appearance once a week at the very quiet and sparsely attended early service. Leslie had heard him attribute these changes to his age and health, but suspected that the humiliation of his wife's behaviour was the real cause.

Preoccupied by all the unsettling events of the day, Leslie found it impossible to concentrate on anything. He knew Bennett was trying to work, but he could not help himself from interrupting whenever the latest thought or speculation came to him. In the end Bennett looked up and sighed.

"For God's sake stop fussing, man," he said wearily. "I've got deadlines to meet and an editor on my back. How am I supposed to—"

Leslie waited for no more. Feeling wounded and guilty in equal measure, he put on his coat and went outside. There were so many strange things going on, it was too bad that Bennett wouldn't stop work for five minutes to talk about them. That he should be working at all so soon after his heart attack was already a constant source of worry to Leslie. Whenever he suggested going away somewhere to convalesce, Bennett dismissed the idea, and carried on as though he had never been ill.

In a fever of agitation, Leslie made for the antique shop. Vintage Dartonleigh had very capricious opening hours and had been shut earlier when he'd gone to spread the news of their prowler. Audrey and Phil had, of course, heard all about Leslie's night-time adventure by now, but they were happy to hear it again over a cup of tea at the shop counter. Leslie sat back, his head resting between a plaster bust of Shakespeare and a brass birdcage, and related the story. They enquired after Bennett, and guessed that he hadn't been upset by the episode. Next Leslie regaled them with the story of Daniel and the cakes at The Woodman. Audrey and Phil exchanged glances.

"I think that may explain something," said Phil.

"Yes," Audrey agreed. "I went out a little while ago and Daniel was getting on his bike; obviously going home. 'You're off early today, love', I said. Do you know what he replied?"

Audrey leant forward and lowered her voice, even though there were no customers. "He said, 'I've been sent home. I've been *bleep bleep* sent home'. I won't repeat his language. He was in a right state."

"That's a bit harsh," said Leslie. "It wasn't entirely his fault. Perhaps I should go in and explain. I was a witness, after all."

"It is odd," commented Phil. "Annie's great, and she's always so supportive of her staff, especially the youngsters. Perhaps it was after Jackie's boy last summer; perhaps she thinks she needs to get a bit tougher on these lads."

"You mean Jamie," said Leslie. "He was rather a nightmare in the tea shop, I've heard. Perhaps you're right; even Annie's goodwill must have a limit."

Finishing his tea quickly, Leslie made his way to The Daffodil next door. The little tea shop was still quite busy, and Leslie waited patiently until Annie had a moment to spare between serving cream teas, dealing with bills and clearing tables. He explained why he had called in, and when he had finished Annie looked upset and said, "It's not as simple as that. I'd like to explain but I can't leave the shop now; without Daniel we're already one down. Can you pop in tomorrow morning?"

Agreeing, Leslie took himself home, another unresolved issue agitating his mind. The kitchen afforded some relief to his restless mood and he made poached salmon for dinner, with French beans and new potatoes, one of Bennett's favourite meals. Bennett, in turn, opened a decent bottle of wine. These tokens of reconciliation exchanged, Leslie felt emboldened to raise again the puzzling events that had recently occurred. They sat by the French windows in the lounge after dinner and, as Bennett poured them each a glass of port, Leslie itemised the perplexing problems. First, there was the arrival of Robert the unconvincing hiker, then the prowler in the night. Next was George's unexplained shock, and now the mystery reason for Daniel being sent home early from the tea shop.

While Bennett gazed silently at the ceiling, Leslie turned the questions over and over, trying to guess the possible motive of the prowler, the real purpose of Robert's visit, the cause of George's shock, and the explanation for Annie's behaviour towards Daniel. At long last he stopped, looking towards Bennett for a response. Bennett said nothing and finished his port. Putting the empty glass on the table, he rose and started for the library.

"Well?" Leslie demanded. "I wish you'd say what you think, for once."

Bennett turned. "Upon the heat and flame of thy distemper sprinkle cool patience," he quoted, leaving Leslie restraining the urge to hurl the port bottle at the closing door.

* * *

29

Leslie awoke early the following day, his mind in the same state of restless agitation, and impatient for George's visit. He breakfasted hastily, expecting George's arrival at any moment and, as the minutes passed, he grew increasingly puzzled by his non-appearance. After clearing away the breakfast things, he took up a vigil at the kitchen window.

It was Sunday morning and people were drifting towards St Mary's for the ten am service. Since retiring and moving to Dartonleigh, Leslie sometimes found it difficult to tell one day of the week from another, but Sunday at least was distinct, marked as it was by the pealing of the bells which started at nine thirty. This was no electronic or recorded peal, but the synchronised labour of six campanologists, four of whom had never touched a bell rope until they retired and moved to Dartonleigh. The services were similarly attended by many who had never set foot in a church, other than for weddings and funerals. But people moved to Dartonleigh to live the village life, and the village life included the church, not to mention the shop, the post office, the tea shop and the WI, all of which they dutifully patronised. 'Use it or lose it' could have been the village motto.

Half an hour passed and then an hour. Bennett came into the kitchen and poured himself a black coffee.

"I think George must have forgotten," said Leslie. "That's not like him. I'll go over to the shop and see if he's been for the paper."

When he returned with the news that there had been no sign of George, Bennett tried phoning him. He received no answer and said, "Why not walk up there, Les? You're as restless as a soul in torment as it is. You might as well go and see what's happened to him."

"You don't want to come as well?" asked Leslie thinking for once of company for himself.

"You'll get on better without me."

This was most likely true as, since the heart attack, Bennett had hardly been out, let alone made a steep climb like the one to Compton Grange. It probably would be quicker to go alone, but Leslie did not relish the prospect. Nonetheless, he wasted no time, and in minutes his jacket and boots were on and he was making his way over the stile and through the wood, the shortcut up to Stag Lane.

This was one of the walks he and Bennett had loved the most when they had come to Dartonleigh for the Easter holidays, year after year, before they had settled here. It had looked then as it did now, adorned with daffodils, primroses, marsh marigolds and lesser celandine; the yellow season. Even the cupped petals of the uninvitingly named Bog Arum were like yellow flames rising from the marshy mud. The path was steep and Leslie was out of breath by the time he reached Stag Lane and then finally the huge mansion that was Compton Grange.

Leslie rang the doorbell twice with no response. He was just about to try for a third and final time when he heard a vehicle travelling very fast up the lane. Turning, he saw Clarissa's car swing round into the drive and she sped past him across the driveway. He caught a glimpse of her signalling him to wait, and heard her pull up behind the house and enter through the back door. Presently the front door opened.

"You'd better come in," Clarissa said in a low voice, and she turned and walked back into the house, giving Leslie no opportunity to explain his visit or decline the invitation. Shutting the front door, Leslie took off his boots which were dirty from the walk, before making his way through the great hallway and into the sitting room. It was a large room, with a high ceiling and massive fireplace; a masculine room, largely unchanged from the days when George lived here alone. Clarissa was already starting to pour a glass of wine, and she turned quickly as he entered, as though she had forgotten him. In the light of the huge bay window she looked like a startled animal. "If you've come to see George, you're too late," she said without warning. "He's dead."

31

4

The news of a sudden death is always shocking. Leslie had prepared himself for bad news, he thought, but still he felt his head reeling and he clutched at the sideboard to steady himself. Fortunately Clarissa was busy with her drink.

"I'm so sorry," said Leslie as soon as he could respond. "What a terrible shock. Whatever happened?"

"He went in his sleep," Clarissa replied, speaking rapidly now. "When I got up this morning I was surprised that he wasn't downstairs already; he always got up before me. We've had separate rooms since his illness." This might have helped explain George's apparent ability to ignore Clarissa's irregular hours. "Have a drink," Clarissa said distractedly, picking up the bottle and looking around for a second glass. Her hand was shaking.

"No, thank you," replied Leslie. "I won't stay long, I'm sure you have a lot—"

Clarissa interrupted him, her manner suddenly agitated. "You must stay," she said in an urgent tone. "At least for a bit. I never could stand being in this house on my own and now... Well, it's intolerable. That's why I've just been to Temple to..." she hesitated for a moment, "to get someone to come and stay with me. They're on their way now."

If it was the boyfriend, as Leslie supposed, it was in appalling taste, and would surely annul any sympathy that Clarissa might otherwise have received from the village. Leslie could hardly say so, and he replied instead, "At least he didn't suffer. But how dreadful for you. It must have been very sudden; I saw him only yesterday."

Clarissa described the trepidation with which she had entered George's bedroom, the horror of finding his body, the phone call to the doctor, and soon afterwards the doctor's arrival. While she was speaking, Leslie looked round the opulent room. Everything was obviously still as it was from the previous evening: there was George's solitary glass and the bottle of port and his old-fashioned fountain pen on the little table by his chair, and the brown checked blanket thrown over the arm. Leslie pictured George sitting in solitude in his final hours, drinking alone and with the blanket over his knees, and he felt overcome by the pathos of the situation. Then he noticed the chess set, George's beloved chess set, and the thought that Bennett and George had played their last game together was almost too much.

"What a terrible shock for you," Leslie said again kindly. Loathsome as Clarissa was, sympathy got the better of him, as it always did.

It was a relief to hear the sound of a vehicle turning into the drive. Clarissa turned eagerly towards the window as the car drove past and round to the back of the house. Anxious to avoid an embarrassing encounter, and relieved to be able to go, Leslie jumped up and bade a hasty farewell, shoving his feet into his boots and lacing them as quickly as he could. This time Clarissa made no effort to delay him, and was still standing by the window, rigid and alert, when he left the house.

Leslie went home along the lane. It was a longer walk, but he suddenly had no energy for stiles and muddy footpaths, and he wanted time to think. It was impossible to guess what effect the news would have on Bennett, but Leslie was sure that, whatever his feelings were, Bennett would keep them to himself. For Leslie though, all sentiments were eclipsed by an overwhelming sense of regret. The knowledge that George had gone to the grave with the burden of an undisclosed problem was one that could never be resolved, and he blamed himself for not having been more persistent the previous day. If only he had persuaded George to speak to Bennett then. He should have tried harder. What was he thinking of, abandoning him to Edgar like that? It was with a very heavy heart that Leslie made his way down the road.

Bennett was standing by the French windows when Leslie got home, looking out into the garden. Sombre music was playing in the background; a movement from Mozart's requiem, Leslie thought. "It's bad news, I'm afraid," he said sadly. "In fact, it couldn't be worse."

"Dead?" Bennett turned to face Leslie as he spoke.

Leslie nodded.

"I guessed as much." Bennett sounded matter-of-fact, but there was a melancholy look in his eyes. "George was a stickler for punctuality and always reliable. When he didn't even phone, I knew it had to be serious. Shall I pour you a drink?"

"No, it's all right," replied Leslie, "I think I'll put the kettle on," and he retired to the sanctuary of his kitchen. A few minutes later he reappeared with a tray bearing a cafetiere for Bennett and a pot of camomile tea for himself, and he went through the morning's events in full detail. "There's something very odd about Clarissa," Leslie said thoughtfully.

"I think we already know that, but what was it this time?"

"It was her reaction," replied Leslie, "I can't quite explain it. She didn't try to play the grief-stricken widow I'm glad to say, though she certainly seemed stunned. But there was something strange about her response; something I can't quite put my finger on."

Both men sat quietly with their thoughts for a time.

"Standing there by the window, she looked like a frightened animal," he said after a while. "She did say she hated being in the house alone, so perhaps that was it," he said, doubtfully. "I started to feel sorry for her, but then I heard the car arrive, presumably with the boyfriend. It couldn't really have been him, could it?" exclaimed Leslie, with sudden outrage. "George can't have been gone twelve hours; surely even Clarissa wouldn't stoop that low?"

"Who else from Temple would Clarissa invite to the house?" asked Bennett.

"I don't know when I've ever been more disgusted." Leslie got up and walked restlessly across the room. He stared out into the garden and felt another surge of remorse that he had not persuaded George to divulge his secret.

"While you're over there," said Bennett, "would you pass me the phone? I'm going to ring Paul. I need to see him."

"Are you feeling bad?" Leslie could feel the panic rising. Paul was one of the local GPs, now semi-retired, but the only doctor in the practice Bennett would ever consent to seeing. "It's not chest pain is it? Perhaps it's the shock. If it's your heart I'll call an ambulance."

"You'll be the one having a heart attack in a minute," said Bennett without emotion. "I'm fine." He took the phone from Leslie. "Damn," he muttered. "It's Sunday and the surgery will be shut. I suppose I'll have to bother him at home."

Leslie knew that Paul never minded being bothered by Bennett, as the relationship between them was more as friends than of clinician and patient. In fact, Leslie and Bennett had started as different sorts of clients of the doctor, renting a holiday cottage from him in the village every Easter. Some of their Easter breaks had been eventful, with the men calling on Paul's services for tonsillitis, a sprained ankle and, on one alarming occasion, a peculiar and violent allergic reaction. In return, a strange coincidence of circumstances one year had resulted in Bennett unexpectedly solving a mystery for the doctor and saving him from potential litigation. They had got to know each other well.

Six years ago, when Leslie and Bennett had arrived in Dartonleigh on Maundy Thursday, Paul had greeted them with the unwelcome news that he was selling the cottage as he was retiring from full-time practice. It would be their last holiday there. This news fell like a blow to the two men. Their Easter holiday in Dartonleigh was always an oasis in the year, and that year they had particularly needed its respite. Disenchanted with their jobs, Leslie suffering relentless bullying from an inadequate manager and Bennett disillusioned by academia, it was the last thing they needed. Quickly, however, the disappointment had generated an idea which then materialised into a plan. By the Easter Monday they had put in an offer for the cottage. Now here they were; it was their home. Over the subsequent years mutual respect between them all had mellowed into friendship and the doctor now found any excuse to call in on the two men.

"Good to see you both," said Paul, arriving half an hour later. "You're looking well, Bennett. I put my bag in the car, despite what you said on the phone, but it looks like I won't be needing it. Now, spill the beans, man. I know you haven't brought me over here for nothing."

"It's George Harrington-Thomas. You've heard he's dead?"

"Yes. Very sad. They rang me this morning. He'd been my patient for years."

"He was coming here this morning to talk to me about a shock he'd had. Les can tell you about it."

Leslie, still ignorant of why Bennett had summoned the doctor, obediently recounted the story in detail. Paul sat listening patiently, and when Leslie had finished speaking Bennett resumed.

"There may be no connection," said Bennett, calmly, "but about six weeks ago, the last time George came down here for a game of chess, he told me that someone was trying to blackmail him."

"What?" exclaimed Leslie, astonished at this news, though not that Bennett would have kept it a secret. "You never mentioned it."

Bennett made no answer and Paul said, "Did he know who it was?"

"I don't believe so," said Bennett.

"Did he go to the police?" asked Paul. "And have you any idea what they were blackmailing him about?"

"I don't know any more. He didn't say," replied Bennett.

"I don't suppose you even asked him," exclaimed Leslie in exasperation.

"You're right, I didn't," replied Bennett.

"I suppose you're wondering about the cause of death now," said Paul. "Is that it?"

"Yes," answered Bennett, "especially as it seems very sudden. He was well enough to be at The Woodman, having a drink and being shocked by something, yesterday."

The doctor sat thoughtfully for a while. "I must admit," he said at last, "I was surprised that he'd gone so quickly, but I didn't think too much about it. It does happen like that sometimes. I don't know which doctor attended him; I believe Clarissa phoned through at about a quarter to seven this morning so it would be whoever was on call last night." He drank his coffee thoughtfully. "You don't know if the body was still at the house when you were there, Leslie, or where it had been taken?" he asked.

"I didn't give it a thought," replied Leslie, shuddering with horror as he did so now. "Could he have been left in the house? Don't they send paramedics out to try and revive the person, even if it seems hopeless?"

"If the case is terminal and a plan has been agreed, the deceased is fortunately spared those indignities," said Paul.

"Yes, of course," said Leslie.

"I think I'll go and pay our Clarissa a sympathetic visit," the doctor said, thoughtfully. "I'll go straightaway. Please don't give any of this another thought, either of you. I don't want you worried by this, Bennett, just when you're on the mend. Nor you, Leslie; you've had quite enough to cope with. If this matter needs following up, you can leave that to me."

"While you're at the house, there's a photograph of George I'd like to have," Bennett said rather unexpectedly. "I'll take a copy and return the original to Clarissa, of course. It's in the sitting room on a table with some other photos. It's an old picture of George when he was up at Oxford, holding a trophy. I sat opposite it whenever I went there to play chess. I must have looked at it for many hours over the last few years."

"I'll ask Clarissa. I'm sure she'll let you borrow it."

Moved by Bennett's request, Leslie started to feel overcome again and was glad that the doctor had finished his coffee and was now standing up to go.

"I'll let you know what happens," he said as he took his leave, "but I don't want either of you worrying."

* * *

About half an hour later, Leslie answered the phone. "That was Paul," he said when the call was over. "He's been to the house and the body isn't there. But there's a strange thing: nor is that photograph." According to the doctor, Clarissa knew exactly which picture Bennett wanted but, when she went to fetch it, it had gone. She had seemed very surprised, and couldn't remember when she saw it last. "Clarissa is going to ask Jackie Thackeray, the cleaner, and give us a call if it turns up," said Leslie. "She also said to go up any time you like and you can take another one." Leslie smiled wryly at such an idea, and then his thoughts turned back to the reason that the doctor had gone up to The Grange. "Do you really think that George's death might not have been natural?" he asked.

"Perhaps," replied Bennett, "but we'll have to wait and see."

There was a pause and then Leslie said, "I take it you don't think that George took his own life?"

"Highly unlikely, with his beliefs."

"Then that would mean he'd been murdered," Leslie said, aghast at the thought. "Why would someone murder George? Why would anyone murder a dying man?"

5

From his vantage point in the kitchen, Leslie could see all the comings and goings outside as he prepared lunch. A couple of old chaps were heading for The Woodman, and they passed the time of day with two ladies, strolling towards the shop. The whole of Dartonleigh, he knew, would be preoccupied by now with the news about George which undoubtedly would have spread throughout the village. Leslie guessed that had he called in at The Woodman, he would have observed the old men drinking their pints more silently than usual, in morose contemplation of their own mortality. In The Daffodil, tea and cakes were no doubt being served up along with philosophical reflections on the brevity of life and the unpredictability of its termination. In the shop, the speculations would very likely be directed at the terms of the will and the future of the lovers.

Lunch was a sombre affair, with Bennett absorbed in his thoughts and Leslie wrestling with a multitude of unhappy feelings. After lunch Leslie went across to the shop and, as he had anticipated, George's sudden demise was the only topic of conversation.

"I can't believe it," said Janet. "It was so sudden at the end. I knew something was amiss when he didn't come down for his paper this morning, with him being so regular in his habits. Then Leslie came in asking after him, didn't you, Leslie? I had a feeling then. I know he looked rough the previous morning, but not as you'd expect him to go like that. Very breathless, but he'd been like that for a while."

Bearing knowledge that he couldn't share, Leslie said as little as possible. For the time being, information about blackmail and unexplained shocks would have to be kept to himself and, unlike Bennett who divulged nothing unless he had to, Leslie's nature was far from secretive. He maintained an uncomfortable silence but this passed unnoticed amid the thrill of gossip.

Vera had evidently come into the shop simply to talk today and was not even pretending to buy anything. She was full of news. "When I was in the post office yesterday, I heard that there had been a row during the morning between George and Jeff Clayden. Veronika told them all about it. A right ding-dong it was, by all accounts."

It was no secret that there was no love lost between George and his neighbours Jeff and Veronika. At any other time, an altercation between them would have barely caught Leslie's notice, and he would have dismissed most of the details as speculation. But today it held his attention.

"Everyone's saying that it finished George off; a strain on the heart. Of course, Veronika's playing it down today, and making out it was only a little tiff, but that's not what she was saying yesterday."

"What was the row about?" asked Irene. "Do you think George found out, at last, about Clarissa's affair with Jeff? Or maybe he knew all along and just couldn't put up with it any longer."

"I don't know if she's still at it with him now that she's got the artist," said Vera. "But anyway, the argument wasn't about that. It was about the planning permission."

"It seems such a shame to fall out with neighbours," Janet sighed. "Live and let live, that's my motto."

"I don't blame George one bit," replied Vera energetically. "From what I heard, Jeff wants to build a big modern house right on the boundary of the two properties. Apparently it would stand directly between Compton Grange and the view across the moor. No one in their right mind would put up with that."

"Jeff is a builder, after all," said Irene. "What can you expect?"

"It makes you wonder why Jeff didn't just wait for a bit." Janet absentmindedly rearranged a row of local jams on the counter as she spoke. "Everyone knew George only had a few months left, and Clarissa wasn't likely to bother. She'll probably sell up anyway; it's well known that she hates the house."

"Veronika and Jeff have money problems. Didn't you know? It's being said that they need the planning permission quickly," said Vera.

"Then how can he afford to build a new property if they're short of money?" Irene asked.

"Someone said he was selling the plot of land with the planning permission," said Vera. "I don't think he was going to build on it himself."

"I don't suppose Clarissa will be interested in taking up the case," said Irene.

"Absolutely not," laughed Vera. "Now she's got the lover-boy installed, the only part of the house she'll be interested in is the bedroom."

Another vilification of Clarissa's character began, and Leslie, tired of it all, politely interrupted them to pay for the vegetables he had come in for and took his leave.

Back at the cottage, Bennett had retreated to the library in what seemed to be a sombre mood. Leslie took consolation in cooking. He set to work on the Sunday roast in the reassuring knowledge that Bennett, who rarely seemed to be comforted with words, would at least take solace in eating. North Dartonleigh Farm had supplied the chicken, and Leslie put from his mind the disquieting thought that he had perhaps once seen it happily scratching about in the field along the lane. He started preparing it for roasting, toying briefly with the idea of removing the fatty skin, in deference to Bennett's arteries, but this was the tastiest part and Bennett would surely notice. Instead, he brushed it with the merest spoonful of olive oil, rubbed in dried herbs instead of salt and placed it on a rack in the roasting tin to allow the fat to drain away during cooking. Next, he prepared the stuffing; he always enjoyed making his own. He chopped onion and apple finely and pulled a few leaves of sage from the plants on the window ledge, rinsed them, and set to work with his best knife. He scraped the mixture into a bowl and stirred in the breadcrumbs, adding a beaten egg. The bowl was put aside to stand while he attended to the vegetables.

As he peeled and chopped and stirred, Leslie considered the perplexing events of the last twenty-four hours: the mystery shock, the secret of which George had taken to the grave, and the astonishing news of the blackmail threat. Who on earth would want to blackmail George? And what skeleton could have been rattling round in George's cupboard with which he could be threatened? Leslie wasn't in the least surprised that Bennett had not confided his knowledge of the blackmail threat to him, but that did not prevent him from wishing that he had. There was the sudden death itself and Clarissa's indecent behaviour in bringing her lover straight into the house. The more he thought about it, the more he tormented himself with the recollection of how close he had been to knowing what had disturbed George. Just one sentence more, that was all. What a time for Edgar to come blundering in. Bennett was right, Edgar was a fool; a complete and utter imbecile. Then Leslie remembered the prowler. Was that only the night before last? It seemed like months ago.

Later, these issues were still preoccupying his mind as he brought coffee into the sitting room after dinner. He paused in the doorway. "Bach?" he enquired, screwing up his face at the orchestral music issuing from the speakers.

Bennett nodded. "Not in the mood?"

"You know I find Bach agitating at the best of times," said Leslie. "Too many notes."

Bennett silenced Johann Sebastian mid-phrase and, a minute later, the melodious sounds of *Clair de Lune* filled the room. The music, combined with the satisfying roast dinner, had the desired therapeutic effect, not least because Leslie knew that Bennett had chosen a piece which was to Leslie's, not his own, particular liking. After a while, the two men returned to the only possible topic of conversation.

"Do you think there's any connection between any of these events, Bennett?" Leslie asked when he had gone over everything that was on his mind.

"Let's wait until we hear what Paul has to say." Bennett went to the sideboard, poured two glasses of Madeira from the decanter, and passed one to Leslie.

Leslie swilled his glass round pensively. "I could kick myself that I didn't try harder to persuade George to say what was on his mind, or to convince him to come back here and speak to you. I feel so bad that he died without having had the chance to share his problem. If there's any way I can find out what he was going to tell us, I mean to try. I feel I owe it to him." He spoke rather defensively, expecting Bennett to dismiss the idea.

Instead, Bennett replied, "You think that the shock he mentioned had happened not long before he spoke to you? He didn't sound as though he was talking about something that had happened earlier in the day? Nothing to do with that row between him and Jeff that they were talking about in the shop?"

Leslie had, as always, regaled Bennett with the story in verbatim detail. He considered Bennett's question as he took a sip from his glass. "I'm almost certain it had happened in the pub just before I saw him," he said. "He looked awful, still with what looked like the physical effects of a shock. His face was a terrible colour and his hands were shaking."

"Who was in the pub when you went in?"

Leslie thought for a moment. "The snug was packed, but George was down the end in the lounge bar which was pretty deserted. I think there was another table occupied but I didn't notice the people. Daniel was at the bar explaining the cake disaster to the landlady. I think that was it."

"Did you see anyone coming out as you went in?"

There was another pause. "Only Kenny. I think he was coming from the gents so he must have passed through the lounge." Leslie was thoughtful for a while. "I'm certain that George would have said nothing to Edgar about the shock after I left. He clammed up the minute Edgar appeared. I'll only ask Edgar as a last resort; it would be round the village in five minutes."

"George wouldn't disclose anything to Edgar," agreed Bennett. "Who did you say was behind the bar when you went into the pub?"

"It was Cheryl. She was talking to Daniel, presumably about the cakes he was supposed to be delivering."

"It's possible she saw something," said Bennett, helping himself to a handful of nuts from the bowl on the sideboard.

He cracked a walnut, oblivious to the fragments of shell that flew onto the carpet. "Why not speak to her? You might be able to find out if anything had happened."

"Why don't you come as well?" said Leslie half an hour later, as he was putting his jacket on. "It'd do you good to get out for a change." Bennett declined, just as Leslie had expected he would, and he reluctantly took himself off alone. It had been a very long day and he wasn't in any mood for socialising, but he was galvanised by determination to find out what it was that George had so nearly told him.

In the pub it was easy to fall into conversation with the landlady, and it was natural enough to talk about George. "I can't believe he's gone," said Cheryl as she handed Leslie his drink. "He was one of my regulars. He used to come down for a bit of company, I think. And for it to happen so sudden like that. He seemed fine, all things considered, when he came in yesterday lunchtime. I was just saying so to Jackie."

"It's funny you should say that," said Leslie, "because when I came in, he was looking quite peaky. Really rather unwell, in fact, and not himself at all. I was wondering if something had upset him."

"I didn't see anything, but I was busy serving the snug, this side, most of the time. George was back there in the lounge," said Cheryl nodding towards the lounge behind her. The bar was in the centre of the pub and served both rooms. "Didn't you ask him what the matter was?"

"I was about to, but Edgar joined us, and I didn't really like to then."

"You're thinking that maybe something happened to upset him, and that's what finished him off?"

Leslie was spared answering this as Cheryl excused herself to serve another customer. Leslie sat with his drink, disappointed that his investigation seemed to have come to such an abrupt end.

Returning to Leslie, Cheryl said, "I've just thought – that new woman was in the lounge bar yesterday when George was in there. You know the one I mean. She's opened that weird health shop in Temple – the woman with the hair and beads. She was in here with a friend. They might have seen something."

"You mean Gloria?" said Leslie. "Of course, I remember now seeing her when I came in. She was sitting with a younger lady in the opposite corner to George. Perhaps I'll ask her if I see her." Leslie spoke rather cautiously. Gloria had recently moved into the neighbourhood, opening an alternative therapy shop in Temple Ducton. She was large and exuberant and, although she lived a few miles out towards Temple, she had joined everything in Dartonleigh that could be joined. The few encounters Leslie had had with her had been somewhat overwhelming.

A middle-aged man now came into the snug. He spotted Leslie and joined him, perching up on a bar stool at the counter next to him.

"Evening, Martin," said Leslie. "Hello there, Cromwell." This last greeting was to the dog which accompanied him, a wiry grey lurcher. Cromwell ambled across and, after a cursory snuffle at Leslie's shoes, set about scavenging for scraps dropped by earlier patrons. "We were just talking about George," Leslie said, as Cheryl came over to take Martin's order. "Dreadful business."

"Poor old sod," Martin replied gloomily. "Decent chap, too."

"Leslie was just saying he looked like he'd had an upset in here yesterday, but I didn't see anything," said Cheryl. "Now if it had been a few days earlier, when Jeff Clayden was in here, I shouldn't have been surprised if he'd dropped dead on the spot."

"Whatever happened?" asked Leslie.

"They were having a right set to," Cheryl said.

"Apparently Jeff was rowing with George yesterday morning as well," said Leslie. "Someone said it was about the new house that Jeff wants to build; the planning permission for it."

"That's exactly what they were arguing about in here. I had to tell Jeff to pack it in; raising his voice to George like that. I can't have that in the pub." Cheryl handed Martin his pint. "'Rich bastards like you fink you rule the bleedin' place'. That's what he said," said Cheryl in a greatly exaggerated imitation of Jeff's London accent. "'You've cost me a fortune, an absolute bleedin' fortune, money I can't afford, and you won't even be alive by the time the property's built. It won't even affect you, you selfish bastard'. It was all very upsetting, but you should have heard George's reply. Calm and dignified, he was. 'I care about what happens to my estate after I have gone', he said. 'I don't know if you are capable of understanding that. I care about Dartonleigh, about the environment, about the Dartmoor National Park, and about cowboys like you lining your pockets at the expense of the countryside. It's not about me, it's about something far more important: it's about principles, it's about what's right'. It was quite a speech. 'Winston Churchill eat your heart out', I thought at the time."

"I wonder what Jeff meant about it having cost him a fortune," said Leslie. "I suppose he must have paid an architect to draw up the plans."

"I don't know," said Cheryl. "It wasn't those exact words, of course, but it was something like that." She broke off to serve another customer.

"George was quite right," said Martin. "We've got to stand up against all these new-builds in the area. There are new houses, absolute monstrosities, springing up everywhere. My wife works in the planning office in Lymeford and she's really worried about some of the decisions that are being made. Have you seen that eyesore on the road into Stretton Cross? It's completely out of keeping with the area. I can't believe it was allowed, and I know that George had raised his concerns with the council about it. There aren't enough people with principles, like George. We'll miss him."

"He'll be missed at the chess club too, I expect," said Leslie.

"Yes, he was a bloody good player. Not as good as Bennett, of course, but probably the only person in the club who could really take him on." Martin was being modest for Leslie knew that Bennett enjoyed playing him, a sure sign of a good opponent.

"While we're on the subject," said Leslie, "why don't you come round to the house for a game with Bennett some time? I know he'd appreciate it, especially now he's lost his regular chess partner."

"He'll slaughter me. He always does," said Martin glumly. Then he laughed. "Of course I'll come round, I'd be delighted, if only for one of your legendary cakes. Get him to message me."

"How is the club going?" asked Leslie. Since George's health had declined, Martin had taken over as club chairman.

"Pretty good; it's growing all the time," Martin answered. "People who retire to the village want something to do and there seems to be no shortage of folk moving here. That's why people like Jeff Clayden are tempted to stick up houses where they've no business putting them."

Cheryl had re-joined them now, and she leant over the bar and spoke in a lower voice. "As Jeff was storming out, he said a terrible thing to George. He turned and said, 'It's bad luck about your illness, George; bad luck it didn't kill you six months ago'."

"Bastard," said Martin with feeling. He reached down and stroked Cromwell's grizzled back, and the men sat on in a gloomy silence until their drinks were finished.

On his way out of the pub Leslie's attention was arrested by a photo on the wall. It was a picture he had walked past hundreds of times, but this evening it caught his eye. It showed a group of men and women, Bennett among their number, standing in proud and cheerful company at a presentation ceremony, with George in the foreground holding a trophy. The photo had been taken about a year after Bennett and Leslie had moved to Dartonleigh. The caption read: *George Harrington-Thomas, Dartonleigh Chess Club chairman, receives the Devon and Southwest Championship club trophy.*

Leslie plodded home.

6

It wasn't until breakfast the next day that Leslie was able to recount the evening's events. Bennett had taken himself off to bed by the time Leslie had got in and did not stir, having a capacity for sleep that Leslie envied.

"Jeff is a nasty piece of work," said Leslie, having related the whole story. "What a terrible thing to say to George. By the way, I suggested Martin came round. You'll be needing a new chess partner."

Leslie added the last sentence with some hesitation, Bennett being unpredictable about having arrangements made on his behalf. He was relieved when Bennett replied, "Good man, I'll give him a call."

As he was clearing away the dishes, Leslie suddenly exclaimed that he hadn't been back to see Annie at The Daffodil, to find out what was behind the incident when Daniel was sent home early. The distressing events of the previous day had put it out of his mind. "I'll hurry across there now," said Leslie, hanging up his apron. "I should catch Annie before the customers start arriving." He was, therefore, surprised to see a gathering of ladies already around the counter when he went in.

"Leslie, Leslie!" exclaimed Marian, vigorously beckoning him. "It was murder!" she hissed. "Murder! George didn't die, he was murdered!"

Although he and Bennett had been the ones to raise the alarm, it was still distressing to hear the word spoken. For the second time in two days, Leslie felt his head swim. Clutching a chair for support he said, "Never!"

"It was poison," Marian whispered with grim delight. "Clarissa poisoned him with arsenic."

"Never!" Leslie repeated, this time with complete incredulity.

"Well, that's what Angela said in the post office," Vera interrupted. "But Irene heard that George caught Clarissa with the boyfriend, and there was a fight, and George's heart gave out on him."

"Where did all this come from?" asked Leslie.

"Jackie went up to the Grange this morning," said Marian. "It's the day she does for them. The place was crawling with police and there was blue tape across the entrance. They told her she couldn't go in; it's a crime scene. Clarissa and the artist, the boyfriend, have been taken to the police station in Lymeford. They must have done him in."

Leslie was still reeling at this news when Annie cut in. "Come on now, ladies," she said. "I'd better be getting on. There'll be customers in soon and I won't be ready for them at this rate." She skilfully ushered them from the premises, still chattering and whispering and exclaiming as they went. "What a crowd of witches," Annie said when they were out of earshot. "I don't believe a word of it. It's probably some routine police procedure following a death, and they've made a complete three-act drama out of it."

Leslie, who had knowledge about George's death that was unknown to Annie, was relieved that he was spared responding, for she was already making her way towards the stairs. "Let's go up to the flat where we won't be overheard," she said. "Laura can manage on her own down here for ten minutes or so; there won't be many customers in for a while."

Annie occupied the rooms above the teashop while it was open from March to October every year, after which she fled the British winter and joined her husband in some hot country where he worked – Dubai, Leslie thought. It seemed a strange way of going on to Leslie, for whom the short separation from Bennett when he was in hospital had been agony, but it seemed to suit Annie well enough.

He followed her up the narrow staircase and into the lounge, a beautiful and very quaint oak-beamed room with a low crooked doorway, thick casement windows and a perilously uneven floor. On any other occasion Leslie would have been utterly charmed by it, but today, with his mind distracted from everything except the macabre events surrounding George's death, he struggled even to bring his thoughts to bear on the purpose of his visit.

"I'll be glad to tell you why I sent Daniel home early," Annie began, "but it does involve some information I've been keeping confidential."

"Please don't feel obliged to tell me anything," said Leslie hastily. "I'd hate to—"

"No, it's all right," Annie interrupted. "In fact it would be a relief to tell someone, and I know I can trust you with what I'm going to say. I'll have to start at the beginning, though, so please bear with me."

Leslie waited while she marshalled her thoughts.

"Daniel is the son of Linda, a very old friend of mine," she began. "Linda has sent him down here to stay with his aunt who lives just outside Temple while he retakes his exams. He failed them all at school last summer and, according to Linda, it's because he got in with the wrong crowd. He went back to college in September and, straightaway, he seemed to find another bad crowd to fall in with. Linda is determined that he's going to get to university, so she took him out of college and moved him down here. He goes to evening classes at the college in Tiverley. He has to work during the day to pay for his keep with his aunt, and for the first couple of months he had a job at The Imperial Hotel, working in their leisure club. He's quite a sporty type and he used to help in the pool and fitness centre.

"Just before Easter I had a call from Linda, to ask if I had any work available, because he wasn't needed at The Imperial any more. Daniel had told her that there were a lot of changes in the hotel and they were laying off all the temps. I was desperate for seasonal staff at the time so I jumped at the offer and agreed to take him on. I didn't think to ask for references, or anything like that, what with Linda being an old friend.

"Soon after I'd agreed to take Daniel on, I was surprised to receive a call from his aunt. She's a nurse at the hospital in Tiverley and I get the impression she's a bit of a Tartar. She wanted me to know that things weren't quite what they seemed. Daniel had actually been asked to leave the leisure club – sacked, really.

He wouldn't admit it to her at first, he told her the same story as he told his mother, but the aunt could see through him. In fact, she'd been having a few problems with him since he went to stay with her. There's a nightclub in Tiverley and he'd been missing his evening classes, staying out late and then wasn't fit to go to work the next day. He'd been absent and late for work several times and in the end he admitted that's why he'd been dismissed."

"Oh dear," said Leslie, "he seems to have a talent for getting in with the wrong crowd."

"Quite," said Annie. "I obviously thought twice about taking him on after that but, to be honest, I was pretty desperate for staff at the time. I'd had to turn away Jackie's boy, Jamie, who was a complete liability last summer, and I'd had no other replies to my job ads. In any case, I thought I'd give him a chance."

"Well, that does explain a few things," laughed Leslie. "Bennett and I had been wondering what he was doing here. It's hardly the usual thing a lad like that does for a gap year."

"I know," sighed Annie. "He's been telling everyone, especially the girls, that he has a place next year on a sports science degree course at Loughborough. He's very plausible. The fast and furious cycling is all part of his training, according to him; nothing about having to be at evening classes on time, or at home for tea with the aunt."

"It's good of you not to give him away."

"I wouldn't do a thing like that," said Annie. "I believe in giving people a chance; we were all young once. In any case, I do genuinely feel for the boy. His father buggered off with another woman when Daniel was in his early teens. Soon after that Linda was diagnosed with cancer, and she's been fighting it on and off for years. He goes about with that swagger, but it's all a front. Many times I've caught him off guard, and underneath I believe he's a bag of nerves.

"But, for all that, unfortunately I've been having trouble with him myself, and that's what the fuss was about when I sent him home early. Nothing to do with the cakes. That was an accident, though if he'd made two journeys across like I told him to, it wouldn't have happened. No, this was about money; the tips, to be precise. All gratuities given by the customers here are split between the staff. They're put straight into a moneybox behind the counter and shared out at the end of the week. The cash tips don't usually amount to much these days, but it all adds up, so they still go into the box. I made that quite clear to Daniel on the first day. Soon after, Laura, the young waitress, came to tell me that Daniel was pocketing any tips he took. I challenged him about it, and he claimed he didn't realise that they were to be shared. I asked him what he thought the damn great moneybox behind the counter was for, and he made a cheeky comment about having been worked too hard since he'd been here to notice it."

"Oh dear." From what he'd seen of him, Leslie could imagine Daniel brazening it out.

"Yes," agreed Annie, "I would have preferred an apology. As you can imagine, I've been watching him like a hawk since. It's been hard to catch him at it, because he's been putting some of the tips in the box, but I knew he was still keeping most of the money. The other day, when he went across to the pub with the gateaux bases, I made him take his apron off. I thought there was something funny about the way he folded it up and put it out of the way. When he'd gone, I picked it up. The front pocket was full of cash; he'd obviously picked up quite a few good tips. Naturally he said he'd intended to put it in the moneybox later, he just hadn't got round to it, but there was no question in my mind that he was lying. It was his dishonesty that bothered me, not the money which wasn't really enough to be bothered about. I sent him home, as you know, and when he came in yesterday I gave him a final warning. He won't be waiting at table, or be anywhere near the money, from now on." There was a pause. Annie pursed her lips and looked grim. "I might as well tell you the rest while I'm about it," she said. "It's not the only trouble there's been with him. He hadn't been here a week when George came down to the teashop to tell me he'd caught Daniel smoking cannabis in the woods up by Stag Lane. George said he'd given him a ticking off, and threatened to tell his aunt if he caught him at it again, but he wanted to warn me. I dare say it's common practice among youngsters, if I did but know, but I don't have to like it."

"And you're going to keep him on?" Leslie queried.

"I need the staff," said Annie, more emphatically this time. "But there's another reason. Daniel's mother is in the middle of another course of cancer treatment at the moment. As I said, she's a really old friend and I just couldn't worry her right now. She's already at her wits end with Daniel, and blaming herself because she thinks her illness has made him the way he is. I know that the aunt hasn't told her about his late-night drinking and clubbing or that he was really sacked from the leisure club." Annie sighed and shook her head. "I wanted you to know. I'd hate you to think me capable of punishing the kid because he dropped a few cakes." She stood up, suddenly brisk again and ready to get back to work. Leslie followed back down and into the teashop. He went to the counter to buy a loaf. There seemed to be nothing but trouble at the moment, and that called for hot, creamy soup for lunch. Some granary bread would be the perfect accompaniment.

"Don't forget it's mahjong tomorrow evening," Annie said as Leslie was leaving. "Marjory is hosting it at The Cedars. Do come; no excuses. We all need cheering up a bit at the moment."

7

There was no leisure for Leslie to contemplate the morning's astonishing developments for, as he turned towards his cottage, he saw a couple of policemen walking up the front path. They were, to his dismay, the same officers who had called only two days earlier. Hurrying across the road, he arrived at the gate as Bennett was letting them in. "Good morning, gentlemen," Bennett was saying suavely. "To what do we owe the pleasure of this return visit? Perhaps you have come to tell us that you have identified the prowler who disturbed us recently. If not, I am afraid we are rather busy."

The policemen seemed to be unperturbed by these audacious remarks. Ignoring Bennett's comments, the taller policeman, PC Overton, spoke. "We're here in connection with the death of George Harrington-Thompson," he said.

"Harrington-Thomas," corrected Leslie.

"As I said, George Harrington-Thomas," replied Overton.

"So, it was murder after all," said Leslie. "Everyone's saying so in the village. It's hard to take it in."

"We are here to ask you about the call you made to the local doctor." PC Overton had adopted a pompous air today. "I understand that one of you contacted him with some information."

Leslie grudgingly showed them through into the sitting room. He had taken a great aversion to these two officers and fancied that PC Overton was surveying the room like an estate agent valuing the property. He felt an irrational resentment when Overton, on being invited to take a seat, made himself at home in Leslie's favourite armchair. PC Dunn, the shorter man, perched on the settee.

"We received a report that you contacted the local doctor regarding the deceased," said PC Overton. "Why was that?"

Leslie began by explaining his encounter with George in the pub, and PC Dunn silently took notes.

"You didn't get any clue about the nature of this shock, then? He gave you no idea of the cause?"

Leslie replied in the negative.

"What about this blackmail threat, then?"

"Bennett can tell you about that," said Leslie.

The tall officer turned to Bennett.

"It was just over six weeks ago that George told me about it," said Bennett, and gave the exact date. "George had come here to play chess, as he often did. He played badly and the game was over quickly. He apologised, saying something like, 'Sorry about the rotten game I'm not quite myself. The truth is I've had a threatening phone call – a blackmail attempt'. I said that if there was anything I could do, and so on. He replied, 'Thanks, just keep it to yourself. I don't want a thing like that getting about'."

"The threat was made by phone, was it, not a letter or any kind of message?"

"That's what he said," said Bennett.

"Oh!" exclaimed Leslie, "you might be able to trace his phone calls if he'd had the blackmail call on the same day he came to play chess." PC Overton gave Leslie a withering look, and Leslie was irritated with himself for stating the obvious and giving the policeman the pleasure of despising him. He felt fated to make a fool of himself in this man's presence.

"And the blackmailer was a man?"

"I believe so. George said 'he'."

"But he didn't say, or even hint, who he thought it might be?" said the officer.

"No."

"Do you know if he took any action? Did he give this blackmailer anything, or do whatever it was the blackmailer wanted?"

"I have no idea," said Bennett.

"He didn't give you any more information?"

Bennett shook his head.

"Did he say anything to you?" said the policeman, addressing Leslie.

"Oh no, I wasn't present," replied Leslie. "I don't play chess. I'm a mahjong man."

"Mahjong?"

"Oh yes," replied Leslie. "Mahjong club. We play most weeks at different houses, or sometimes at The Woodman."

PC Dunn paused uncertainly in his notetaking, and Overton spoke to Bennett again. "And did you see Harrington-Thompson again after that?"

"Harrington-Thomas," Leslie corrected again.

"I only saw him once more," continued Bennett. "It was the following week. I played chess with him again, up at the Grange that time."

"Did he say if he'd had any further threats?"

"No."

"Did he mention the blackmail?"

"No."

"You didn't ask him about it at all?"

"No," repeated Bennett.

The officer seemed unconvinced that George had disclosed nothing further to Bennett, but he turned to Leslie. "Did you speak to—," he checked his own notes and said with ostentatious care, "Harrington-Thomas about the blackmail?"

"Oh no," replied Leslie. "I didn't hear about it until after George's death. The first I knew about it was when Bennett told the doctor the other day."

There was another pause and this time PC Dunn spoke. "Do you know if Harrington-Thomas had any enemies?"

"It would certainly seem as though he did," remarked Bennett.

Dunn ignored this comment and turned to Leslie. "Anyone you can think of who might blackmail him or—" He caught a warning glance from his colleague, "Or anything?"

Distrust overwhelmed Leslie's strong natural openness. In the last twenty-four hours there had emerged no shortage of people who had unfriendly feelings towards George but, in any case, none of them, surely, could have a motive for blackmail or murder. He shook his head. The police would have to hear about them from someone else.

"And neither of you have any idea of what the nature of the blackmail threat might have been?"

Both men answered in the negative.

There were a few more questions before the two policemen got up and made their way to the front door. As they were about to leave Bennett said, "I suggest that you make enquiries about a man who has been staying at The Woodman for the last few days."

PC Overton raised his eyebrows.

"Who's he?" he asked.

"That's what I have been wondering," responded Bennett.

"Why do you mention him?" said the officer, unable to disguise his impatience. His irritation was hardly surprising, Leslie thought; Bennett could be very provoking.

"He arrived here three days ago pretending to be a walker," replied Bennett, "but he isn't one."

"I'm not sure what you mean," replied the officer, guardedly.

Bennett impassively pointed out the coincidence of the young man's arrival and George's decease and stated that if Leslie said he wasn't a walker, then that was good enough for him. He declined any further explanation.

The officer asked for a description of the man.

"He's slim, with light brown hair, about five-foot ten, and he's about twenty-three, I'd say," replied Bennett. "But he's staying at The Woodman at the moment so I'm sure they'll be able to help you."

"Is this the same young man who was prowling in your garden the other night, or a different young man?" said Overton, and there was that same, barely perceptible, exchange of glances between the two policemen, as Leslie had seen on their previous visit.

"It's not the same person," Leslie replied, ignoring their impudence, this time. And then to Bennett, "Surely he hasn't got anything to do with this?" He felt an irrational sense of loyalty to the young man he had temporarily befriended, but caught the look of the two officers and said no more.

After a few more cursory questions, the two policemen left.

When they were back in the sitting room Leslie rounded on Bennett. "Why on earth did you drag Robert into it like that? What can that boy have to do with it?"

"You don't think there's anything coincidental about Robert's appearance a day or two before George's death?" Bennett asked.

"Why shouldn't it be just a coincidence? In any case, they've arrested Clarissa and the boyfriend, haven't they?" Bennett made no reply and Leslie stomped off into the kitchen to make coffee, infuriated by this maddening mood of Bennett's. It was one thing to wind up the two policemen who deserved to be baited, but it was unjustifiable to do so at the expense of an innocent person. He stalked back into the sitting room and put the tray on the coffee table. "If you'd wanted to set those stupid police officers on a wild goose chase, you could have sent them after Jeff and Veronika. Or how about Daniel, or Jamie, perhaps?"

"What do you mean?" asked Bennett.

"Jeff and Veronika have an obvious grudge against George over that house they want to build, to say nothing of the fact that Clarissa has been having an affair with Jeff, if rumour is to be believed. Daniel – he's the new boy serving at The Daffodil – had a run-in with George." Leslie related the story he'd just heard from Annie that morning about George finding Daniel smoking cannabis. "And the other day Jamie hinted at some problem he'd had with George, though I never found out what it was." Leslie suddenly laughed. "I can't see Jamie as a blackmailer or murderer, poor lad, can you? But still, you see my point; there are plenty of others with flimsy pretexts for suspicion."

"The police will have time to question Jeff, Daniel, Jamie and anyone else living locally if they need to. Robert's a visitor and will be leaving soon; he might be missed."

"But I still don't see what you've got against him other than the unfortunate timing of his visit to the village," said Leslie stubbornly. "And there must be dozens of other visitors staying in and around the village at the moment so why pick on him? You could tell from talking to him that he isn't a murderer or a blackmailer." Leslie tried to dismiss the recollection of Robert's awkward self-consciousness and his erratic behaviour outside the pub when he'd collided with Daniel.

"Think about that first conversation you had with him, Les, when he was heading off on a walk," Bennett replied.

"He needed directions out of the village, but there are plenty of people who can't read a map, " said Leslie defensively.

"But remember where he wanted to go."

Leslie furrowed his brow in recollection, then his face changed. "Oh Lord," he said quietly, "he wanted to find the path that leads to Stag Lane." He paused. "It comes out just below Compton Grange."

8

Glad of the distraction, Leslie set to work preparing lunch: chicken soup, homemade from what was left of Sunday's roast. Before long the kitchen was filled with a mouthwatering aroma, and while the events of the last few days were no less tragic or perplexing, they seemed, for a while, less all-consuming. Cooking almost always had the ability to transport Leslie, and he was never surprised that wizards and witches were so often depicted stirring cauldrons; he knew what magic could be conjured up from a bubbling pot. It seemed to him nothing short of a miracle that a handful of ingredients – a few herbs, some bones and leftover meat, an onion, a couple of root vegetables – all unpromising in themselves, could combine into this soul-satisfying and nourishing food.

They sat in the kitchen, dipping thick slices of granary bread into their bowls, and Leslie told Bennett all about the events of the morning. "Do you think Clarissa did poison him?" Leslie asked. "Arsenic is a ridiculous suggestion, but there was his medication."

"We'll find out when the postmortem report is released. Until then, it's rather pointless speculating," Bennett replied.

"I know, but it's impossible not to," Leslie sighed. "Tampering with his pills is certainly more likely than Irene's suggestion of a fight with the artist."

"Stabbed with a sharpened paintbrush, perhaps," said Bennett.

"George was certainly on plenty of tablets," continued Leslie, ignoring the remark. "I remember him telling me that he took a little white heart tablet, a little white blood pressure tablet, a little white water tablet and a couple of big white painkillers. He said, 'My life seems to revolve around white tablets nowadays, but so long as I keep taking them I should keep going for a bit, yet'. It would be ironic if that's what finished him off."

Bennett, who found it perfectly easy to resist the urge to speculate, attacked his bread in silence. Undeterred, Leslie continued, "I think he was on the same heart tablets as you, Bennett – Ramipril. I bet they would be lethal in an overdose."

"I can tell you one thing," said Bennett, reaching for another slice of bread, "Clarissa couldn't have got away with slipping anything into his drink. His palate was far too good."

* * *

Later that evening, Leslie took himself across to the village hall for choir practice. Dartonleigh and District Choral Society was of an excellent standard, attracting members from far and wide. If the choir had a fault, it was that it took itself rather seriously and rehearsals were exacting. However, Gloria had joined the choir and Leslie, weary though he was, couldn't miss the opportunity of speaking to her while events might still be fresh in her mind, for she was the lady who had been in the pub when Leslie had last seen George.

Leslie arrived early and, as the minutes went by, he was irritated to see that there was no sign of Gloria. It was tempting to sneak back home again, but instead he seated himself in his place among the tenors and tried to avoid getting caught up in the frenetic gossip. There was, of course, only one topic of conversation, for the news of a murder in the village had already spread beyond Dartonleigh, and those from the neighbouring towns and villages were eager for first-hand information. It was unusually difficult for the conductor to call the rehearsal to order and, just as he had settled everyone down and was about to begin, Gloria made a grand entrance, gushing her apologies as she squeezed her way into the centre of the sopranos. Even once the singing began, the normally impeccable discipline gave way to whispering as covert conversations continued:

"*Miserere nobis*— Who exactly was it who was murdered?"

"*Qui tollis*— That chap from Compton Grange. *Peccata mundi*— They're saying his wife did it— *Suscipe*— That woman with, you know, the reputation."

61

"*Suscipe deprecationem nostram*— I can't believe it!"

"*Qui sedes ad dexteram Patris*— Me neither. Poor old chap— *Miserere nobis*— He'd been ill as well."

In the end the conductor, having exhausted charm and charisma, gave way to wrath, and the gossip stopped until its proper time, afterwards in The Woodman.

At first it was impossible for Leslie to speak to Gloria on her own as she moved from group to group making loud and exuberant conversation. Eventually it was Leslie's turn and, once he could get a word in, he said, "I think I saw you in here yesterday afternoon, sitting at the table over there."

"I say, what an observant man you are," she said, fluttering her eyelids in a misplaced attempt at flirtation. "Fancy you noticing me. I was with my daughter – she was staying with me for a few days."

Leslie ignored her coquetry. "I was talking to a friend at that table by the window," he said. "I don't know if you saw him?"

Gloria's attention was waning.

"Actually, he was the man who died; was murdered," Leslie put in.

"Really?" exclaimed Gloria, her interest instantly rekindled. "Now that I think of it, I do remember seeing him, though I was sitting with my back to him. Just fancy that – I could have been one of the last people to have seen him alive. Not that I really saw him, as I said, because he was behind me."

"That's a shame," said Leslie. "I was wondering if you'd seen him talking to anyone."

"You sound like a detective," said Gloria, "as if you're investigating."

"No, not really," said Leslie hastily. "He was a friend, that's all. When I came in, he seemed upset about something. He never got around to telling me what it was, and so I was wondering if you saw anything."

"You are investigating, I know it," said Gloria wagging her finger at him playfully. "But it will be our little secret. I'll ask Gina, my daughter. She was sitting opposite me, so if there was anything to see, she would have seen it. But don't worry, I'll be ever so discreet."

Leslie doubted this, but it didn't really matter now that the whole village was saying that George had been murdered.

"You will be careful, won't you?" Gloria was suddenly serious.

"Yes, of course," said Leslie.

"Don't forget, it does look like murder," Gloria continued. There was now no trace of caprice in her manner. "I know they've taken his wife and Antonio in for questioning, but what if it turns out that it wasn't them? The murderer might still be on the loose and they might not take too kindly to you asking questions."

"Antonio? That's the name of the artist, is it? Do you know him?"

"Not really." Gloria gave a little giggle. "Perhaps just a teensy bit. His shop is across the road from mine in Temple Ducton. I've been in there once or twice." Gloria flushed. "He's very good-looking," she said girlishly, then she looked puzzled. "I can't imagine why he's taken up with that woman, Clarissa; she must be nearly old enough to be his mother. I know she's pretty good for her age, but he could have the pick of all the young women and girls around. The shop's always full of them. It's good to see so many young people taking an interest in art."

Leslie started to give a wry smile, and then realised that there was no trace of irony in Gloria's remark. Before he could think of anything to say, Gloria renewed her promise to speak to her daughter, gathered up her many scarves and, resuming her extrovert manner, made a conspicuous exit.

Cheryl came out from behind the bar to collect the glasses. "Did she see anything?" she asked.

"No, unfortunately not," said Leslie. "She was sitting with her back to George. I'm not sure she's the sort who notices other people, anyway."

"I know what you mean," said Cheryl.

"Is that young fellow, Robert, still here?" Leslie couldn't help asking. He'd been worrying ever since Bennett had mentioned him to the police.

"Oh, that's very odd," said Cheryl. "He's gone. He checked out suddenly yesterday morning even though he'd booked and paid for the room until tomorrow. The police came in asking about him. I think he's a suspect for the murder. It's horrible. I'm trying to keep it quiet. I don't fancy all the tittle-tattle if it goes about that we've been hosting a murderer in our rooms."

"Surely the police have to make enquiries." Leslie tried not to sound as defensive as he felt. "Just because they ask about someone doesn't make them a suspect. He seemed perfectly harmless to me."

"That's what I thought at first, until he went peculiar. It might turn out that he was a homicidal maniac. God, he could have done us all in."

"Whatever do you mean?" said Leslie.

"He seemed OK when he first arrived, a bit nervy perhaps, but nothing you'd worry about," said Cheryl. "But on Saturday evening he came back really late. I was waiting to lock up. I never give guests a key unless they particularly ask. Mostly our guests are walkers and they usually turn in long before we've closed up. More often than not they spend the evening in the bar or maybe go into Temple or Lymeford, but they're always back long before we finally lock up for the night. I was starting to get really worried about him, thinking he'd gone out and got himself lost on the moor or something.

"When he finally turned up, he looked done-in. He was full of apologies when he realised that I was waiting for him; he just said he hadn't realised the time, which was ridiculous, of course. I asked him where he'd been and he said that he didn't know. The next day he came down to breakfast but hardly ate a thing. He went out and then came back shortly afterwards and said he was leaving. Just like that. I thought it must be a mental health issue at the time. It wasn't until we heard that George was murdered, and then the police came, that I started putting two and two together."

"Haven't they still got Clarissa and the boyfriend at the police station?" asked Leslie.

"As far as I know."

"So the boy probably had nothing to do with it," Leslie declared, defiantly. "There could easily be another explanation for his odd behaviour."

"Well, how about this," said Cheryl, playing her trump card. "The police came back to check that they'd taken his details correctly. They couldn't find anyone of his name at the address he had given me, and the telephone number was wrong too. They wanted to trace him through his bank details but, guess what? He'd paid for every single thing here in cash."

9

Leslie was full of stubborn indignation when he got home. Despite everything, he still trusted his instincts and was neither willing nor able to relinquish the belief that Robert was entirely innocent. Cheryl's account aroused in him an irrational feeling of resentment.

Bennett was sitting up in bed reading when Leslie went in. Leslie felt so defensive that he very nearly kept Cheryl's story to himself, but he knew that he was being ridiculous. In any case, secrecy was not his gift and it was second nature to tell Bennett everything that happened. "They've still got Clarissa and Antonio in for questioning," he said after relating the details, "so I'm standing by my opinion that Robert has nothing to do with George's death. If they catch up with him, they'll find there's an innocent explanation for what he's done."

"Are you going to pace up and down the room all night?" asked Bennett placidly. "There's nothing more you can do at the moment. I've poured you a drink." He indicated the glass on the bedside table. "Get your book and come to bed."

"I'll never understand you," said Leslie, suddenly angry. "How can you sit there as if nothing's the matter? George is dead, murdered, you've implicated Robert, quite unnecessarily, and you think a glass of whisky and a book will solve everything."

"You're tired out," said Bennett.

"And you're bloody annoying," said Leslie, storming off downstairs. He stalked into the kitchen to make himself a hot drink. Bennett, he knew, would turn the light off and go straight to sleep. There was no chance that he would lay awake for so much as five minutes, let alone follow Leslie downstairs to try to mollify him. Leslie stamped about the kitchen in grumpy resentment itemising to himself all his grievances. It was all too bad. Leslie prided himself on his judgement of character and he was confident that he knew an innocent person when he met one.

If Robert ended up in trouble with the police, thought Leslie, he would insist that Bennett got him out of it. Bennett was always so jolly clever, having the answer to everything. Well, let him sort that out.

The hot milky drink was comforting and Leslie was glad of its warmth. It was a chilly night and he had come downstairs without his dressing gown. He spotted Bennett's cardigan abandoned on one of the kitchen chairs and picked it up, catching sight of the label. That retailer had gone out of business twenty years ago, surely. Leslie pulled the shabby item round his shoulders and thought of all the new cardigans and jumpers that he'd bought for Bennett each birthday and Christmas. There was a drawer full. Bennett was saving them, he said, for when his current ones wore out.

As he sat with his drink, Leslie turned his annoyance on himself for overreacting again. He really must have a word with the doctor. His nerves were getting worse and he was letting everything get out of proportion. After all, as far as he knew Clarissa and Antonio were still in custody, and Robert had not been found, let alone accused of anything. And if Robert had an innocent explanation for his behaviour, as Leslie was asserting, he would exonerate himself.

By the time he went back up to bed, Leslie felt considerably calmer, but as he dropped off to sleep, he could not ignore the nagging feeling that Robert had been wrongly implicated and that they had been largely to blame.

* * *

The men were late getting up the following day and it was nearly mid-morning by the time they breakfasted. A night's sleep had restored Leslie's mood, and Bennett never voluntarily referred to any altercation, so the day had started peacefully enough. Leslie was taking croissants out of the oven when he saw the doctor pull his car up in the little layby beside The Daffodil, and head for their gate. Hastily putting another croissant in the oven, he called out to Bennett who went to the door.

The doctor came into the kitchen and joined them at the table where breakfast was set. "I wanted to check up on you both," he said. "And to take your blood pressure." This was directed at Bennett. "I just found out that you haven't been to the surgery once since you were discharged from hospital, despite being told to make an appointment. So I thought that if Mohamed wouldn't come to the mountain..."

"This is awfully good of you," said Leslie. "Bennett doesn't deserve a home visit if he refuses to go to the surgery. I didn't even know he was supposed to have seen anyone, but I'm not surprised since he never tells me anything."

"And Bennett doesn't deserve you looking after him, either," said the doctor in mock severity. "You're a lucky man, Bennett."

Bennett held his hands up in simulated surrender, but did not look in the least bit contrite.

"Seriously, though," said Paul, "I also came over as I know you'll want to be kept up-to-date on what's been happening about George. Not that I know much yet."

"Did Clarissa poison him?" asked Leslie. "That's the rumour. Or can't you say?"

"I'm waiting to hear the official results of the postmortem," said the doctor, "and the toxicology reports always take a while to come back. What I can tell you is that when I examined the body, there were definite signs of suffocation. It's not exactly a secret, the police will make a statement soon, but it's probably a bit premature to be made public yet."

"Horrible," said Leslie. "We won't mention a thing about it."

"Any idea of the time of death?" asked Bennett.

"That's always difficult," said the doctor. "Doubly so when a patient has a chronic illness. He had certainly been dead for several hours, probably between eight to twelve hours, before the attending doctor examined him. Of course, he didn't examine him with forensic accuracy, as you know. The postmortem may narrow it down some more, if we're lucky."

"How did that doctor miss the signs of suffocation?" asked Leslie.

"One of the first rules I learnt at medical school was, if you don't look for it, you won't find it. The on-call doctor would have known the status of George's health, and I guess that after a long night on call, he came at it with the assumption that death was from natural causes. He would certainly have had no reason to suspect foul play. I'd like to think I'd have been a bit more diligent and observant, but I can't guarantee I would have done anything different. There but for the grace of God..."

They fell into general conversation and Leslie went on to tell the doctor about the police visit, their questions and their impudence. Paul looked concerned and said that he hoped that they hadn't been too bothered by it. Then, finishing his coffee and croissant, he insisted on listening to Bennett's chest and taking his blood pressure, both of which satisfied him. As he was getting ready to leave, Bennett asked, "If Clarissa had wanted to poison George, I suppose she could have used his heart tablets to overdose him, could she? I know he was on the same medication as me - Ramipril. We had a conversation about it."

"That will all be investigated," said Paul, picking his case up and making for the door. "But I've no reason to think that anything other than suffocation will come up at the postmortem." The doctor opened the front door to go. "Good Lord!" he exclaimed. "What the devil's going on?"

"We seem to have been invaded," said Bennett. "Wherever the corpse is, the vultures will gather."

The normally quiet street outside was obstructed by vehicles with strange devices on their roofs, and clusters of men and women with microphones, cameras and headsets.

"I'm off while I can still get my car out," said the doctor, fleeing. He hurried away, ignoring a group of journalists who were homing in on him.

***

Leslie spent most of the day imprisoned in the cottage, and the deserted street outside suggested that everyone had gone to ground, save a few bemused visitors. It was clear that the whole village had closed ranks. Garrulous as they were with one another, by tacit agreement a wall of silence was drawn up against the press. Everyone despised Clarissa and was disgusted by her behaviour and was horrified that she, or some other felon, had murdered George. But it was Dartonleigh's own scandal and they resented the intrusion of these incomers to feast at their banquet. Even the most ardent gossips were constrained by their native distrust of comers-in.

"I think they've given up and gone into The Woodman," said Leslie, looking out of the window just after two o'clock. "I'll sneak across to the shop now; there are one or two things we need."

It seemed as though everyone in the village had the same idea for, as he hurried across the road, other residents were starting to emerge, like rabbits from their burrows after a storm. An excited chattering group had already gathered in the post office as Leslie passed on his way to the shop.

"I've been marooned in my own cottage," he said to Janet, as he arrived, puffing, into the shop. Vera was already in situ, perched on the stool by the counter.

"I know, Leslie dear," Janet replied. "I'm sure everyone's been the same. There's hardly been a soul in today, other than those, what-do-you-call-them, 'media people'. Mind you," she continued, lowering her voice, "I'm not saying I haven't done a good trade." She gestured towards the deli counter, which was nearly empty. "I'm clean out of pasties and sausage rolls, and Irene's been making sandwiches like there's no tomorrow." She leant forward and dropped her voice to a whisper. "I've marked them up well – double the price. They jolly well deserve it, scaring off all my regular customers."

"I dread to think what stories they'll concoct," sighed Leslie.

"They'll probably drag our village into the gutter," said Vera complacently. Before they could indulge in further speculation, the gaggle of ladies that Leslie had seen in the post office crowded into the shop.

"Have you heard the latest?" exclaimed Marian breathlessly. "Doreen," she said, addressing the lady in the centre of the group, "Tell them what Stan saw."

Doreen stepped forwards to claim her moment of glory. "Well," she said slowly, "my Stan was out walking the dog on the night Mr Harrington-Thomas passed."

"Was murdered," interrupted another lady. "Don't forget it's murder now!"

"All right," replied Doreen. "On the night poor Mr Harrington-Thomas was murdered, my Stan was out walking the dog as usual. As he was coming down Stag Lane, he saw someone coming away from Compton Grange. It looked like a young man. And he was running."

"What? Did he see him actually coming away from the house?" interrupted Vera.

"Not exactly. He was running down the lane, just as if he'd come out of the drive when Stan caught sight of him. And he thinks it was a young man. He couldn't absolutely swear to it though as it was dark and he was a little way away."

"What time was that?" Leslie asked.

"It would've been very close to ten o'clock or just a few minutes after. He always goes out with the dog the same time every night, does Stan. Very regular, like. He puts his coat on the minute the ten o'clock news comes on. He can't stand all that doom and gloom at bedtime; gives him nightmares, he says."

"Has he reported it to the police?"

"Yes, we had the police round this morning. You see, we didn't know there was anything suspicious about poor Mr Harrington-Thomas passing on until yesterday evening, and then it wasn't until this morning that Stan mentioned to me having seen this young fellow. He's a bit slow like that, my Stan."

"Who do you think this man was?" asked Vera. "I bet it was Clarissa's toy boy. I knew they were in it together."

"It can't be him," said Irene, whose curiosity had drawn her from the storeroom. "He's got an alibi. My neighbour works at The Imperial and that... that disgusting man was there from eight pm until the next morning. The police have checked the CCTV of the entrances and he didn't leave the hotel."

"You don't suppose it was the same man who was creeping round your garden the other night, do you, Leslie?" asked another of the ladies.

"I wish I knew," he replied. Before he could say anything else, there was a shush from one of the ladies who nodded towards the door and, at the sight of a journalist, probably only coming in for a bag of crisps or a bottle of water, they departed on mass.

10

Leslie lost no time in relating the latest developments to Bennett, who went so far as to look up from his papers and grunt at the news. "I wonder if it was our prowler," said Leslie. "I've a mind to have a word with Stan, myself. Who knows what else he might have seen? I think I'll have a walk up there now."

"Which way are you going?" asked Bennett. "Don't forget that the lane will be full of reporters."

"Damn," said Leslie. "I don't want to get caught up with them. I suppose I'll have to go up past Edgar's and cut through the top of the woods."

The village was still eerily deserted when Leslie set off and he saw hardly a soul as he passed the church and then turned into Broomhill Lane. Edgar's ramshackle house was on the left and Leslie hurried on, lest Edgar should spot him and come out. The road was quite steep and, once safely out of Edgar's range, he stopped to catch his breath before turning onto the path that led through the woods. Leslie eventually emerged into Stag Lane, high above Compton Grange and turned off into the unmade road that led to Stan and Doreen's house. The rather strenuous walk was rewarded for, as the house came into view, he could see Stan in his garden, broom in hand.

Stan turned round and Leslie raised his hand in greeting. To Leslie's surprise, as soon as Stan caught sight of him he put his head down and hurried into his house without returning Leslie's acknowledgement, as though he was trying to avoid him. This was rather disconcerting but, hoping he had misread the reaction, Leslie continued to the front door. The impression, however, was reinforced as despite knocking twice, there was no response, other than the sound of a barking dog somewhere inside. Leslie suddenly felt indignant. While Stan had no obligation to answer, it was hard not to be offended, and he hammered on the door for a third time.

Leslie had plenty of opportunity to take in the scenery. The house, aptly, if unimaginatively, named Moor View Cottage, looked out onto miles of open moorland, rugged, wild and, even on a bright day such as this, rather forbidding. Leslie's attention was attracted, however, down the lane, for Moor View Cottage stood on high ground and gave a perfect view over the back of Compton Grange and the neighbouring house belonging to Jeff and Veronika. Compton Grange was an impressive mansion, with large and beautifully landscaped gardens, looking out across the moor to Harrier's Tor. From here it was easy to see how a property built on Jeff's land might ruin the idyllic outlook from Compton Grange.

The most striking feature of Compton Grange today, though, was the presence of numerous uniformed police officers and plain-clothed personnel prowling about the place, and the chilling sight of two men in what looked like white space suits coming out of the back door. Shuddering, Leslie made his way round to the back of Moor View Cottage. The dog heard him and hurled itself at the back door barking furiously. Leslie was not afraid of dogs, but he instinctively withdrew a little from the house. Behind the door there was a crash and a clatter and for a moment the dog was silent, satisfied, apparently, at having created mayhem. The unseen mishap brought Stan to the window at last, scowling through his glasses. His expression changed. "Oh, it's you," he shouted above the din of the dog which had found its voice again. "Hold on." The dog was removed and there was a short delay while Stan cleared up behind the door, and Leslie was finally admitted to the house.

"I don't know how many times I've told Doreen not to put this recycling bin by the back door," Stan grumbled. "I thought you were one of those pesky newspaper people. I've had dozens of them knocking on the door about the trouble down there," he said indicating in the direction of Compton Grange. "I thought you were another one. I can't see far without my glasses on and I don't wear them when I'm gardening. Pesky things fall off my nose all the time."

They went through to the sitting room, and the dog, a large black Labrador, hurled itself at Leslie with exuberant friendliness.

The sitting room, filled to bursting with trinkets, ornaments and family photographs, had large picture windows looking down the lane over the two great houses below.

"Bad business that," said Stan, nodding towards the Grange. "Is it what you've come about, or is there something else?"

"Sort of," said Leslie. "I was in the shop this morning and Doreen said that you saw someone in the lane. We had a prowler in our garden the other night. I don't know if you heard about it, but I wondered if it was the same person."

"I told Doreen to hold her tongue," exploded Stan. "Women! Tittle-tattle, tittle-tattle, all day long. That's where she'll be now – in that cafe, eating cake and gossiping, or in some woman's cottage doing the same. I told her to say nothing about it. The newspaper people have been trouble enough already, without this as well. You wait until they hear about it; we'll have them camped in the garden."

"Perhaps not if you let this fellow out," smiled Leslie, stroking the dog's head which was now resting across his knee.

"Fat lot of good Cassius would be, the old softy," said Stan. "He could lick them to death, I suppose. But I don't think I can help you with your prowler. I don't wear my glasses when I'm walking the dog either, so all I saw was a figure ahead of me. I'm guessing from the way that he was moving, running in fact, that it was a young man. The clothing was on the dark side, but that's all I can tell you. It might've been your prowler if that fits the description, or it mightn't have been."

"Oh well," replied Leslie, clearly disappointed, "thanks, anyway." Leslie started to get up to go, but Stan, having taken so long to admit him to the house, did not now seem anxious to let him go.

"This was her dog, you know," he said, unexpectedly. "That besom down there."

"Clarissa's? Oh yes, I remember now that they had a dog for a little while."

"Yes," replied Stan. "One of her fads, it was. She strutted about the village in green rubber boots but the novelty wore off in a week or two. Mr Harrington-Thomas took it on then but it was beyond him, with his health so indifferent. He's a fine strong dog, is Cassius, and he needs a lot of walking. They had a terrible row about it when she wanted to get rid of the dog. Mr Harrington-Thomas had become attached to him."

"How do you know?" asked Leslie. Moor View was much too far away to overhear even the most acrimonious argument.

"I'm their gardener. Didn't you know? You overhear things when you're gardening." Stan paused and shook his head morosely. "She's a nasty piece of work. Everyone's saying they can't believe she's done the old man in, but I can. Do you know what she said when they were rowing about the dog? 'I don't care where it goes or what happens to it. Take it to the vet and have it put down if that's the only option. Just get rid of it'. Anyone who could say that about this lovely fella would be capable of anything." Stan stroked the dog's head affectionately. "In any case," he continued, "I offered to have the dog. The old man was over the moon. I used to take Cassie down there sometimes, when the missus was out, which was most of the time."

"Can I share a confidence with you, Stan?" Leslie ventured. "It's not something I would like spread around the village." It was clear to Leslie that Stan liked a good gossip just as much as Doreen, but the opportunity was too good to miss.

"I can keep my mouth shut. I'll not say anything to the wife."

"Nor in the pub?" added Leslie cautiously.

"What do you take me for?" Stan sounded injured. "I'll not say a word."

Leslie told Stan about encountering George in The Woodman and the unexplained shock. Leslie confided his own frustration that George had died before being able to disclose his secret. "George was a good friend of ours," said Leslie, "and if there was anything that you'd noticed in the days or weeks leading up to his death, anything that might have been connected with it, it might just help to make sense of the tragedy. Maybe even something you wouldn't bother to tell the police about. It's really playing on my mind that he so nearly told me something that might have been significant."

Stan shook his head. "I can't think of anything that might be to do with a sudden shock. You know about all her love affairs, I suppose. I saw her take that artist bloke in that hut there with her. She waited until the old man went down to The Woodman but people like her don't notice a gardener. And I can see what goes on from up here as well; I wear my glasses indoors all the time!" He laughed mischievously. Stan got up and went to the window and Leslie joined him. Stan was right; it was an excellent view over the back of the Grange. On the edge of George's land, right next to Jeff and Veronika's large house, stood a wooden summer house.

"That studio is very close to Jeff and Veronika's house, isn't it?" said Leslie. "If you didn't know otherwise, you'd think it was theirs, not George and Clarissa's."

"Very convenient for the builder bloke to hop over the picket fence," said Stan, looking deeply disgusted. "She's not content with one at a time, that one. All those la-di-dah ways but she's actually no better than a whore. I usually say live and let live, but to carry on like that and with a husband not long for this world, it's beyond me."

"So it's true about Clarissa and Jeff? I'd heard talk of it, but wondered if it was just a lot of gossip."

"It's true all right," said Stan. He suddenly laughed. "It's a funny thing: for all her tittle-tattling, the wife, Doreen, never saw any of it. She never looks out of the window; spends all day watching that pesky television and all the rubbishy daytime shows. I've said nothing about the goings-on down there. She'd be wild if she knew what she'd been missing."

The two men fell into silence watching the distant police activity at the Grange. To Leslie, the whole business suddenly felt unbelievable – fantastic and surreal. It was as though he was watching a film. Any minute now the camera would zoom in and he would be able to see exactly what that officer by the summer house was doing, and hear the conversation being carried on between the two policemen by the wall. He turned from the window, restoring himself to reality. "Well, thanks for your time, Stan," he said.

Once again, Stan didn't seem in a hurry to be rid of him. "I'll tell you something else, since you're interested." Stan indicated for Leslie to sit down again. "I don't see that it has to do with old Harrington-Thomas having a shock or anything like that, mind," he continued. "It was something I overheard a couple of weeks ago, I can't remember exactly when. I was working in the rose garden, down at the foot of the grassy bank. Suddenly I heard raised voices so I looked out to see what was to do. It was Mr Harrington-Thomas leaning over the fence at the bottom having a right old ding-dong with the neighbour, the builder. I thought at first they were rowing about the builder wanting to put up a new house on the land, as I could only catch bits of what they were saying. But then I heard Harrington-Thomas shouting at him, 'Don't think I don't know what you've been up to, because I do. You won't get away with it, I'll make sure of that'. That made me wonder if he'd found out about him carrying on with his wife. The builder stamped off indoors without even looking round, and I went back to my work."

"Are you going to tell the police?" Leslie asked.

"We've already called the police up here once," Stan sighed, "and I don't know that I'd have bothered with that if Doreen hadn't insisted. It was all questions, questions that I couldn't answer. Did I see the person actually coming out of the Grange? No, just running down the lane. What age was he? I don't rightly know, I didn't see his face. Could I describe him? No, I didn't have my glasses on. What colour was his jacket? I couldn't tell, it was a dark night. Did I see anyone coming or going at the Grange that night? No, I pulled the curtains just after seven pm and there was nothing unusual. Both their cars were there, but I saw no one about, and I saw nothing after that on account of the curtains being drawn." Stan got up and went to the window again. "Do you really think I ought to tell them what I overheard?" he said. "Do you think it's important?"

"It's probably nothing, but I think perhaps you should tell the police and let them decide."

"Maybe I will," said Stan sighing even more deeply. "But there's something else as well, and this isn't for the police. You asked me to hold my tongue. If you can hold yours, I'll tell you."

"I won't say a thing," said Leslie, then added with his customary honesty, "but I always tell Bennett everything."

"So long as it goes no further," said Stan. "There is someone who will very likely be able to give you a full description of the person I saw running down the lane the night George was murdered."

"Go on," Leslie urged.

"Pete Parkin," said Stan, "the chap who works at the Stretton Cross garage."

"I know Pete," said Leslie. "He looks after my car."

"He came up the lane on his motorbike just before I caught sight of the person running down the lane. Pete must have just driven past him, seconds before I saw him. Stands to reason he must have seen him."

"Why can't you tell the police?"

"Ah, now that's the tricky bit," said Stan. "Pete, you might know, lost his licence just before Christmas. Speeding again, I dare say. So he didn't ought to have been on his motorbike at all. I often see him go past in the evening on it, but he keeps to the back lanes and isn't doing anyone any harm. You can't blame the bloke; how else can he get about here? The police aren't likely to take that view, though, so I kept quiet about it. If Pete wants to come forward to the police with information, that's his lookout."

"If I speak to him about it," said Leslie, "he's bound to ask how I know."

"You can tell him it was me; he'd probably guess anyway. He always gives me a hoot and a wave as he goes by. He knows I won't grass on him to the law."

Leslie eventually took his leave but, as he was going, Stan said, "I hope you don't think I'm poking my nose in, but if you want my advice, I'd leave any sleuthing to the police."

"Oh, I'm not sleuthing," said Leslie hastily. "I'd just like to find out what it was that had upset George that day."

"Sleuthing, finding out – it's all the same. You want to be careful. If it was his wife that did him in, who knows, she might have had an accomplice who is still out and about. If it turns out it wasn't her, then who was it? Watch your step; you don't want to be next."

With these chilling, if fantastical, words echoing in his head, Leslie took his leave and hurried home.

As he breathlessly related the new developments in minute detail, Bennett sat back in his chair and stared at the ceiling without comment.

"I think I'll take a drive to the garage tomorrow and see if Pete is there," said Leslie. "I can think up some excuse. I just hope he wasn't driving too fast to see the man running down the lane."

"And that he's prepared to talk to you," said Bennett.

Leslie went on to repeat the row that Stan had overheard. "He heard George saying to Jeff, 'I know what you've been up to, and I'll make sure you don't get away with it'," Leslie repeated. "I wonder what he meant. The most obvious explanation is the affair between Jeff and Clarissa, of course. But you don't suppose Jeff could be the blackmailer, and he was referring to that, do you?"

Bennett continued to stare up at the ceiling. "That's what I was wondering," he replied.

"If he was," said Leslie, "and he thought that George had rumbled him, he'd have had a good reason to wish George dead."

11

Marjory Hastings had set two tables for mahjong in her large conservatory. It was a lovely room in a lovely house, with a magnificent view along the Dartonleigh valley. Dusk was falling and the lights in Temple Ducton twinkled in the distance. Leslie had even drawn a pleasing set of tiles. If it wasn't for George's death and the disturbing events unfolding since, it would have been a perfect evening.

Leslie sorted his mahjong tiles on the rack. He had two dragons which he would hold on to in order to thwart Marjory, who was seated to his right, for she always collected the dragons. To his left sat Gloria, wearing a brightly coloured kaftan-style dress and, as usual, many beads and flowing scarves. She was a dark horse, this being her debut at the mahjong club. She claimed to have played just a teensy bit of mahjong before and insisted she was an absolute novice. Sitting opposite Leslie was Edgar. He was obviously in a state of nervous agitation and, more than once, he knocked his tiles from the rack.

Annie smiled at Leslie from the other table. She had brought two friends with her, which was just as well since she was seated with Jeff's wife, Veronika, who was not the easiest company. Veronika was Latvian, and with her strong accent and irregular grasp of the English language, conversation could be a challenge.

But there was rarely a dull moment with Veronika. On one occasion, she and Jeff had engaged in a blazing row outside The Daffodil Tea Shop, and she had seized a flowerpot, complete with budding begonia, from a front garden and hurled it at his receding figure, hitting him smack on the back of the head. This was witnessed by the fascinated clientele of the teashop and the astonished morning congregation leaving church. The sympathies of the onlookers were entirely with Veronika, as Jeff was an unpopular man – surly and argumentative. Veronika's appearance was equally striking. This evening she sported a very short dress in a gold material which clung so tightly that it looked as though it had been painted onto her, a sparkly fur bolero and white high-heeled boots.

While Marjory was helping Edgar with his tiles, Gloria leant casually across to Leslie and, with surprising discretion, said quietly, "I've some news. Can I call round tomorrow, perhaps late morning?"

"Of course," whispered Leslie as he studiously rearranged the tiles on his rack. "How about lunch?"

Gloria hissed an eager acceptance. Leslie sighed. He was a martyr to his innate, almost involuntary, sense of hospitality and he wondered what Bennett would have to say about lunch with the eccentric Gloria.

"I can't get over this business with George," Annie was saying in consternation. "I keep thinking there must be some mistake. We all know what Clarissa is like, but surely she can't have committed this dreadful act. Why would she do such a thing? Why would anyone? After all, the poor man was not long for this world."

"Perhaps it was an accidental overdose," said Marjory. "That would make more sense."

"Of course she done it." Veronika's strident Latvian accent came from the other table. "She is a wicked woman. George was a very nice neighbour – gentleman – until he marry that flossy."

"I think you mean floozy, dear," corrected Marjory.

"Floozy, flossy – *nesvarīgs*! We had no troubles until she come along and make poison in his mind."

There was clearly considerable animosity between these neighbours and Leslie wondered how much she suspected, or indeed knew, about Jeff and Clarissa's affair.

"I tell you what I can't believe!" exclaimed Veronika, getting excited now, and stabbing a scarlet-nailed finger towards Marjory. "They have the big cheeks to forbid our planning permission, when they have erected artist studio the size of Buckingham Castle at top of their garden, right in front of our living room. 'It is temporary structure', George says. 'No planning permission needed'."

"Very trying, dear," said Marjory briskly. "Perhaps we should get started with our games now, and you can tell us afterwards."

But Veronika was not to be stopped so easily. "It is not artist studio, anyway. She use it to try and steal my husband away. She wait until my husband is watching from the window and she throw open the door of the studio." As she spoke, Veronika stood up and demonstrated the action with a dramatic gesture. "She stand there wrap in nothing except, how do you say, a cloth, a big scarf. I watch from the upstairs window and she don't see me. I watch her let the scarf—" Another piece of mime suggested a flowing scarf slipping back from the shoulders. "She stand there, vlaunting her fake boobies."

"Doing what with her what?" exclaimed Marjory in consternation. Gloria, sitting next to Leslie, drew out a large handkerchief and mopped her forehead. Annie and her friends were studiously avoiding eye contact with each other.

"She have booby job done. It is obvious they not real. In a woman that age, real boobies, very droopy." Veronika illustrated her remark with a graphic hand gesture. "Hers – they look like, I don't know, like a couple of fakes. She vlaunt them before my husband."

"Flaunt, dear, flaunt," said Marjory faintly.

"She say it is her garden, she can wear what she like. I tell her straight: not when you are flashing in my husband's face. Then she say is for art. She say she is in nude for that artist to paint her. Paint her? Huh! She is a wicked woman, and now I hope she go to prison."

"You don't mean she was sitting for Antonio in the nude in that studio?" Gloria's face was puce. "Not with George in the house?"

"Antonio? Is that his name?" interrupted Annie, her face also rather pink, but from the effort of self-control. "Very exotic."

"Sitting? Huh! I don't think so," snorted Veronika. "In any case, she wait until George go out before she bring her lover back there. The rest of the time she's having it over with him at that hotel."

For a moment it looked as though Marjory was going to correct this idiom but, to everyone's relief, she refrained from comment.

"Did you know," said one of Annie's friends, "after she murdered him, if it really was her, she went and spent the night at the hotel? My neighbour's daughter is a receptionist at The Imperial and she was on duty the night it happened. She told me this morning. The police have questioned them all about it, and they've looked at the hotel CCTV. Clarissa actually spent the night with that artist at the hotel; she left early in the morning. She was lying when she said she was at home and found George dead when she got up in the morning. The CCTV shows Clarissa walking through the hotel door at nine minutes past ten that night and leaving the next morning at twelve minutes past six."

"How horrible," said Gloria.

"But there was that man seen in the lane at about ten o'clock," said Marjory. "I wonder what he has to do with it. Perhaps he was an accomplice. Or perhaps he did it and it wasn't Clarissa after all."

Leslie maintained an uncomfortable silence lest he should let slip anything that he had learned from Stan that morning. Fortunately a distraction came as Edgar knocked his tiles over again and, in his efforts to retrieve them, sent Gloria's glass of wine flying across the table. His hands were shaking as he tried to retrieve the glass and collect up his tiles.

"Edgar, dear," said Marjory, who looked relieved at the distraction, despite the mess. "I'm sorry. You were an old friend of George's – I was forgetting. I think perhaps we had better change the subject."

"It has cut me up, I must admit," muttered Edgar, sitting helplessly while everyone mopped up around him.

"Well then, let's get started with our games," said Marjory, but again Veronika ignored the hint.

"Well, there was no one at the house at half past ten, or at least no one who could answer a door," said Veronika. "My husband, he called at the house then and got no answer."

"What was he doing there at that hour?" asked Leslie in surprise.

"He had a little quarrel with George in the morning. Then, on his way out to the bowls club in Lymeford in the evening, he decide to call on George to make it up a bit. I tell him to do that. There is no way George will agree to planning permission if we have quarrels. So I tell Jeff to call in on way to bowls and be nice to him. So he go there at seven o'clock. As he turned in the drive he saw someone going into the house. So he put it off until on his way home at ten thirty, but no answer."

"Jeff saw someone going into the Grange at seven o'clock? Did he see who it was?" asked Leslie.

"Just a man. Maybe," said Veronika with astonishing indifference. "He only see the person's back for a second as they went in through front door."

"Do the police know all this?" asked Leslie.

Veronika flapped her hand in a dismissive fashion. "I don't know. I advise my husband not to get involved with police. I don't know what he decided. He don't tell me."

"Well, Veronika," said Annie, "at least you should be able to get on with your planning permission now, without George inconveniencing you." The sarcasm was wasted on Veronika.

"No such thing!" she exclaimed vehemently. "If he had died six months ago it would have helped us, but this is no good. Now everything will stop while they decide what to do. They have no procedure for what to do when someone who was objecting is decease. They have now to make up procedure. All delay, delay, delay. Jeff kept saying the old man would die at wrong moment."

"How very inconvenient for you," said Annie, acidly, turning her attention to her mahjong tiles, and at last they got down to the purpose for which they had gathered.

Gloria won every game, dismissing it each time as beginner's luck, and when the mahjong sets were put away for another week, they sat round with drinks and the conversation reverted to the only topic of interest.

"I'm very surprised," said Annie. "I thought it was all a lot of hysterical nonsense at first, but it does seem now that the police are treating it as murder."

"I'm still hoping they find it was an accidental overdose," said Marjory with stubborn denial, "or natural causes."

"I wonder if the police have identified the young man seen in the lane yet," said one of the friends. "Perhaps it was a robbery that went wrong."

"It can't be that young man," said Edgar suddenly standing up and looking about him wildly. "Or Clarissa, for that matter."

"Oh, I say!" whispered Gloria under her breath, as they all stared at Edgar in bewilderment.

"It can't be either of them," Edgar repeated. "I know, because I was with George until ten fifteen. I had some business to do with him and I didn't leave him until then." He sat back down heavily in the chair, and there was an uncomfortable silence.

"Why, Edgar," said Marjory, at last, "you must have been the last person to have seen George alive."

12

The mahjong evening had finished on a strained note after Edgar's strange outburst and Leslie arrived home in a state of high tension. As he opened the front gate, however, his feelings underwent a seismic change. He could hear Bennett singing at the piano. The only time Bennett sang these days was when he was in a rare demonstrative mood, happy or sad, and even he would not be singing Gilbert and Sullivan if he was feeling miserable.

Such was his volatile mood that Leslie felt like running in and embracing Bennett but, not wishing to break the moment, he opened the door quietly and stood in the hallway enjoying the experience. Bennett had a beautiful baritone voice, as good as a professional, Leslie thought, and he accompanied himself well on the piano.

It was singing that had brought the two men together, in the Light Operatic Society at the university where Leslie had worked in HR and Bennett as an academic. The LOS had been a wonderful meritocracy, with the security officer cast in the lead role and the dean relegated to the chorus. Leslie and Bennett met during the production of *HMS Pinafore* and it was *Fair Moon to Thee I Sing* that Leslie could hear now. They had been such good times, and for one precious moment Leslie was transported back.

He stood in the doorway of the library and, as the song finished, Bennett looked over his shoulder at him and smiled.

"Don't stop, please," said Leslie, walking over to the piano and putting a hand on Bennett's shoulder. Bennett took another piece of music from on top of the piano. It was a handwritten arrangement, the pages worn with use. He looked at Leslie and cocked his head on one side in enquiry. Leslie recognised the sheet immediately – it was *The Best of Times is Now*. It had been their song in those early days and it was a long time since they had sung it together. Bennett played the familiar introduction and the years vanished as they sang. It was a moment of rare affection, and Leslie could have wept with joy.

Bennett closed the piano and they went into the sitting room where Bennett poured drinks. "There's nothing like a death for reminding one," said Bennett, "that the best of times is now. Don't worry," he laughed, seeing Leslie's emotional response, "the mood's sure to pass. And I've also managed to get this week's copy off to the editor. That's always a load off my mind."

"You've started working again far too soon," said Leslie, anxiety flooding back. "It can't be good for your heart. I keep telling you that you should have taken far more time off."

"And I keep telling you," said Bennett calmly, "that the worst thing about being incarcerated in that damned infirmary was the interminable boredom. You know I'd go mad without any work, and it's hardly demanding."

"The work may not be, but those daily and weekly deadlines are. I've been thinking about it. I'm sure I could get some sort of a job. There must be—"

Bennett interrupted him. "We've been through all this before. What do you want me to do instead? Can you really imagine going out to work and leaving me to keep the house?"

"OK, OK," replied Leslie, who could imagine it. "I just worry, that's all. The pressure every week can't be good for you." He went into the kitchen, and brought through the cheese board, a rare luxury these days, while Bennett poured out port, and they sat by the French windows in the sitting room. There was a lot to tell: Veronika's graphic disclosures, Annie's friend's gossip from the hotel, and Edgar's startling revelation.

"Edgar hasn't told the police he saw George late in the evening. I don't think he realised the significance. He promised to tell them tomorrow. To be honest I'm really worried about his mental health. He's a nervous wreck at the moment. I'd forgotten until this evening that he knew George years ago. I think they were neighbours in Surrey or Sussex, or somewhere." Leslie took a crumbly chunk of Cheshire cheese onto his plate. "I think, though," he continued, "that he must have something else on his mind. He was very agitated the other day when I had coffee with him in The Daffodil, and that was before George died. I expect it's the business and problems with Kenny. Perhaps I'll invite him for dinner one evening. Can you put up with him?"

"The man's a perfect fool," said Bennett, though more benignly than usual. "I suppose we'd better have him over."

"It certainly seems to have narrowed the time of the murder right down. Edgar was with George until ten fifteen, when he was still alive, but Jeff called at ten thirty and there was no answer. Presumably George was dead by then."

"Perhaps," replied Bennett.

"Perhaps?" queried Leslie "Why only perhaps?"

"We've only Edgar and Jeff's word for the times they were there and I'm not sure how reliable either is," replied Bennett.

"But surely in these circumstances they'd be careful to be accurate?" said Leslie. "After all, they've both put themselves in rather a vulnerable position by admitting that they were at Compton Grange on the night that George died."

"That's true, but even supposing both their accounts are precise," said Bennett, "it doesn't mean that George was dead at ten thirty just because Jeff got no response. George was a man who could easily ignore someone knocking on the door if he didn't want to answer."

"That's very true," Leslie conceded. "Jeff would probably be the last person he'd want to speak to, especially if he'd just had to put up with Edgar. Or perhaps he thought it was Edgar back again for something he'd forgotten, and couldn't face another minute of the man. Come to think of it, it may have been as simple as George not hearing the door, with his deafness." Leslie took some more cheese onto his plate and added a spoonful of homemade chutney. "I wonder what Edgar was doing there," he said thoughtfully. "What kind of business would have taken him to Compton Grange at that time of the evening?"

"I was wondering that, too," said Bennett.

"Still," said Leslie rather gloomily, "even allowing for some inaccuracy in Edgar's account, it now looks like it can't have been Clarissa who committed the murder. She was captured on CCTV at the hotel just after ten o'clock, and didn't leave again until the morning. Antonio too; he was there from even earlier in the evening."

Bennett cut himself a wedge of stilton and took another cracker. "It's not looking good for the mysterious young man, Robert, I'm afraid," he said.

13

It was extraordinary to see Dartonleigh all over the media the next day. The shop sold out of newspapers almost immediately and residents drove to Temple Ducton and Lymeford, buying half a dozen copies to give to disappointed neighbours. Some were even seen buying the low-brow tabloids. It seemed that the reporters had not yet caught up with the sighting of a young man running away from the house, for there was no mention of it.

Leslie paid an early visit to the shop to collect his paper and some groceries. Not only had Edgar agreed to come to dinner, but he also had to cater for Gloria at lunchtime and she looked like a woman with a good appetite.

"I saved you a paper, Leslie love," said Janet, reaching under the counter. "They've nearly all gone, but I've put a few aside for my regulars. Would you be a dear and take these over to Annie for me? She always has newspapers for the customers to read in the teashop. Irene usually takes them across but she's not coming in until later and I'm sure, today of all days, Annie will want to have the papers first thing."

It was never difficult to persuade Leslie to go to The Daffodil. The teashop was still empty of customers and Leslie soon found himself sitting at a table with Annie, drinking camomile tea and eating fruit cake. Annie picked up one of the copies and gasped as she opened it. She turned it round for Leslie to see and there on the centre spread was a huge photograph of The Daffodil. The photographers had had a field day in the picturesque village, and as Annie turned the page, there was Leslie's thatched cottage, the church, the village shop and the post office. The contrast between the idyllic setting and the heinous crime which had been committed there was exploited to the full.

"It seems unreal," she said unhappily.

"I know. Such a horrible reason for the village to have its fifteen minutes of fame."

"I still expect to see poor George go across and get his paper in the morning." Annie looked close to tears.

To change the subject Leslie said, "How's Daniel getting on?"

Annie raised her eyes and made a despairing gesture.

"Has he been sulking out in the kitchen?" Leslie asked.

"Far from it," Annie replied. "The boy is incorrigible. He came back in the day after I sent him home early, and was strutting about as though nothing had happened. Then yesterday I caught him skiving out the back when he was supposed to be washing up in the kitchen."

"What was he doing? Having a crafty smoke?"

"I wouldn't put that past him, but no, he was round the side talking to Edgar's son, Kenny."

"Kenny?" said Leslie, surprised. "I wonder what Daniel can have to do with him? I hope Kenny's not up to no good. I don't trust him."

"I know what you mean. I was surprised to see them deep in conversation, but I can hardly pry into the boy's affairs. He did at least have the decency to look shamefaced when I called him back in."

"As well he might," said Leslie. "I hope he comes to realise how lucky he is and how well he's been treated."

"Some hope," said Annie. "But at the moment, I just want to avoid rocking the boat, if I can. There seems to be enough trouble in the village without adding to it. I lay awake for hours last night thinking about what Edgar said at mahjong. If he's right about the day and time he saw George, and surely even Edgar can't have got something as important as that wrong, it can only mean one thing: Clarissa and that man, Antonio, couldn't have been responsible for George's death. So there's a murderer out and about, and we've no idea who it is, or what their motive was."

Although this thought had not escaped Leslie, it was gruesome to hear it spoken, and he was not sorry that customers were starting to arrive as he was terrified that he might let slip some piece of information that he was supposed to be keeping secret. He hurried off, galvanising himself for the task of driving to the garage to speak to Pete, in the hopes that he could shed some light on the identity of the young man seen running away from the Grange.

There had been a time when Leslie had enjoyed nothing better than a leisurely drive in the country, but the car had been used with decreasing frequency since they had moved to Dartonleigh. Bennett had not driven for many years, and the narrow twisting lanes, populated as they were by farm vehicles, tourists and kamikaze locals, made Leslie's nerves bad these days. He had come to enjoy the bus ride into Lymeford for shopping, and he rarely ventured any further. As a result the car stood for weeks, sometimes months, without moving. In truth, there was little point in keeping the vehicle but she was a classic, a vintage Rover, and he could not part with her. Bennett, he guessed, was equally attached to the car, though he would never admit it. On one occasion, when Leslie had idly commented that perhaps they should think of selling her, Bennett had come up with some surprisingly persuasive arguments against the idea.

The car was in pristine condition; the bodywork was gleaming, the red leather interior as good as new and the wooden dashboard was polished to perfection. Leslie was wryly aware that the cost of maintaining the car could hardly be justified, but perhaps this was true of many a classic car owner. "Wake up, Gertrude," Leslie said patting the grey wing affectionately. "We're going for a ride to see your friend Pete." A wave of anxiety came over Leslie as he turned on the engine, though not this time provoked by the thought of the narrow lanes. It was brought on instead by the recollection that the last time he'd taken the car out was on a journey to the hospital when they had phoned him in the night to come quickly. The memory was so acute that he felt quite ill and he had to put it out of his mind and pull himself together before setting off.

The route took Leslie past Lower Stretton Farm and its glorious farm shop. Leslie had shopped there regularly when they first moved to Dartonleigh but, as his driving had diminished, so had his visits. Impatient though Leslie was to speak to Pete, it was impossible for him to drive on past, and he pulled into the farm and parked in the neat cobbled courtyard. Once inside, all thoughts of murder and blackmail, of heart attacks and hospitals, temporarily left him as he browsed the shelves and cabinets. He feasted his eyes at the fresh meat counter and his favourite recipes came to mind: beef wellington, stuffed breast of lamb, moussaka, cannelloni, and curries of every kind. He chided himself for neglecting the shop for so long. He loaded his basket with bread, ham and a particularly fine truckle of oak-smoked cheddar, and was just moving eagerly to the delicatessen counter, when he heard his name. Turning, he saw Veronika appearing from behind a grocery cabinet. She was clad in a leopard-print fur jacket, a very tight short skirt and black patent leather high heel boots, topped off with a mauve beret. It was no wonder that the shop boy was gawping at her.

"What are you buying today?" she demanded, by way of a greeting.

"Oh, just a few things for lunch," said Leslie vaguely. "I'm still looking around. I don't come here very often."

"Nor do I. The prices is a scandal," Veronika replied at the top of her voice. "But is the only place round here to get the pork belly slices. They don't sell it in village shop – all sorts fancy foods but no pork belly slice. I get it for Jeff. He's in such bad moods just now and I get it to try cheer up."

Leslie had a strong desire to flee before he was subjected to further unsavoury details of Veronika and Jeff's private life, but there was also the possibility that Veronika, as George's neighbour, might give away something of importance, as she had the previous evening. He made the sacrifice and put down his shopping basket. "Things must have been a great strain, recently," he said.

"You don't know, Leslie, you don't know. I did not say last night." Veronika lowered her voice. "I don't tell those people my business. Is money matters, and I don't discuss with those people."

Leslie cast his mind back to the previous evening's disclosures. Veronika certainly had her own unique brand of discretion.

"The fact is," she continued, "we have police round our house, asking about Jeff's bank accounts. They ask permission to see his accounts at the bank. Why? They won't say. Jeff refuse, of course. He say that he have nothing to hide, but this is a free country and he refuse to behave like it is some communist state. I agree with him. But when he go out, I think I have a little look at his accounts myself. Is not that I don't believe him but, you know, I wonder. Jeff don't know I have his password. He thinks he hide it, but I know where he write it down." Veronika looked around suspiciously, and despite there being no one in earshot, she lowered her voice to little more than a whisper. "When I look into account, I expect to see nothing unusual. But I get greatest shock. Two big, big sum of money. I cannot understand it. I know nothing about these sums."

Leslie felt his heart racing. Two large sums of money. He had already suggested to Bennett that Jeff might be the blackmailer and this seemed to corroborate his suspicions. Trying not to sound too interested he said, "Really? When was this?"

"First was twentieth February. Second was nineteenth March. I remember exact," and she tapped her temple with her scarlet-nailed finger as she spoke.

Leslie suppressed a shiver. Those dates seemed to reinforce, if not confirm, Jeff's guilt. It seemed certain, though, that Veronika knew nothing of the crime. "And you haven't asked Jeff where the money came from?" he ventured.

"From? No, no, no, you misunderstand. This is not money going into account. Huh! Would I be complaining if it was money in? No! It is money out of account. This the big problem. No wonder we overdrawn big-time if he is taking money from account like this. I tell you, is big sums of money. Not like he spend it on a fancy woman, no. More like money you spend for very big holiday abroad, or very big purchase. I can't ask Jeff the reason – he would be very mad if he knew I look at his account. Maybe I find out some other way. Maybe I question him after we have nice plate of pork belly."

Leslie was silent for the moment, trying to process this new information, and it seemed that Veronika had nothing further to say, for she departed abruptly in search of her purchases. Leslie paid for his shopping, puzzling over the reversal of his ideas about

Jeff. As he left the shop he could hear Veronika haggling with the butcher over the price of his meat.

The garage was on the road to Stretton Cross, just beyond the ugly new house which Martin had been complaining about. Leslie slowed down as he passed it. It was certainly an oddity, quite out of keeping with the other local properties, but Leslie thought it not nearly as unsightly as some of the farm buildings he had passed with their corrugated and rusting roofs, nor indeed the garage that he was heading for, and no one seemed to complain about them.

The first person Leslie saw as he pulled up outside the garage was Pete and he greeted Leslie with a smile.

"Morning, Mr Mountfield. I was working out the front here and I saw you coming along the road." Pete patted the car's bodywork affectionately. "What can we do for you? No problems I hope, Mr Mountfield?"

"Oh no, none that I know of," said Leslie. "She seems to be running well. I've just been to the farm shop and I thought I'd come along the road and see you as there's something I wanted to ask."

Pete looked a little surprised. "Well, fire away."

"Actually," said Leslie, lowering his voice, "it's rather a private matter. It won't take a minute. Is there somewhere private we can talk?"

Pete hesitated, looking perplexed, but then glanced behind him at the oily workshop, devoid of any amenities. "There's nowhere there," he said, doubtfully. "Tell you what, I'll tell the guv'nor that you think your car's making a funny sound, then we can drive down the road and you can tell me. How about that?"

A few minutes later, Leslie was pulling the car off the road onto a verge by the gate into a field. It was a sloping field strewn with granite boulders where dozens of little lambs were leaping and scampering close to the grazing ewes. It was a picturesque scene, and it seemed so incongruous with the reason he was here.

At home, Leslie had thought carefully about how he was going to approach the subject, but now his mind was blank and he felt doubtful. Pete was a cheerful, friendly person, but Leslie didn't know him beyond the attention he gave to the car, and he didn't know how he might react. He was also a big man, about six foot tall and muscular. In this lonely place, Leslie could not help but feel rather vulnerable.

"I'm hoping you might be able to help me," he ventured. "I don't know if you heard that we had a prowler in our garden a few nights ago. It was a youngish man. Yesterday, I found out that a young man had been seen running away from George's house the night he'd been murdered. I was wondering if he was one and the same person."

"What's that to do with me?" said Pete tersely, his manner suddenly quite different to normal.

"I went to see Stan yesterday, up at Moor View Cottage. He's the one who reported seeing the young man running away from the house. He couldn't identify the man because he didn't have his glasses on. He told me, in confidence, that you went past him and must have seen the young man." Leslie felt Pete shifting uneasily in the passenger seat. "Stan assured me," he continued hastily, "that he'd never tell the police about it. Nor will I, I promise you. I just wanted to know if you knew who the young man was or if you could describe him."

"I dunno," said Pete shortly. "I dunno that I was there, do I?"

Leslie waited for a while but Pete was silent. "I can understand your position," said Leslie at last. "It's OK, I won't press you for an answer." He switched on the engine.

"Hang on a minute," said Pete. "Just give a bloke a chance to think, will you? Switch that engine off, and let me think."

Leslie obediently switched off the engine and sat in silence for a few moments more.

"If I get found out I'll lose my job, for certain," Pete said, at last. "When I had my licence taken away, they were very difficult about it. They don't need a mechanic who can't take a vehicle on the road. It's only because I've been there so long and I'm a good worker that they kept me on, but if I got caught again I wouldn't get a second chance. I've been pretty stupid by going out on the motorbike, I know, but I only do a short run up the back lanes in the evening. It's my mam, you see, she's on her own and I've always gone in most evenings to see her. My wife doesn't drive, so she can't take me. It's hard living here without transport. I use the pushbike as much as I can, but you've no idea what some of those hills are like, Mr Mountfield. You really won't say anything, will you?"

"Of course not," said Leslie. Smiling, he added, "If they fire you, who on earth will look after Gertrude for me?"

Pete smiled back. "OK. Well I don't think I can tell you much, anyway. I was going a bit fast, to be honest, and it was dark. All I saw was a young guy running straight down the lane. Early twenties probably, but he had a hood up and I only got a quick look at him. He was a bit taller than you, maybe about five-foot eleven or so. I saw enough to tell you that he wasn't anyone I know; no one from round here, I don't think."

Leslie shivered. "You say it wasn't anyone from round here. Do you know the young chap serving in The Daffodil at the moment, Daniel? He's quite new. I'm wondering if it was him. He's a bit of a fitness fanatic. Perhaps it was him out jogging."

"I don't know him. Do I look like someone who takes afternoon tea?" Pete laughed. "But this guy wasn't out for a jog. He looked like he was late for his grandmother's funeral."

"You've been really helpful and I do appreciate it," said Leslie. "I wonder if you'd do one last thing for me. Is there any chance that you could pop round on Saturday? We can walk over to The Daffodil. They do a good sandwich if afternoon tea's not your thing. You can tell me if Daniel was the one you saw. I'll make it worth your while."

"You're fixing up an identity parade, are you? But sorry, I can't do Saturday, I'm working."

"Never mind." Leslie tried to keep the disappointment from his voice.

"Tell you what," said Pete, "I finish at four tomorrow. I'll come down to you after that, but we'll just go in and buy something and come away. As I said, I'm not really a one for tearooms and all that stuff."

They drove back to the garage in silence, both of them deep in thought. As they pulled up, Pete said, "What exactly is it that you're trying to find out, Mr Mountfield? You started out by telling me that you were trying to identify your prowler and see if the young man running away from George's house matched up with him. But you know your prowler wasn't this Daniel, don't you, so where does he fit into it?"

"He probably doesn't," said Leslie. "He probably has absolutely nothing to do with it. But George was a friend of ours and I can't help wondering who was the young man seen running away from his house on the night George died."

"You're sure you don't want to leave that sort of thing to the police?"

"If I leave it to the police to find out who it was, or who our prowler was, I think I'll be waiting for ever," Leslie replied rather defensively.

"I know what you mean. If the cops stuck to catching real criminals and not hounding drivers, we might all be better off," complained Pete bitterly.

Leslie made some noncommittal noises; it was not the moment to voice his opinion of speeding motorcyclists in country lanes.

"OK, I'll see you after work tomorrow," said Pete. He got out of the car, but before he closed the door, he bent down and put his head back in. "I can tell you one thing about that boy," he said. "I caught sight of his face as he was running past me, and he looked as though he'd seen the devil."

14

Delayed by his outing to the garage during the morning, and with the diversion to the farm shop, Leslie was still busy preparing lunch when Gloria arrived. Bennett let her in and Leslie came through from the kitchen as the lady was making her entrance into the sitting room, bearing a bouquet of flowers so extravagant that it would have been excessive as a gift at a full-blown dinner party.

"I say, what an absolutely adorable house," she gushed. "It's quite the loveliest house in Dartonleigh. I said so to Gina when we were going to the pub. I said, 'That is my favourite house in the whole of Dartonleigh. I wonder who lives there'. And now, only a few days later, here I am inside. How extraordinary life is!"

"Yes, quite," said Leslie.

"This room.... So elegant, so charming! It's all simply adorable!"

"I'm rather fond of it myself," said Leslie faintly, exhausted already by her effusions.

"You must show me round the whole house." Gloria made a sweeping gesture with her arm and the many bracelets jangled like a wind chime.

"Of course," replied Leslie. "But perhaps you would like to eat first?" and he ushered her in the direction of the food.

The table was laid for the three of them. Gloria observed it and, looking round, said, "Is it just the two of you living here?"

"Yes," replied Bennett. "We got rid of the others."

"Others? What others? Oh, you're teasing me!" She wagged a finger roguishly at Bennett.

The lunch Leslie had prepared was, in his view, much improved by the addition of the ham and cheese, and the large white farmhouse loaf, from Lower Stretton Farm Shop. The apple and walnut chutney, however, was his own creation and, though he wouldn't have admitted it, he had never tasted better. Gloria helped herself generously.

"I know you're dying to hear my news," she said, and she leaned forward conspiratorially, her beads trailing in the chutney on her plate. She paused and carefully licked them clean. She turned to Leslie as she was about to resume her speech, and in doing so she managed to sweep the cutlery to the floor with her enormous bosom. Leslie crawled about under the table gathering up knives and forks as Gloria dispensed a profusion of thanks and apologies. Clean ones were fetched from the kitchen and eventually she continued speaking. "Gina said she did remember seeing your friend, George, when we were in the pub that afternoon, and she did remember seeing him in conversation. In fact, she remembered at least three people talking to the poor man. From her description I believe that you, Leslie, and Edgar, were two of them. Now, the other one..." Gloria broke off temporarily and took a bite of thickly buttered bread. She chewed it with slow deliberation and Leslie suppressed an urge to leap up and strangle her with her scarves.

"The other one," she eventually went on, "was, according to Gina, a rather attractive young man." Gloria giggled like a teenager, her face flushing. "He was tall and slim, wearing jeans and a navy top. He wasn't there for long, Gina said, and she didn't think he looked very happy."

Leslie started to say something but Gloria interrupted him.

"That's not all," she said, her voice rising. "I haven't finished. You haven't heard the most important bit. Gina went out to the ladies', and as she was coming back she heard George say, 'I can see you at seven o'clock'. She heard him quite clearly. The young fellow was much quieter but he answered something like, 'All right, I'll be there at seven'. How about that! She didn't hear anything else, and by the time she got back to the table and sat down, the young chap had gone."

"This seems awfully important," said Leslie. "Do you think you ought to—"

"Oh, I know what you're going to say," interrupted Gloria airily. "I should inform the police. I was just coming to that."

Gloria took another bite of the bread, chewing it thoughtfully, and Leslie pressed a hand to his stomach. He was convinced that he could feel a stress ulcer developing.

"I had a visit from the police this morning," she said at last, "if you could call those two adolescent boys policemen. They came into my shop in Temple. I believe they'd made enquiries at the pub, and the landlady put them on to me. They had a very odd attitude, quite offhand I thought. They asked if I'd seen George Harrison-something-or-other, whatever the poor deceased man's name was, in the pub that afternoon. I replied that I thought I had. Then they asked if I'd seen anyone with him. I said that I hadn't, and paused, and before I could continue they just said, 'OK, thank you', and left. Just like that! I'm afraid I let them go. Very naughty of me, I know, but I really didn't feel like chasing after them."

"They had the same effect on me," said Leslie. "I didn't want to tell them anything."

"I'm glad it wasn't just me," said Gloria. "Anyway, I knew I would be seeing you today and that you would follow it up if you think it's important. I've got a lot more faith in you than in those two constables. Now, perhaps I'll have one more piece of this bread; it's simply divine, and it would be a crime to waste it. A crime – now there's a pun!"

Leslie brought through some slices of pear and ginger pudding cake. It was only the remains of the previous day's dessert, but it was received with rapture by Gloria. After her fulsome praise of Leslie's 'heavenly baking', conversation resumed during which, to Leslie's vexation, it became clear that Gloria fully expected him to investigate and solve the crime. He made several attempts to eschew his role as a detective, but Gloria dismissed it, through a mouthful of cake, repeating her appeal for Leslie to be careful. Wiping her mouth she then said, "I hope you don't mind me rushing off now. Rather rude of me I know, but I have to get back to the shop. The girlie who helps me is very inexperienced. I'm training her up but it's early days and I don't like leaving her on her own. Yesterday I caught her trying to sell someone yohimbe for insomnia! Whatever next!"

Leslie and Bennett followed in her wake towards the front door. She paused on the doorstep to thank them again and insist they come and have tea with her at her shop in Temple Ducton. "Dartonleigh is such an adorable place; I'm sorry I don't live right here in the centre of the village." She was thoughtful for a moment. "I'm wondering if I could run my Tai Chi classes in the village hall. Do you think people would come?"

"My dear lady," said Bennett, "this is the kind of village where, if you advertised a class in Sumatran nose fluting you would get a full house."

Gloria looked startled for a moment before throwing her head back with a whinny of delight. "I say, you're such a card," she squealed, and headed off towards her car and Temple Ducton.

* * *

It was a lovely afternoon and, after clearing away, Leslie ventured into the garden to recover from Gloria's visit and ponder on the latest developments. He was impatient to discuss with Bennett the astonishing news of the encounter between George and the young man who perfectly fitted Robert's description which Gloria had just told them about, not to mention his conversations during the morning with Veronika and Pete, but Bennett had some work calls to make and had gone straight back into the library. It would have to wait and Leslie resigned himself to solitary contemplation. He was just getting started on the herbaceous border when he heard his name.

"Mr Mountfield!" It was the unmistakable voice of Jamie.

Leslie's heart sank, but he forced a smile onto his face and turned round. Jamie was leaning over the side gate, holding a large folder.

"I've brought my artwork for you to see," he said. Adding in a slightly accusing tone, "You did say you'd like to see it. I've nothing to do today so I brought my portfolio for you to look at."

Leslie was certain he had never made such a rash request, but resigned himself to his fate. He opened the gate, and they sat together on the garden bench.

"Did you see the papers today?" the boy asked ghoulishly. "Your house was in most of them. Ours wasn't in any." He sounded disappointed.

There was a long pause and Jamie seemed in no hurry to open the folder he was holding. Leslie looked at his trowel, abandoned by the flowerbed, and suppressed his impatience. He was about to get up to make them both a coffee when Jamie suddenly wheeled round.

"The police have been questioning people," he said, a wild look in his eye. "I was questioned."

"I'm sure it's nothing to worry about," said Leslie. "You probably know that someone reported seeing a young man in Stag Lane, so I suppose the police have to speak to all the young men in the village. Now, let's see this artwork of yours." Jamie passed the folder across to Leslie. As Leslie turned to the first page, he was unprepared for what he was to see. He gasped involuntarily at the first picture and then turned the pages slowly and speechlessly. The pictures, mostly charcoal line drawings, were horrific and brutal, the uniting theme being violent death.

"Well," said Jamie, belligerently, "what do you think of them?"

Leslie did not dare to say what he really thought about the pictures, or the state of the mind that could have produced them. He struggled for something honest. "They're very clever and... er... evocative," he said tentatively. At once he wished he had just lied, for Jamie leapt up.

"You don't like them. You don't, do you?" he shouted, snatching the portfolio from Leslie.

"Perhaps they're not meant to be liked," suggested Leslie, slowly standing up to join him. "They're very disturbing, but art is often disturbing."

"You think there's something wrong with me, don't you? You, too. I thought you would understand, Mr Mountfield, but you're just the same as the others." And with that he hurled the heavy folder forcefully at Leslie, who dodged to one side. The portfolio flew past Leslie and, as it skidded along the ground there was the shattering sound of breaking gnome. Leslie looked round and Arthur was in a thousand pieces.

The patio door opened and Bennett appeared. "Hello? What's to do?" he demanded.

Jamie was as white as the shining chunk of ceramic by the pond, which had once been the inside of Arthur's hat. "Mr Bennett, I'm sorry. I didn't mean it... I didn't mean to— I'm sorry."

"I don't think it's me you should be apologising to," said Bennett and retired indoors.

Leslie retrieved the portfolio and brushed dirt and gnome dust off the cover. It was otherwise unscathed and he returned it to the terrified boy.

"Oh, Mr M-mountfield," he stammered. "Your gnome! I didn't mean to. It's the police. They've upset me."

If it was the same two officers, Leslie thought, they were capable of sending anyone over the edge, especially this nerve-ridden boy. Leslie went inside and put the kettle on, presently returning with mugs of coffee and a plate of chocolate cake. He was a firm believer in the therapeutic effect of food. They sat in silence for a while but, after he had taken a few gulps of coffee and eaten most of his cake, Jamie said, "It was the police questions – they were asking me about the night Mr H-T passed. That's Mr Harrington-Thomas," he explained, as if Leslie may not fathom the abbreviation. "That's what Ma calls him. That's what we call him at home."

"Harrington-Thomas is a bit of a mouthful," agreed Leslie. "What were you saying about the police questions?"

"I told them that I was indoors babysitting my sisters, as I always have to when Ma's working at the pub."

"What was wrong with that? Didn't they believe you?" Leslie could imagine PC Overton's supercilious stare.

"Yes, they did, but..." The sentence tailed off.

"You weren't?" prompted Leslie.

"Well, sort of," Jamie replied hesitantly, but volunteered nothing further for a while.

Leslie sipped his coffee patiently until Jamie continued, "When the girls go up to bed, I sometimes go out."

"Go out? Where to?"

"I walk about in the dark. It doesn't matter where. Sometimes I don't even know where I've been. It's how I get ideas for my drawings. I walk about in the dark and think about my next one."

"Does anyone know you go out?"

"Oh no," said Jamie. "Ma would go berserk if she found out I left the girls. And I feel really bad about it. Guilty, you know. But I have to get out. I have to. But I'm scared in case anyone saw me."

"Even if you were seen, I'm sure the police wouldn't think you had anything to do with George's death," said Leslie more reassuringly than he really felt. He would not put anything past the two policemen he had encountered. "What reason could you possibly have had?"

"That's just it," said Jamie. "Not long before he passed, I think it was only a few days before, I was in a terrible row with Mr H-T. Ma does the cleaning up at Compton Grange, but that day my sister was ill. Ma sent me up instead to see if there was anything I could do – she doesn't like letting people down. I knew it wouldn't work out; cleaning's not really my thing. I knocked a table over, well, not even right over, but it had Mr H-T's chess set on it. He went off his head."

"I expect he was in the middle of a game. These chess players take it rather seriously."

"He told me it was a game he was playing with Mr Bennett," said Jamie miserably. "He said he'd been waiting until Mr Bennett was well enough to play again, but it could never be completed now. I've thought of that over and over. It was like an omen."

"Now you're being silly," said Leslie. "Knocking over a chess game, which was just an accident, had nothing to do with George's death."

"Then I heard Mrs H-T saying nasty things about me to Mr H-T. I was in the kitchen, they were in his study and you can hear every word from there, especially as Mr H-T talks so loud. 'What can you expect if you let a kid like that in the house?' she said. 'You can see what he's like – he's not all there'.

"When I went home and told Ma, she was furious at what Mrs H-T said," Jamie continued. "She said if it wasn't for the fact that Mr H-T was dying she'd have given in her notice. I said

I thought that should make him see that a stupid chess game isn't that important and that I wished he was dead. And now he is. It was another omen." Jamie got up as if he was about to go, but instead wandered over to the pond and started scraping the pieces of the broken gnome into a pile with his foot. Without turning round he said, sullenly, "Are you going to tell the police about me, Mr Mountfield? Are you going to tell them that I lied to them?"

"I don't think so," said Leslie, "not if you promise me that you won't leave your sisters on their own again. That seems a more serious matter. And not if there isn't anything else that you haven't told me."

Jamie continued scraping with his foot for a while without responding. Leslie forbore to interrupt this irritating action, suspecting that Jamie had something more to say.

"There is something," the boy said, at last. "On the night of the murder, I saw someone else in Stag Lane, near to Compton Grange. I couldn't tell the police, could I, because I'd told them I was at home. I don't know exactly what time it was, but it would have been somewhere around ten because that's about when I go out. It was someone on a bike." He paused for effect, with an expression on his face that Leslie could not read. "It was Daniel."

"Are you sure? Quite sure it was Daniel?" said Leslie.

There was a slyness about Jamie's manner and it was difficult to tell if he was lying, or simply pleased to be casting doubt on the boy who had stolen his job at The Daffodil.

"Oh yeah," said Jamie. "It was him all right. I've seen him hanging round there before."

15

When Edgar came to dinner that evening, Leslie was shocked at his appearance. His trousers were crumpled, and his jacket, which was missing a button, looked two sizes too big.

Leslie served dinner straight away. It was a simple fish pie with vegetables. He had chosen the meal with care, unsophisticated and comforting food. White sauce and mashed potato, which topped the dish, were what Bennett described as nursery food, though he always ate it with evident enjoyment. Edgar devoured the dinner as if it was the first proper meal he'd had for a long time.

During the meal, Leslie kept up a monologue of small talk. Bennett sat in silent contemplation and Edgar seemed oblivious to everything except his own inner troubles. Afterwards, they went through to the sitting room for coffee.

"Are you looking after yourself, Edgar?" asked Leslie. "I think you've lost some weight. You mustn't neglect yourself."

"I must admit, I've been a bit cut up about George," replied Edgar.

"It must have been a bit of a shock, being the last person to have been with him," said Leslie. "You have told the police now, haven't you?"

"Yes. I had to go to the station in Lymeford and they kept me there for hours," said Edgar, sounding aggrieved. "I think they were trying to pin his death on me. They were making an issue of the fact that I knew George before. I told them, I hardly knew him really. We just happened to live in the same village. We were both widowers, and that brought us together for a bit, but when George moved away, we didn't keep in touch, or anything. It was a complete surprise to see him when I moved here; I'd no idea he lived in Dartonleigh."

"Difficult for you," said Leslie, "but I suppose they have to ask questions."

"I've been thinking about it, and it has to have been Clarissa who committed the murder," Edgar went on vehemently. "I was with George until at least ten fifteen and there was no sign of any young man. We were sitting quietly round the fire drinking coffee, and I'm sure no one came near the house; we'd have heard them on the gravel path. Well, I would have done; I know George was a bit deaf. No, it was Clarissa all right. She was after his money and she's put him out of the way so that she can have that other fellow. She could easily have slipped back from that hotel during the night. I've always been surprised at how George came to marry someone like her. His first wife was such a nice woman, a proper lady."

Leslie did not want to get into a discussion with Edgar about Clarissa's alibi and the CCTV evidence, so he said, "Perhaps George got to an age where he felt he needed some company. Clarissa's a good-looking woman, and quite a bit younger than him, but I don't suppose he realised what she was really like."

"Yes, yes, I can understand that side of it," said Edgar, his voice suddenly heavy with self-pity. "After a long time on your own, loneliness gets the better of you. You do things you'd never have done years earlier. Stupid things, and you wish you could turn the clock back." He sunk into morose silence.

"I dare say the police will get to the bottom of it eventually," said Leslie, trying to sound more convinced than he felt.

"Not if it's the ones who wasted half a day questioning me, they won't," said Edgar bitterly. "Fortunately I had evidence, of a kind, anyway."

Leslie looked at him enquiringly.

"I'd gone to see George on a business matter and I'd taken some documents for him to sign. There was one that wasn't quite in order. Kenneth had had it drawn up and I could see that it wasn't quite accurate. It gave a rather optimistic view of our business capital. I'd removed this document and was going to get it redrafted, but I gave George the other papers which he signed. Without his signature on that final document though, the deal is worthless. The timing couldn't have been worse from my point of view. I stand to lose a great deal, a very great deal, by George's death.

"I showed the police the paperwork. I didn't, of course, tell them the real reason for the paper which had been missing. I said that I'd forgotten to take it with me when I had my meeting with George. It took me sometime to convince them that George's death at this precise moment means ruin for me. The police officer took the papers away. I was awfully glad that I'd destroyed the, er, irregular paper."

"What terrible luck for you," said Leslie, ignoring the little matter of Edgar's deceitfulness.

"That deal meant everything to me," said Edgar, looking down into his lap. "It was a trifling sum to George, but without his input, I'm finished – ruined. I've spent my life building up the business. Last year I had to buy out my business partner to give Kenneth a chance. I took a risk. I thought it would be worth it. Kenneth's had such a hard time and has found the world of work difficult. He was so keen to join me; I thought we'd really turned a corner at last."

Leslie poured more coffee, and he and Bennett sat in silence while poor Edgar unburdened himself.

"He was always a highly-strung child, and he suffered badly from the death of his mother. I did my best but every boy needs a mother."

Leslie stole a glance at Bennett, whose childhood had been blighted by a similar fate, but he made no visible reaction. At least Kenny had not been sent to boarding school a month after his mother's death.

Edgar was still speaking. "He dropped out of school and has never really held down a job. I was so pleased when he suggested coming into the business. I thought he was ready to settle down at last, but it hasn't been easy. Some of his decisions have been rather strange. I suppose he wanted to put his own stamp on it. Lack of experience, as well. I've tried to get him to listen to me, but I've never really been able to get him to respect my opinion. I was relying on George's agreement to buy into the business as it would have given us time to get back on our feet. But now this has happened. I'm ruined."

"You've taken advice, I suppose?" said Leslie. "You're sure it's as bad as that?"

Edgar sat bolt upright. "As bad as that, you say? Bad? It's worse. It's far worse than you can imagine. You really can't understand." As he shot out the final few syllables, he banged his fist on the side table with a crash, causing his coffee cup, fortunately empty, to leap in the saucer. Leslie jumped up and moved the crockery out of harm's way, while Edgar sat rigid, staring fixedly ahead, and clutching the arms of the chair until his knuckles were white.

* * *

Discussing it later that night, Leslie said, "I think I'll give Paul a ring in the morning. Edgar's had a complete breakdown."

"Good idea," said Bennett.

The two men were propped up against the wooden headboard of the bed, pondering the evening's events.

"There's no point trying to speak to Kenny about his father," said Leslie.

"No," agreed Bennett. "He seems to be the problem rather than the solution."

Leslie had walked Edgar home late that evening, and gone into the house with him. The house was in a squalid condition, filthy, with unwashed mugs and plates on every surface. The bins were overflowing and Leslie had shuddered when he opened the fridge. The grimy shelves were bare, but for an ossified lump of cheese and two half empty bottles of sour and separated milk. There was no sign of Kenny who supposedly lived at home but, according to Edgar, would sometimes be away for days or weeks at a time 'on business'.

It was tragic that Edgar invested so much in such an unworthy son, but Leslie could see that he could not help himself. Leslie had no children, but he understood how one could involuntarily become so committed to another person, particularly one's offspring, whatever they were like.

"What age do you think Kenny is?" Leslie asked Bennett.

"Late thirties, I should say."

"It's odd, isn't it," said Leslie. "Edgar speaks of him as though he's just starting out in life; as if he's a son just leaving university."

"I keep telling you," said Bennett, taking off his glasses and turning off his bedside lamp, "the man's a fool. A complete fool."

111

16

The following morning, Leslie was surprised to receive a visit from Jamie's mother. He knew her to pass the time of day with, as one knew everyone in the village, and also because she sometimes worked behind the bar in The Woodman. She stood self-consciously on the doorstep, holding an envelope.

"I've come to apologise about the damage, Mr Mountfield," she said. "Your garden gnome. Jamie told me last night." She held out the envelope. "I hope this will cover a replacement, but please let me know if it's any more; it's just that it might have to wait a week or two."

"There's absolutely no need for that, Mrs Thackeray," said Leslie, "it was just an accident, and please do call me Leslie."

"I'm Jackie," she responded, still holding out the envelope.

Seeing that she was not easily going to take no for an answer, and sensing that she had more to say, he invited her in. Showing her into the sitting room, he went through to make a pot of tea. Leslie was pouring the tea when Bennett came through from the library. Taking a cup of tea and a shortbread, he seated himself by the French doors.

"I'm really sorry about what happened," she said. "Jamie hasn't been himself for a while now. He's never really got over his father leaving, and it's been worse since he left school and can't find work."

"I suppose the village is rather isolated for a lad of his age," said Leslie.

"It doesn't help that he has to look after his sisters a lot while I work, especially in the evenings. It's the only way I can make ends meet. I get nothing from their father," she said rather bitterly, "and when he left I vowed I wouldn't lose the house. I do cleaning jobs in the day and work at the pub in the evenings and at weekends."

"Jamie told me he babysits his sisters," said Leslie.

There was an awkward pause and then Jackie said cautiously, "I think he told you that he went out the other night when he was supposed to be watching them. And you know that was the night that a young man was seen near the Grange. Before poor Mr Harrington-Thomas passed."

"He did mention it, but he said that you didn't know."

"He told me everything yesterday. He was terribly upset about breaking your gnome, and it all came out when he was telling me. He never was any good at keeping a secret. As it happened, I knew already. Lisa, his sister, knows he goes out and she'd told me."

"Didn't you challenge him about it? Weren't you worried?" said Leslie, and instantly regretted his tactless comment.

"Of course I was worried," she replied, sharply, "but you can't have any idea what it's like. He gets so wound up and upset about the smallest thing sometimes, and I feel guilty enough as it is making him stay in nearly every night. To be honest, Lisa's got twice the sense of her brother. She's got her phone and she can ring me if she's worried about anything. I know it's not very good, but honestly, Leslie, you've no idea what it's like." She clutched her cup of tea tightly as she composed herself. Feeling chastened, Leslie did not dare say anything else.

"I wanted to know if you were going to report what Jamie told you," she continued. "I can understand if you feel you have to, but I just want to know."

"I didn't have any plans to tell anyone about any of it," said Leslie. "But surely the police wouldn't think he had anything to do with what happened up at the Grange."

"I'm not so sure," replied Jackie unhappily. "He showed you his drawings; what would anyone make of those? They might think anything. And then there's his father. He left, or rather I threw him out, because of his violent temper. The police have all that on record, not that they were much help to me at the time. I was seriously worried when Jamie went to stay with his father recently and I'm not surprised he didn't stay long. I tried to discourage it, but he wouldn't listen. I don't really know what went on between them but Jamie's been much worse since then. Of course, the police don't know about that but there is another thing that would go against him. I have a key to Compton Grange; I've cleaned there since long before Mr Harrington-Thomas got married. I have keys to a lot of the houses I do for. Jamie knows where the key is; he could get in anytime he wanted to. Perhaps you can see why I'm so anxious."

For a moment Leslie wondered if Jackie Thackeray actually suspected her son of the crime.

"I've tried to persuade him to see the doctor," she continued, "but he just goes off the deep end and says that I'm trying to get him locked up. Even if I could convince him to go, you never know who you'll see at that surgery in Temple. The only one I'd trust is old Dr Seymour, but he's hardly ever there."

"We know Dr Seymour quite well," said Leslie. "If you'd like me to, I could ask him to call you. I'm certain that he would. There must be something he could do to help."

"I suppose it wouldn't do any harm if I spoke to him," she said, sounding unconvinced. "He might be able to suggest something."

They sat quietly finishing their drinks and then Jackie got up to go, and the argument over paying for the gnome resumed.

For the first time, Bennett spoke. "My dear Mrs Thackeray, your son did me the greatest favour in smashing that hideous object. I forbid you to give Leslie any money. He will only feel obliged to buy a replacement, and then there may be another murder in the village." With that, he retired to the library, and Jackie, smiling for the first time, took her leave.

17

When Leslie had things on his mind, he generally resorted to cooking. At times of high anxiety, Bennett was the beneficiary of some of his most superb meals. Leslie's repertoire these days was restricted by anxiety for Bennett's heart and he sorely missed being able to add liberal doses of cream, butter and salt to his cooking, but he did his best. The omissions were all made by stealth, though, as Bennett resolutely opposed any dietary or lifestyle changes.

Leslie had assembled the ingredients to make a chicken and mushroom casserole for dinner later, and was chopping a shallot, when he saw with interest and then surprise, a tall, thin, silver-haired man striding along the pavement, then turning in at their gate.

"Bennett!" called Leslie. "There's a man coming to the cottage."

"I've already got one man in my life, I don't need any more," Bennett called back wearily. "Send him away."

"I can't do that," Leslie exclaimed, rinsing his oniony fingers and wiping his hands on his apron as he hurried to the door. "He looks important."

"An important man – that's all we need."

Bennett had now joined Leslie in the hallway and if his reply was clearly audible to the man now standing at the open door, he betrayed nothing. The visitor produced a warrant card from an inside pocket which bore the name and title 'Detective Chief Inspector Charles Ridgeway'. He extended his hand to each of them in turn, and they introduced themselves.

"Is it convenient?"

"If it's about the television licence," said Bennett, stepping back to allow the detective chief inspector to pass, "we were going to get one next week, honestly."

Ridgeway hesitated.

"Take no notice of him," Leslie said hastily.

"I had a call," Ridgeway began, "from Dr Seymour – Paul. I know him well. We play golf together. He told me that you'd raised the initial concerns about George Harrington-Thomas's death."

"That's right, Chief Inspector," Leslie replied, taking the man's jacket and showing him into the sitting room.

"I understand from Paul that you've just come out of hospital," Ridgeway nodded towards Bennett. "He also told me that a couple of our chaps had been round and, to be honest, he gave me a bit of an earbashing about it. I understand that their behaviour was—" He paused, briefly, "their behaviour was far from correct. I'd like to offer my apologies and assure you that such conduct isn't tolerated."

"We weren't planning to make a complaint," said Leslie, "but thank you, anyway. In fact, we were quite surprised to get a police visit about the man in the garden, considering it was such a minor matter. Obviously George's death is more serious."

"We needed to speak to you again about that, but I'm under Paul's strict instructions that you aren't to be bothered. As it happens, I was on my way from a meeting in Lymeford, so I thought I'd call in myself. But," he gave a rather forced laugh, "I'm under doctor's orders not to upset you!"

Leslie's offer of coffee was accepted and when he came back through with the tray, the chief inspector was standing with Bennett at the French windows admiring the garden. Bennett was speaking.

"Leslie's the one with the green fingers, the garden is all his work. And the house, for that matter. I wouldn't know where to begin."

"I was just admiring those beautiful azalea bushes," said the chief inspector to Leslie. "That's one thing that won't grow in my garden, I'm sorry to say. Wrong sort of soil."

"They are rather stunning," agreed Leslie. "They're a variety called fireball."

Leslie watched in wonder as the chief inspector, skeletally thin, heaped three spoonsful of sugar in his coffee and helped himself to a giant slice of cherry cake. They fell into easy conversation and before he knew it, Leslie was talking to Ridgeway about Clarissa and George.

"George was on his own when we first moved here," said Leslie, "a widower. His wife had died long ago, when he was living in Surrey or Sussex, I can't remember which. He's lived here in the village for over twenty years. About five years ago, to everyone's astonishment, Clarissa appeared on the scene, and they were married very shortly afterwards. Internet dating it was, if rumour is to be believed. They seem ill-suited to each other now, but perhaps it wasn't such an unlikely match at the time. Clarissa's attractive, and it's understandable that a man of that age would be flattered by the attentions of a younger woman."

"No fool like an old fool," supplied Bennett, through a mouthful of cherry cake.

"I'm afraid it seems to have turned out that way," Leslie continued. "George was a good-looking man for his age before he became ill, and exceedingly rich, and most people think that Clarissa fancied herself as lady of the manor, with an eye on the will. Unfortunately I don't think she was prepared for George's quiet and stuffy lifestyle. In the early days she came to all the village functions, but you could see that she didn't enjoy them for what they were; she paraded about as if she was royalty. You can imagine how that was received in the village. She got involved in the amateur dramatics society at Lymeford, but that didn't last. According to village gossip she was thrown out when she had an affair with the leading man. She bought a dog, a beautiful Labrador, and went about in a Barbour coat and green wellies for a few weeks, but that was all too much trouble. She took up golf and a few other things, but they were all five-minute wonders. She even went to the WI once.

"Earlier this year she started art classes at the studio in Temple Ducton. That hasn't been a five-minute wonder – more's the pity, some would say. As you undoubtedly know by now, Clarissa's having an affair with the artist. I gather that she was with him at The Imperial Hotel on the night of George's death."

"Have my men been blabbing?" said Ridgeway.

"Oh no," replied Leslie, "I didn't get anything from them. You're forgetting, Chief Inspector, this is a village and the hotel is one of the main employers in the area. People talk."

"They may talk to each other, but they don't seem to be so keen on talking to my men," said Ridgeway wryly. "What do you know about this artist chap, Antonio?"

"Hardly anything," replied Leslie. "I've never seen him. Gloria Fairweather's the one to ask. She has a shop in Temple. It's some sort of a health store, and apparently it's directly opposite the art studio."

The chief inspector made some notes. "Doesn't it seem a bit odd that Clarissa should have been so indiscreet about this affair?" he said. "Surely there was somewhere more private they could have chosen for their rendezvous, somewhere not staffed by half the village?"

"I thought as much myself," said Leslie, "but the general opinion is that Clarissa has courted the publicity. She wanted it known; she was proud of being attractive to a younger man, especially as she now found herself as the wife of an ageing invalid. That's the expert opinion of the ladies in the village shop."

"Perhaps I'll call in at the shop," said Ridgeway. "It sounds like it's the nerve centre of the village."

"You're right, there," said Leslie. "Bennett sometimes refers to it as the Dartonleigh GCHQ."

Ridgeway smiled and finished his cake.

"But surely Clarissa and Antonio are in the clear now," said Leslie, returning to the subject. "From what we've heard, Edgar Barr was with George until at least ten fifteen pm; there is CCTV evidence that Clarissa arrived at the hotel before that. Antonio was there all evening and neither of them left the place until Clarissa came back to the Grange in the morning."

"You've acquitted them very decisively," laughed Ridgeway. "Tell me, who are the other likely suspects in the village?"

"I don't know that I'd call them suspects," said Leslie cautiously, "but George had fallen out with his neighbours." He told the chief inspector about Clarissa's affair with Jeff; the dispute over planning permission, and of Veronika's claim that

Jeff had tried calling in on George on the night of the murder, and had seen someone going into the Grange at about seven pm, and could then get no answer at ten thirty pm. He then wrestled in his mind over whether to mention Jamie or Daniel, both having minor grudges against George and both possibly having been in the vicinity on the night of the murder. He decided against it. He felt certain they were just two silly boys and he had more or less told Jackie Thackeray that he would say nothing about Jamie. The police could make their own discoveries about them, if there was anything to discover. He certainly was not going to break his word to Stan and Pete Parkin, and say anything about Pete being a potential witness.

The chief inspector looked at Leslie enquiringly.

"I was just thinking," said Leslie hastily, "I wish it was Kenny Barr." He gave the chief inspector a few details about the unpleasant man. "Apart from Clarissa, who I'm sure is devoid of concern for anyone except herself, he's the only person in the village I could imagine doing a really wicked thing. As far as I know, he's got absolutely no connection with George and no motive, but that doesn't stop me from wishing it was him!"

"Are you aware that George was rather deaf?" said Bennett to the chief inspector. "Not stone deaf, but he had certainly become noticeably hard of hearing, and he wore no hearing aid."

"Ah, is that so?" said Ridgeway, making another note. "He might not have heard someone coming into the bedroom, then, especially if he was asleep." Turning to Leslie, Ridgeway said, "You reported earlier that George had told you he'd had some sort of a shock. Have you had any ideas about what that could have been?"

"Perhaps," said Leslie. "We know that he was talking to someone just before that." Leslie related everything that Gloria had told him and said, reluctantly, "There seems little doubt that it was Robert, the young man who has now gone missing."

"Ah, well, I have some news that will interest you. I'm not breaking confidentiality by telling you but—" The chief inspector hesitated.

Leslie, anxious not to miss this snippet, said quickly, "We won't repeat a thing until we hear it officially."

119

"That's appreciated. Stories have a habit of growing legs," said Ridgeway. "What I was going to say, is that this Robert has turned up again!"

"Never!" exclaimed Leslie. "However did you find him?"

"We didn't," Ridgeway replied ruefully. "He found us. I'm told that he saw in the news that he was a wanted man and he reported to his local police station in Surrey."

"There!" Leslie exclaimed again. "I knew he was honest; turning himself in like that."

"Leslie is convinced that he is not your man," said Bennett.

"Really?" said Ridgeway. "Any particular reason?"

"No," said Leslie. "I spoke to him a few times and, I know it sounds stupid, but I'm certain that he wouldn't have murdered someone."

If he thought this naïve, the chief inspector did not say so. Instead he said, "They're bringing him down to us now so we'll know more once we've questioned him. One thing I do know is that he's really called Robin, not Robert."

Bennett then said, casually, "You know that he's George's son, do you? Born out of wedlock, presumably."

Both Leslie and Ridgeway started in astonishment.

"How the devil did you know that?" said Ridgeway. "I only found out myself when they rang me an hour ago. Did George tell you about him?"

"No," Bennett replied. "George never said a word about having a son."

"Paul told me you had a knack for discovering things, but he didn't say you were clairvoyant!"

"Nothing paranormal involved," said Bennett. "The boy's the living image of his father at that age. There's a photo up at the Grange of George as a young man, and the other day the son was standing across the road, in just the same pose. The resemblance was uncanny. Someone else presumably thinks so too. The photo's gone missing."

"So that's why you wanted the picture," said Leslie. "Just when I thought you were becoming sentimental."

"The photo's gone missing, has it?" asked Ridgeway. "That's interesting. You also told my officers that George had a blackmail threat."

Bennett recounted the same sparse details that he had given previously.

"And what about your prowler?" Ridgeway got up and went to the French windows again. "Is this where you saw him from?"

"Ah, so that's why you were looking at the garden," said Bennett.

Leslie joined them at the window. "And I thought you were really interested in my fireballs," he sighed. "But it wasn't this window." He took the chief inspector through to the library, relating the story of the nocturnal visitor. They peered through the patio doors; the garden looked particularly beautiful today. The leaves on the apple tree were unfurling in bright green clusters on the branches, the tubs on the patio were bright with daffodils, narcissi and grape hyacinth, and every flowerbed was about to burst into life. The only impediment to perfection was an empty space on a marble paving. The pond was now gnome-free. Leslie had lost heart after the demise of Alf, Arnold and Arthur.

"I suppose the prowler must have been a would-be burglar," said Leslie doubtfully.

As they turned to go back into the sitting room, Ridgeway spotted Bennett's chess set. "Paul told me Bennett was a chess player. In fact, he said he's the best chess player in the West Country."

"Oh yes," said Leslie. "He's very good. He's always winning things. Do you play?"

"Not as much as I'd like to. I'm a bit rusty, I'm afraid. Perhaps Bennett would give me a game one of these days."

"Bennett," said Leslie as they came back into the sitting room, "we're to invite the chief inspector round one evening for a game of chess. Paul told him how good you are."

Bennett looked up from his newspaper but made no reply.

"Here's my card." Ridgeway handed it to Leslie. "If there's anything else you think I should know, you can contact me directly."

Leslie fetched the chief inspector's jacket and showed him to the door. As he was about to leave he turned to Bennett and said, "Paul also told me you are a crossword puzzle setter for the newspapers."

"Did he?" said Bennett.

"Bennett sometimes tries the clues out on me," said Leslie. "He doesn't like it if I can solve them because that means they're too easy. But it's not just crosswords. Bennett does all sorts of different puzzles."

"I wondered what name you write under," Ridgeway asked diffidently. "I'm a bit of a crossword addict myself."

Bennett sighed heavily. "I'm afraid I'm bound by an oath of secrecy," he said solemnly.

Ridgeway smiled uncertainly and took his leave. Leslie knew that the only oath of secrecy binding Bennett was his own, but a Trappist's vow of silence would be broken sooner.

"No wonder that George said he'd had a shock," said Leslie, as they went back into the sitting room. "His secret son turning up like that, presumably out of the blue."

"The chickens, or should I say chicken, coming home to roost," said Bennett.

"That whole episode makes sense now," said Leslie. "Remember, Robert, or rather Robin, came rushing out of The Woodman like a wild thing and collided with Daniel. Then I went into the pub and George looked like he was about to have a stroke."

"Quite unmanned in folly."

Refusing to indulge Bennett by querying this obscure quotation, Leslie gathered the mugs and plates on a tray and started for the kitchen. He stopped as a thought suddenly dawned on him. "You might have told me that you guessed the boy was George's son. Especially when you realised, as you must have done, that his appearance must almost certainly have been the cause of George's shock. You let me torment myself with not knowing what it was about."

"I couldn't be entirely sure," said Bennett, as though this was the only criterion for sharing the information.

"You do make me cross," said Leslie and stomped into the kitchen, thoroughly aggrieved at Bennett's secretive behaviour. The abandoned casserole ingredients lay on his chopping board and he set back to work quickly, to make up for lost time. Soon the chicken pieces had been browned and set aside, and the pot was sizzling with chopped bacon and shallots. The aroma in the kitchen was mouthwatering, the more so as wine, mushrooms, stock and the chicken pieces were added. As Leslie lifted the casserole pot into the oven, and set about clearing up, he discovered that his grievances had been overshadowed by the relief of finding out what it was that had upset George, for Robin's sudden manifestation must surely have been the cause. It was, of course, too bad that Bennett had not discussed it with him much sooner, but at least he knew now.

"Did you really realise that Robin was George's son, from that photo?" Leslie asked when he returned, at last, to the sitting room.

"It was a remarkable likeness," said Bennett, "but it wasn't just the photograph. George's reaction after he had been speaking to the young man; the young man's uneasy behaviour; his scouting out Stag Lane, and the fact that the photo has now mysteriously disappeared – it all added up."

"What do you think has happened to that photo?" Leslie asked. "Or are you keeping that to yourself as well?"

"It's probably been burnt or shredded by now," said Bennett, ignoring Leslie's peevish remark. "Someone recognised the likeness, and didn't want anyone else to. Probably George himself."

"That makes sense," said Leslie. "And have you any idea how Robin found George in The Woodman that afternoon?"

"No," said Bennett. "I was wondering about it myself."

Leslie wandered over to the French windows and peered into the garden. "Who'd have thought that George, of all people, had a past that would catch up with him like that, very much at the eleventh hour?" he said. "I'd always thought of him as rather a stuffed shirt, pillar of the establishment, and all that. Remember when we first came here? He was the church warden over at Sacred Heart, leader of the parish council and chairman of the chess club. But I suppose I should have seen there was another side to him when he took up with the glamorous Clarissa in his mature years."

"And I should have known from his chess game," said Bennett. "Nothing stuffy about that, and masterfully unpredictable."

Both the men were quiet for a while, occupied with their own thoughts. At length Leslie said, "I wonder why Robin came to see his father."

"That's a very good question," said Bennett, getting up and moving towards the library to resume his work. In the doorway he paused and said to Leslie, "You haven't changed your mind about him? About the son, Robin?"

"Not one bit. I'm utterly convinced he didn't murder George," said Leslie without hesitation, and he went off to the kitchen to check his casserole.

18

Pete Parkin arrived at four thirty as promised, pink and perspiring from the exertions of cycling. He propped his bicycle in the little front garden but refused any refreshment, or even to go inside the cottage, because of his oily clothes.

"I'm not cut out for cycling," he complained. "Too much muscle in the wrong places; weighs you down on a bike. Bodybuilding's my game."

That explained the physique, and he certainly wasn't a man you'd want to get on the wrong side of, Leslie thought.

Even though it was nearly closing time, The Daffodil was still busy, and they queued at the counter where the remaining takeaway rolls and sandwiches were being sold off at half price. Leslie looked longingly at the fresh cream cakes, also heavily reduced in price, but the thought of his expanding waistline and Bennett's arteries firmed his resolve, and he decided on some wholemeal scones instead.

The young waitress was busy at the tables and Annie was serving behind the counter but there was no sign of Daniel. Leslie suddenly remembered with dismay that Annie was keeping him backstage and that he was not allowed to serve or wait at table. It would be embarrassing if he had brought Pete here on a fool's errand.

Before he could start to fret though, Daniel appeared from the kitchen, in apron and dripping rubber gloves, and collected up some trays from beside the counter. As he was doing so, he glanced up, saw Pete, and his expression changed. It wasn't much, but there was a definite look of apprehension on the boy's face, and he turned quickly and took the trays into the kitchen.

Pete bought a cheese baguette which was nearly the size of a loaf of bread and four jam doughnuts. "Blimey!" Pete exclaimed outside the shop. "Half price? I nearly said to her, 'It's the roll

I want to buy, love, not the shop!' I can't believe people pay those prices. Still, the wife and kids'll be pleased with the cakes, if I manage to get them home without eating them!"

"Let's find somewhere private to talk," said Leslie, aware that here in the village centre a Vera or a Marian might appear at any moment. The two men strolled past the post office and the village shop and down to the orchard park. Two young mothers were in the playground, pushing their excited infants back and forward in the swings; a couple of little girls were chasing each other round the outside of the roundabout, and some small boys were attempting to climb the wrong way up the slide. It was an innocent scene and all so far removed from murder. They sat on one of the benches on the perimeter of the park and Pete tucked into the baguette.

"This'll keep me going until I get home," he laughed between mouthfuls.

"Let me settle up with you." Leslie gave Pete considerably more than the shopping had cost. "It was good of you to come, and I said I would make it worth the trouble."

"Very good of you, Mr Mountfield, but I feel bad taking it," said Pete, pocketing the cash. "I don't think I can be of much help. I'm pretty sure that the lad in the café wasn't the one I saw running down the lane, but it's difficult to be a hundred per cent certain." He finished his baguette, screwed the paper bag into a ball and aimed it, successfully, into a nearby bin. "I'll tell you what's bothering me," he went on. "Although I don't think he was the boy in the lane, I've a feeling I've seen him somewhere before, and that he was up to no good."

"It's funny that you should say that," said Leslie. "Did you see the expression on his face when he saw you?"

"Yes, I noticed that, all right," said Pete. "I think that's what jogged my memory. I thought to myself, 'I've seen that look before'. I wish I could remember when it was."

They were about to stand up when Leslie said, "Just wait a moment, Pete. Do you see that youngster coming in the park now?"

They looked at a morose figure, hands stuffed into pockets and head down, cutting through the park towards the lane at the back.

"Yes. What of him?"

"That's Jamie, Jackie Thackeray's boy."

"Blimey, so it is. It's a while since I've seen him," said Pete. "What about him?"

"Do you think it might have been him you saw running down the lane?

Pete leant forward and peered at Jamie, who was stomping along the path, oblivious of them. "I don't think so," said Pete and he shook his head. "It's harder than you think to be absolutely sure. Like the other one, I don't think it was him, but I probably wouldn't swear to it in court. Sorry I can't be more helpful than that, Mr Mountfield "

As they walked back, Leslie felt rather subdued. He had known all along that the young man seen running away from the Grange wasn't Daniel or Jamie, and now he was cross with himself for dragging Pete out on this time-wasting exercise.

Pete again refused Leslie's offer of hospitality, and retrieved his bicycle for the strenuous ride home. He was just starting to cycle away when he pulled up, turned around and pedalled back to Leslie. "It's just come to me," he said. "I've remembered where I've seen that boy in the café before. It was quite a few weeks ago at the top of Stag Lane. I was out on my bike – this one. I was pushing it up the hill and as I got near the top I saw this lad hanging about in the trees having a fag. As I got closer I could see, or rather smell that it wasn't a fag at all, it was a joint. He gave me such a guilty look, just like he did today. I couldn't give a damn what the boy was doing, he can smoke what he likes as far as I'm concerned, but I suppose he was worried I'd report him, or something. Anyway, that was it. Nothing to do with this business after all, but I'm glad I remembered." And with that, he pedalled off with the carrier bag full of doughnuts swinging from the handlebar.

19

The news was all around the village: Clarissa had been released by the police and was back at the Grange with Antonio in situ. More notable still, she had taken to coming down into the village. It was months since Clarissa had set foot in the shop or post office and far longer since she had visited the teashop, but now she was seen in all of them. She had taken on a pitiful air and appeared to be seeking sympathy in a display of wounded grief. Though many of Dartonleigh's residents gave her a wide berth, there was no shortage of people willing to play along with her, in return for some grisly detail about George's demise or her detainment by the police.

"Clarissa is outrageous," said Leslie to Bennett at lunchtime the next day. "She's got no shame. All these years she's barely passed the time of day with anyone in the village, but you should have seen her this morning. She was sounding off to any fool who would listen to her. She seems to want everyone to know how hard done by she feels."

Earlier, Leslie had walked across to the village hall to sample the treats on offer at the monthly WI coffee morning. In the noise and bustle of the hall, he had not noticed Clarissa, surrounded as she was by an audience of women eager to feed their lurid appetites for gossip, until he was seated at the adjacent table and within earshot. The slice of lemon drizzle cake he had selected was rather disappointing and could do nothing to distract him from Clarissa's oration.

"In all my life I never dreamt that my husband would be murdered, and by a son I never knew he had," she lamented, with convincing anguish. "It was a double shock!" Her tone suggested that she was confiding the agonising secrets of her heart to her closest friends, but Leslie was only conscious that this was the woman who had installed her lover in the house hours after George's death.

"Have they charged the son?"

"Has the boy confessed?"

"Did he definitely do it?"

The questions came thick and fast.

"I don't know if he's actually been charged yet," said Clarissa, "but if not, it's only a matter of time. He turned up in the village out of the blue, and by the next morning his father had been murdered. It hardly needs a confession."

Various expressions of shock and disgust, mixed with prurient fascination, were uttered.

"I don't like to speak ill of the dead," said one lady, "and especially not him being your husband and all, but I must say—" The sentence remained unfinished but, after a moment, the speaker continued, in a whisper, to her friend who was just behind Leslie. "So George was a bit of a lad, after all?"

"Can you imagine what it has done to me?" Clarissa continued dramatically. "To realise that my husband had been deceiving me all those years. I don't think I'll ever trust anyone again."

There were murmurs of sympathy all round; they were eager to hear all the details. It was impossible to tell if Clarissa was aware of the genuine sentiments of her audience, but she continued to play her part.

"And to be accused of murdering him myself! When they caught that bastard son you'd think they'd have let me go right away, but no. They started quizzing me all over again. I don't know exactly what they were insinuating but I believe they thought I'd found out about the son and murdered George in a fit of rage or jealousy. For a long time I simply couldn't make the police believe that I knew nothing about the boy's existence until they told me about him."

"Do they know why his son did it?" asked one of the women.

"God knows," said Clarissa. "He's probably some sort of crazed nutter, come down here to take revenge on his father for abandoning him. Completely unhinged, I imagine."

"Or maybe he's a junkie," whispered another woman, enunciating the noun with gruesome delight. "After his father's money to spend on his next fix."

"I suppose," sighed Clarissa, "that I can only be thankful that my own life was spared. If I'd been in the house he might have done us both in."

Leslie shifted miserably in his chair. He was sickened by all the scandalmongering and by Clarissa's brazen hypocrisy.

"Thank God that some friend of George's called round to see him in the evening before his death. I'm sure those damned policemen were disappointed when they found that the CCTV evidence proved I was elsewhere at the time of his murder and they had to admit that I had an alibi. They'd been determined to pin it on me up until then, even though I had absolutely no motive. 'He was on his last legs', I kept telling them. 'Why on earth would I kill him?'"

Leslie was outraged to hear poor George referred to in this unfeeling way, but it was impossible not to listen. One of the women said something that Leslie didn't catch.

"Oh no, it's all right now," Clarissa replied airily. "I have to stay in the area for the time being, but that's just a formality. They've changed their tune now." She paused to sip at her coffee, then continued in a highly confidential tone. "My solicitor assures me that I'm completely in the clear now that there's evidence I was nowhere near the house when George died. He managed to find out – I don't know how – that the boy confirmed to the police that he'd turned up unexpectedly, and that George was on his own. So the police now see that I wasn't at the house and knew nothing about the boy's existence."

Everything in Clarissa's account reinforced Leslie's opinion of her, and of Robin. That Clarissa should be referring to her absence on the night George died with such complete lack of shame, epitomised her callous disregard for anything or anyone but herself. In contrast, Robin's apparent openness about his movements further confirmed Leslie's instinct that he was innocent.

Clarissa paused for breath at last and a tumult of commiserations and questions followed. Leslie looked up to see Jackie Thackeray coming away from the counter with a tray and looking around the crowded room for a table. Jamie was following a few paces behind with a sullen expression. If ever there was a boy who needed some friends of his own age, it was him.

Leslie caught Jackie's eye and he beckoned her to join him at the table. Jamie hunched himself into the chair next to Leslie. Leslie began to make small talk, but already Clarissa had taken the stage again at the next table and was very difficult to compete with.

"The police also had some insane idea," Clarissa was saying loudly, "that George was being blackmailed."

Leslie sat rigidly in his chair, his full attention caught.

"I really don't know what it was all about," Clarissa continued carelessly, as though she was referring to some trivial matter. "They went through all his bank accounts and, apparently, he made two particularly large cash withdrawals. I told the police that I'd no idea about it; I never discussed money with George and I couldn't remember him buying anything particularly expensive recently. Why would he? They seemed particularly suspicious because apparently George actually went to the bank and took the money out in notes. I suppose that is a bit odd, but I don't see that it proves he was being blackmailed. I'm sure there are still people who prefer being paid for work cash in hand. He certainly didn't tell me he'd had threatening phone calls or letters or anything like that. I don't really know what put the idea into their heads."

Leslie suddenly remembered his manners and turned his attention back to his own table. He fell into conversation with Jackie but was irritated to see that Jamie was listening to Clarissa with what appeared to be avid interest. The party at Clarissa's table was starting to break up and as they did so, Clarissa noticed Leslie. She pulled her chair around to sit next to him, interrupting his conversation and without taking the slightest notice of either Jackie or Jamie. Leslie made an attempt to introduce his companions, but Clarissa had already begun speaking.

"Darling!" she gushed. Leslie realised she probably could not remember his name. "What luck seeing you. I found that photograph you wanted. You simply must have it."

Leslie did not bother to mention that it was Bennett who wanted the picture, but said something about it not being urgent, and not wanting to disturb her.

"No, no, you simply must have the photo. I'm so touched that you want it. You must come up to the house and collect it."

Hastily declining Clarissa's offer to take him in the car there and then, he promised to go and collect the photograph during the afternoon. Clarissa attempted to monopolise Leslie's attention and before he could shake her off, Jackie finished her tea and politely took her leave, with Jamie in tow, leaving Leslie to carry the burden of Clarissa's bad manners.

* * *

"Clarissa seemed very anxious for me to go to the house," said Leslie to Bennett over lunch, when he had finished regaling Bennett with the details of the morning.

"Perhaps she's just after your body," Bennett replied, through a mouthful of sandwich.

"Well, who wouldn't be?" sighed Leslie. "Seriously, it seems to be part of this new role she's taken on: the poor widow."

"Worthy of Dostoevsky, by the sound of it," said Bennett.

Leslie postponed the visit to collect the photo for as long as he could, but a desire to get it over with eventually forced him into action. The church clock was striking three when he set off and it was starting to rain so he took the longer route up the lane, avoiding the shortcut along the muddy woodland path.

By the time Leslie reached the sweeping driveway to Compton Grange there was a steady drizzle. There was no answer when Leslie rang the bell the first, and then the second time. The irritation that he was soaking for nothing was tempered by the desire to forget it and go home, but just as he was turning to leave, the door swung open and Clarissa stepped forward onto the rain-soaked step and seized him in an embrace.

"Darling! Thank you so much for coming to see me. You've come at just the right moment. I'm all alone."

Although she affected her usual gushing manner, Leslie could see that recent events were taking their toll. Her immaculate make-up could not conceal the thick lines around her eyes, and the strong smell of alcohol probably explained the length of time it had taken for her to come to the door. This suggestion was reinforced when she tottered rather unsteadily down the hall and into the sitting room, and made for the mahogany cabinet.

"What can I get you, darling? What's your poison? Wine? A whisky? Or perhaps you'd prefer a beer?"

"Nothing just now, thank you," said Leslie, "it's a bit early for me."

"Oh nonsense." Clarissa gave a little giggle. "You're not going to make me drink on my own." With that, she poured Leslie a huge glass of red wine.

"It's so good of you to come and see a poor widow lady. Everyone else is giving me the cold shoulder. They're being kind to my face, but I know what they're all saying behind my back." She finished her glass of wine in a few large gulps, and poured herself another. "They're all saying," she continued, dolefully now, "no smoke without fire."

Before Leslie could think of a reply she continued.

"It's terrible. First I was locked up at that police station and questioned for hours and hours about George's death. They treated me like a criminal. Me! I know I didn't exactly tell the truth about my whereabouts the night George died, but what could they expect? Did they really expect me to confess that I spent the night of my husband's death with a lover?" Clarissa sounded aggrieved that the truth might have been expected of her.

Leslie made a desperate bid to interrupt before she went any further, but to no avail. She continued undeterred, her voice taking on a pitiful tone.

"I told them that I was so distressed that my poor husband had spent his last hours alone, and I'd felt too ashamed to admit it even to myself. I was in complete denial about the whole thing."

Leslie stared in disbelief at such arrant pretence.

"They still questioned me over and over again. I told them that I'd spent the afternoon helping Antonio in the gallery until closing time. They could check that with the nosey parker in the health store who spends the whole time ogling Antonio through her shop window across the street. Then we went back to Antonio's rooms; he has lodgings just outside Temple. I don't go there very often as the landlady is usually at home, but she went to a concert on Saturday evening so we had the place to ourselves for a while.

"The police asked if anyone saw us, if we had any witnesses. 'Officer', I said, 'if there had been witnesses then you really should arrest us. I'm sure that what Antonio and I were doing would be illegal with an audience'."

Squirming with embarrassment, Leslie tried to break into the conversation, but Clarissa was not to be checked.

"Antonio went on to the hotel ahead of me, and I stayed in his rooms for an hour or so. We never arrived together. He always checked in for the two of us, in his name, and I'd arrive a little later and just go straight up to the room."

Leslie took a large mouthful of the red wine, which was of course excellent, and wondered how he could escape.

"I left early in the morning," Clarissa murmured in a low voice, "and when I came home I found the back door unlocked. George had started getting forgetful about things. He must have gone to bed and left it undone. Anyone could have walked in and murdered him. Only it wasn't anyone, was it? It was that evil son of his."

It was quite clear by now that Clarissa had forgotten the reason she had invited Leslie to the house and he wondered how he could interrupt this monologue, mention the photograph and get away. Every time he tried to speak, Clarissa continued talking over him. There was nothing for it but to drink his wine and wait for the story to run its course. It was a very good Merlot, courtesy of George's cellar. George would have been horrified at Clarissa drinking it with so little appreciation. In her present condition she might as well have been drinking vinegar.

"Actually, it was only when they found out about George's son that they started to believe my story," she continued. "When they first questioned me about him… the shock! I never knew he had a son, I told them. It was humiliating. My husband had an illegitimate child and I never knew about it until some cop at a police station gave me the news. And George had the nerve to lecture me about my behaviour! You can't believe what I've been through."

It was more of the same old hypocrisy that Leslie had overheard that morning and it was no easier to endure now.

"I was so relieved when they let me go, and just when I thought I might be able to start recovering, Antonio has announced that he has to go to London to see an art dealer. I've begged him to stay, but it's about an important deal and he has to see the man face to face. He can't postpone it – it's an Italian dealer and he's only in the country for a few days. I can't stand it; I don't know what I'm going to do. Antonio's at his studio now, and I'm a wreck just being here alone for a few hours." Her face was flushed with the effects of alcohol and agitation. "I can't stand being in this house on my own. I never could before, and now I can feel George's ghost haunting every room."

For the first time that day, Leslie felt that Clarissa was speaking with sincerity. Her fear was palpable and, despite himself, he felt sorry for her.

"Isn't there anyone who could come and stay with you?" he asked.

"Like who?" Clarissa spread her arms in despair. She was, it seemed, alone and friendless in the world, a pitiful and pitiable figure.

"Don't you have a son?" said Leslie, recalling something he had heard in the past. "Could he come for a few days until Antonio is back?"

"Gordon?" she said in disgust. "He won't have anything to do with me either. He's a worse prig than all those sex-starved spinsters in the village. I couldn't even ask him. There isn't anyone who cares about me except Antonio."

Suddenly, the tears coursed down her cheeks, creating two rivers of mascara, and her shoulders heaved as she sobbed. Leslie sat self-consciously clutching his wine glass, wondering quite how to extricate himself from this situation. Clarissa's self-pitying soliloquy was now barely intelligible.

"It's all that bloody boy's fault. That bastard. I hope they bang him up for life. Shame the bloody woman was a Catholic, like George, otherwise she would have had an abortion like any sensible woman and we wouldn't be in all this trouble."

As Clarissa was uttering this disgraceful speech, Leslie heard the front door open and he looked up to see a figure in the hall. A man had come in from the rain with his hood up. He approached the sitting room and looked in. Leslie gasped in shock, and spilled the remains of the wine down his front. He knew that hooded face. It was none other than the prowler with whom he'd come face to face in the night a week ago.

20

Exactly as before, the man's face contorted and then he vanished as quickly as he had appeared.

Clarissa, oblivious of everything except her own misery, said with relief, "Antonio's home, thank God! Toni! Toni, darling! Where is he?"

"I'll be on my way, then," said Leslie, recovering himself sufficiently for speech. "I was wondering if you had that photograph – the one you said you'd found. If it's not handy I can come back another day."

"Oh yes, the photo of George. I have it here." Clarissa swayed unsteadily across the room and, fumbling with a key, unlocked George's desk. She took out a large mahogany box and lifted it onto the coffee table. The key for this box was already in its lock and Clarissa opened the lid, revealing numerous official-looking documents. "I was starting to look through George's things and I found the photo in here, locked away with all this paperwork. I suppose he must have put it here. I can't imagine why."

It looked as though Clarissa had lost no time searching for the will and the insurance policies.

"God, I can't bear to look at it," said Clarissa rather unexpectedly, and she put the photograph down on the table, her stricken expression suggesting that perhaps she did have some feelings, whatever they were, after all. She scrabbled about in the box until she found an envelope and, hastily tucking the photograph inside, hid the face of her betrayed, and now departed, husband.

Leslie hurriedly put the envelope in the inside pocket of his jacket and made for the front door. He had an overwhelming urge to be at home and made a swift exit. The sight of Antonio in the doorway had caused him to relive the shock of the original encounter and his head was swimming. He could not make sense of the situation, but mixed up together in his frantic mind were mysterious night-time prowling, adultery, murder and Antonio.

Leslie set off down the drive at a jog, desperate to get home where he could tell Bennett and marshal his thoughts. Leslie was not cut out for any sort of aerobic activity, even downhill, and he was out of breath almost immediately. Then behind him he heard the slamming of the front door of Compton Grange and, looking over his shoulder, he saw Antonio coming after him.

Seized with irrational panic, Leslie fled down the lane and scrambled over the stile to take the shortcut through the woods. He slithered his way along the path, now wet and very slippery in the rain. He could hear the sound of Antonio vaulting the stile after him and following him down the track. Leslie realised immediately that he had made a terrible mistake in leading his pursuer into a woodland. It was only a small copse but it was densely wooded and completely deserted. He found reserves of energy he would never have thought he possessed.

Just as it seemed that he might make it to the other end of the track before Antonio caught up with him, he slipped on the muddy path, twisted his ankle and fell heavily onto a fallen tree trunk. He lay motionless for a few moments, badly winded and unable to catch his breath.

Antonio arrived and stood over him. Leslie instinctively put his arms up to shield his face, then, wincing, wished he hadn't.

"Hey, man, are you hurt?" Antonio's voice was a smooth drawl. "Nothing broken, huh?"

It felt to Leslie as though everything was broken, but he was too winded to reply. He gingerly eased himself into a sitting position, and then, with great effort, shuffled himself up onto the fallen tree trunk. Antonio, who had watched without offering any assistance, now sat down beside him, as though they were a couple of mates having a rest while out for a country stroll.

"I guess you recognised me, the guy you came face to face with the other night. I reckon I owe you a bit of an explanation as to what I was doing creeping about in your garden."

Leslie was still too breathless to speak, but Antonio carried on nonetheless, in a light-hearted tone, as though he had been caught doing nothing more innocuous than pinching a biscuit from the tin.

"It's a teeny bit awkward as there's another person concerned. I was with a girl, you see, down at one of the houses nearby and, er, someone came home unexpectedly. They started to come after me so I hopped across your wall and was waiting in the shadows until the coast was clear again. It would have been all right only you chose that moment to open the door." He sounded rather put out about it.

All Leslie could muster was a feeble cough, so Antonio continued.

"I know what you must be thinking. It's just that, although I'm stopping with Clarissa at the moment, it's not really, you know, serious. I'm just keeping her company in the house. I'll be honest with you, I'm in a bit of a tricky situation." His tone was now confiding. "I don't really go for the older woman. When she first showed up at the art classes I thought she was lonely. I felt sorry for her. I'd no idea she was married. She never mentioned the old boy until... well, until it was a bit late. Even then I'd no idea she'd get so involved. Now the old boy's snuffed it, she's talking of marriage."

Had Leslie been able to speak he would have been lost for words. He was soaked through, covered in mud and injured, and now had to listen to this disgraceful man's inappropriate disclosures.

"I would have backed off a long while ago but she's been very generous in, er, sponsoring my art gallery. In fact it wouldn't survive without her very generous, er, sponsorship. But you've no idea what I've had to go through. God, those nights at the hotel. So embarrassing."

Leslie could hardly believe his ears. As if sleeping with a woman he didn't care for was not enough, this man, it now appeared, had been prostituting himself in order to fund his little hobby. Every value that Leslie held was offended to the core.

"I don't like being mixed up in this murder business, and now that Clarissa's talking about marriage, that changes everything. My God, man, you don't know what I've been through the last few months."

This vile individual was now seeking sympathy.

"How are you feeling now? A bit brighter, huh? You took quite a tumble." He injected warmth and sympathy into his tone. "I was just wondering, um, what you are going to do about the other night – finding me in your garden. It's not myself I'm worried about; it's the, er, young lady. It would cause her an awful lot of trouble."

The complete altruist.

"I hope you won't want to take it any further," he said persuasively, "now that you know that it was me in your garden and I wasn't really up to anything."

"I'll have to think about it," said Leslie, who had taken exception to the man's presumptions. "I can't make a decision on the spur of the moment." Leslie also felt wary; there was something unpleasantly manipulative about Antonio's manner.

"Yes, yes, of course." The smooth drawl continued. "Look, come and have a drink with me tomorrow in Temple and we can talk it through. I'll be able to explain a bit more tomorrow. It's just that I'll have to speak to the, er, young lady first."

"I thought you were going to London tomorrow, to see an Italian art dealer," said Leslie.

"I was," he agreed hastily, "but I can put it off until later, or the following day. The Italian art dealer that I'm going to see isn't exactly an Italian art dealer." Antonio had the audacity to give Leslie a one-man-of-the-world-to-another wink.

"I can't go into Temple tomorrow," said Leslie. "I have an optician's appointment in Lymeford at eleven."

"Lymeford it is, then!" said Antonio. "Meet me at The Swan after your appointment. No, make it The Plough; the beer is better. And give me your word that you won't contact the police until I've a chance to explain myself."

Quite against his better judgement, Leslie found himself giving his word to this repellent but persuasive man, if only to get rid of him. Antonio got to his feet and set off at a sprightly pace towards Compton Grange, without so much as a backward glance at Leslie, who was struggling to get up.

It seemed a long walk back to the cottage. In an unprecedented state of filth and disarray, Leslie appeared in the doorway to the library where Bennett was working. He looked up, cocked his head on one side and said, "Have you come home across country?"

At that moment, Leslie's jacket fell open, and Bennett's expression changed instantly. He rose quickly from the chair saying, "My God, Les, what's happened to you?" and he took hold of Leslie by the shoulders, peering with anxiety at his chest.

Perplexed, Leslie looked down to follow Bennett's gaze. "That's red wine," he explained.

"For pity's sake, don't do that to me, Leslie," Bennett said. "Coming in here looking like something from the battle front and with a damn great crimson stain on your torso! What the devil have you been doing, anyway? Did you have to fight Clarissa off in the bushes?"

Bennett ran a bath, adding, to Leslie's surprise, just the right combination of lavender oil and calendula to the bath water. A glass of brandy completed the treatment. Bennett sat on the white wicker chair in the bathroom while Leslie soaked his cuts and bruises and reported his encounter with Antonio.

"He sounds a right creep," declared Bennett, "but it does explain his relationship with Clarissa. You aren't seriously going to meet him tomorrow, are you, Les?"

"I don't know how I can get out of it. I'd rather not cancel my optician's appointment, and the town isn't big enough to hide in. He's bound to see me there."

"Are you sure it's wise to go, Les? A lot of strange things have been going on, and we don't know much about this chap. What we do know isn't good. Why don't you speak to Ridgeway about him first?"

"What is there to say to Ridgeway?" said Leslie. "It was only because there was something rather, I don't know, something rather disingenuous about his manner that I didn't agree to drop the matter there and then. After all, his sex life is none of my business. I've certainly got no loyalty to Clarissa if he is two-timing her. If Antonio was hiding in our garden from some enraged husband or partner, it's hardly a police matter. But I gave him my word that I'd go and see him tomorrow, so I feel I must go.

I'll have one drink with him, hear what he has to say, and then come home. I can speak to Ridgeway then, if there's anything to tell. One day can't make much difference."

It was after dinner that Leslie remembered the photograph. His jacket was hanging up to dry in the utility room and he retrieved the envelope from the inside pocket, relieved to see that it was dry and undamaged. He took the photograph out and, stickler as he was for recycling, added the envelope to a neat pile of reusable stationery in a cupboard. Bennett was right, the picture did bear an uncanny resemblance to the anxious young man he now knew to be George's son. He carried the picture through and studied it before handing it to Bennett.

"Whatever anyone says, I'll never believe that Robin is the murderer," he said. "It's just not in his character."

21

The following morning Leslie regretted not having cancelled both his optician's appointment and his tryst with Antonio. Normally he enjoyed the mile or so walk to the bus stop on the main Lymeford Road. It was a pretty little lane and, in any case, it was a small price to pay for living in a quiet village. One of the reasons that Dartonleigh had remained unspoiled and escaped the commercialisation of its neighbours, was its narrow, single track roads which prohibited the tourist coaches from reaching it and discouraged all but the most determined drivers.

Today though, aching and sore from the previous day's misadventures, Leslie was conscious of every painful step. He paused in the lane and considered going back for the car, but parking in Lymeford was notoriously difficult. The car park was often full at this time of year and he had had more than one embarrassing experience unsuccessfully attempting to manoeuvre the Rover into one of the tight parking spaces on the street, holding the traffic up in both directions. Had he not had a row that morning with Bennett, in which he had insisted on keeping the appointment with Antonio, Leslie would undoubtedly have turned back completely. Instead, stubborn pride gave him the determination to go on. Beneath his resolve though, Leslie was aware of a deep sense of unease brought about by Bennett's uncharacteristic persistence in discouraging him from this meeting.

After what felt like a much longer, bumpier ride than usual, the bus arrived at Lymeford. It was an ancient market town and, although large enough to house the local hospital, police station and town hall, it retained a traditional character and charm. The infrequency of the bus timetable meant that Leslie had an hour to spare before his optician's appointment and it would normally have passed quickly and pleasantly in browsing the shops and market stalls. Today, he had the energy to do no more than to make for his favourite coffee shop.

As he rounded the corner into the main street, he could hear a man's voice raised in loud protest. The strident tones sounded familiar and, sure enough, as the complainant came into view, Leslie recognised Veronika's husband, Jeff, engaged in an angry dispute with a uniformed parking attendant.

Before Leslie could make an escape, he had been noticed. Had Jeff encountered Leslie in other circumstances he would undoubtedly have ignored him, but today, incandescent with rage, he turned to Leslie to vent his feelings and enlist support.

"Can you believe what that... that.... stupid bloody fool has done?" he shouted.

Fortunately, the parking attendant had taken advantage of Leslie's arrival and had melted away.

Jeff ripped the parking ticket from the windscreen and brandished it at Leslie. "Look at this! He saw me coming and bloody well ignored me on purpose. I was shouting at him to wait, but he went ahead and issued the ticket."

Leslie made sympathetic noises as Jeff, now quite beside himself, revealed the reason for the depth of his fury.

"It's unbelievable. I had an appointment at nine o'clock with those incompetent morons in the planning office. They kept me waiting for over an hour and then, after all that time, they told me no decisions can be made about my planning permission now that stupid, sodding neighbour of mine has kicked the bucket. Even worse, they don't know when my case will come back on the agenda. I came out to the car and, can you believe it, one of their stupid, sodding parking wardens has slapped a ticket on my windscreen. I told him that it was the fault of the planning officer – that, and their damned antiquated parking system – but he wouldn't listen. I won't tell you where I want to stuff this ticket. The stupid imbecile should be made to pay the sodding fine." As he spoke, Jeff made several unpleasant gestures in the direction of the town hall. "That planning office – full of so-and-so morons who can't make a decision between them. Weeks ago I had a conversation with that planning officer about my planning permission. 'Very likely', I said to him, 'that stupid, interfering neighbour of mine will be dead before you've finished processing the application and then that'll be the end of the objections'."

Disgusted by Jeff's comments, Leslie tried to remonstrate with him, but his protests were unheard as Jeff continued his tirade.

"'Oh no, Mr Clayden', said the planning officer, 'once someone has made an objection, we have to follow it through unless they formally withdraw the objection. We have to complete the process. The process has to be signed off. I'm sure it would get very complicated if the objector was to become deceased'. Completely moronic, of course, but I know what these council people are like. So I made the damnedest efforts to get my case heard by the planning committee straight away. I told them it was absolutely imperative it was heard quickly. They wouldn't budge at first, I would just have to wait, but finally, after nearly killing myself, it was put on the agenda. It was due to be heard next week and I was given to understand that it was going to get the nod." He paused to make a gesture of exasperation and despair.

"Now that bloody fool of a neighbour of mine has died, I'm back to square one. Honestly, if I found out who the hell had murdered him, I'd murder them myself." There was no trace of irony in his remarks, just wild rage. He cast the parking ticket into the gutter, got into the car and drove off.

Leslie hobbled into the café to recover.

The optician's appointment over, Leslie set off for his meeting with Antonio. Lymeford had several pubs. The Swan was conveniently located almost directly opposite the optician, but naturally Antonio had not picked that one. In contrast, The Plough was an inconvenient walk away from the main high street. There was a shortcut to the back of the pub which Leslie took through the park and down an alleyway. The park was deserted, but when Leslie got to the alley he could see a man standing at the end of it. It was a strange place for someone to wait, and Leslie hesitated for a moment, seriously considering whether to turn back and go the long way round. He was, however, too weary, and he knew he was being ridiculous. His nerves were all to pieces; he must make that appointment with Paul when he got home.

He pulled himself together and carried on, but found himself instinctively pushing his wallet and phone further down in his pocket.

Mastering his nerves, Leslie nodded a greeting to the man as he passed, which was returned, and he made his way inside without event. It was a dingy pub, very quiet, and there were only three drinkers in the main bar area. Sitting at one table was a man in his mid-thirties wearing a dark leather jacket, and at another table was a slightly younger man clad in denim. An elderly man was at the bar talking to the lady serving. There was no sign of Antonio.

Leslie walked through to the smaller lounge bar, and when he saw it was deserted he experienced a surge of hope that Antonio would not turn up. He made his mind up to wait no more than a few minutes and then escape.

Leslie returned to the main area and waited, ill at ease, drawing the attention of the woman behind the bar who called across.

"You all right, love? Can I get you something?"

Leslie explained that he was meeting someone. "I'll just wait for a moment if you don't mind, in case he doesn't turn up."

At that moment, Antonio appeared, complete with self-assured smile and apologies for keeping Leslie waiting. He surveyed the silent and barely occupied room, then went across to the little lounge bar. "Let's go into this room," he said. "It's quieter in here, and then I'll get you a drink."

They made for one of the tables in the small room and Leslie sat down. "I'll just have—" Leslie's words tailed off. Two big men were striding into the room purposefully. One of them was the man who had been waiting in the alley, and he had been joined by another. Behind them, the two drinkers from the main bar had stood up from their separate tables and were following them in. The four men advanced towards Leslie as a pack. Terrified, Leslie jumped up and pressed himself against the wall behind him, knowing he had no escape. He tried to speak, to shout out for help, but his voice was silent. He would have no hope against even one of these men, and four of them would surely kill him.

The next thing he knew, the men had surrounded Antonio's chair. One of them produced a warrant card.

"Anthony Mark Spinner. I'm arresting you under Section 9 of the Sexual Offences Act 2003," and he read out a caution.

Antonio, or rather Anthony, attempted to leap up and began a futile struggle with two of the men. He cast a look of hatred at Leslie. "You traitor, you scab, you scum," he screamed, adding some choice expletives, and he kicked a chair towards Leslie. Leslie dodged to one side, losing his balance and falling awkwardly, catching his head on the corner of the table. As he was falling he heard Antonio laugh, until some rough handling by the officers caused another tirade of abuse. Moments later, Antonio and two of the officers were gone, leaving two to deal with Leslie.

He sat, silent with bewilderment, while the pub landlady kindly cleaned him up and gently dressed the gash above his eyebrow with sticking plaster. There had been a lot of blood, but she declared it to be a superficial wound and Leslie refused the policeman's offer to take him to the local casualty department.

Leslie was too shaken to say much to the officers when they drove him home, and they volunteered very little beyond a few sympathetic platitudes for his inconvenience. When he got indoors he burst into the library. "What the hell do you think you were playing at, Bennett?" he stormed with uncharacteristic rage.

Bennett shut his newspaper, turned to face Leslie, raised his eyebrows a fraction, but said nothing.

"It was you, I take it, who contacted the police. You can't know what you've just put me through."

"What's happened?" said Bennett with a calmness that was exceedingly provoking.

Leslie's account took some time to relate and when he had finished Bennett said, "I phoned Ridgeway and told him that Antonio was the prowler and that you'd agreed to meet him. You may have promised Antonio you wouldn't tell the police, but I made no promises. I've no idea how it resulted in what you've just told me."

"I don't understand why you went behind my back," said Leslie. "Why didn't you tell me you were calling Ridgeway? It would have spared me a terrifying ordeal."

"That would have made you complicit. Antonio may think you grassed, but at least you know you didn't. You kept your word and you can have a clear conscience. I'm sorry about what happened but I couldn't have predicted that."

"You always think you're so bloody right," shouted Leslie, slamming the door and stamping upstairs. He took off his blood-spattered clothes, put on his dressing gown and flung himself on the bed. Minutes later, he was asleep.

22

It was after three pm when Leslie woke, to see the doctor standing beside his bed. "Paul?" said Leslie, confused. "What brings you here?"

"Bennett called and told me you'd got a head wound that might need seeing to. And when he said that you were fast asleep in the middle of the day, I thought I'd pop in and make sure you were all right."

"That's very good of you but there was really no need; it looks as though we've disturbed you on a day off again."

"Don't mention it. You've done me a favour; I hate mowing the lawn. Now, let's have a look at this wound, and you tell me what happened."

While Leslie recounted the story, starting with the previous day's events, the doctor cleaned and glued the wound. Leslie took off his dressing gown to reveal the damage from his fall in the woods.

"Dear God, Leslie!" he exclaimed. "Have you seen the state of yourself?"

Leslie shuffled himself painfully into a position where he could admire his injuries in the mirror opposite. The bruising was impressive, it was true.

Paul gently prodded and poked at Leslie's ribcage before saying, "I don't think there are any broken ribs, but I can send you for an X-ray just to be sure."

"No thanks, I'll trust your judgment," said Leslie, having had quite enough of hospitals for the year.

As he continued his examination, the doctor asked Leslie questions about his general health, his eating and sleeping. Before he knew it, Leslie was pouring out all his concerns about Bennett and telling the doctor about his difficulty in falling asleep for fear of finding Bennett dead beside him. To his dismay, he felt tears coursing down his cheeks, and for a while he gave himself up to misery.

The doctor seemed unperturbed. He slowly packed away his case, and when Leslie recovered himself said, "I don't have any medicine that will stop you caring about Bennett. But Bennett's in pretty good shape now, and there's no reason why he shouldn't go on for as long as you, though you know no one can promise you that – we all go sometime. The important thing, old chap, is to not let anxiety about tomorrow spoil today. It's early days; you won't always feel it as badly as this. It's been a difficult time in the village; a lot of folk are feeling anxious at the moment, especially those who knew George. I don't want to start prescribing sleeping pills or anything else like that. If you've had a bad night's sleep, do what you did today: have a lie down in the afternoon. Doctor's orders!"

Leslie heard Bennett and Paul chatting for a while downstairs, then Bennett appeared in the doorway with a tray. "It's a bit late for lunch," he said, "but this should keep you going until dinner."

Leslie wasn't yet ready to give up his anger and hurt, but took the tray of soup and bread with as much good grace as he could muster. He'd really rather have made his own lunch, and he tried not to think about his kitchen and the mayhem that had probably resulted from the preparation of even this humble meal.

Bennett ran a bath for Leslie, but this time he left him on his own to soak, except for bringing in a cup of peppermint tea. This further act of reconciliation was not lost on Leslie, and his wrath, always transient, started to abate. While Leslie was cautiously drying himself, he heard the doorbell, and he strained his ears to identify the visitor. From the top of the stairs he listened again and eventually made out Ridgeway's voice. Leslie's anger resurfaced and, as he gingerly dressed himself, he resolved to tell Ridgeway exactly what he thought, chief inspector or not. He composed some suitable phrases in his head and rehearsed them as he went downstairs. Ridgeway was sitting on the settee in the sitting room.

"Pardon me for calling in unannounced," he said with his usual diffidence, "but I think I owe you an explanation. And indeed an apology."

Sitting opposite this mild and exquisitely well-mannered man, Leslie found that somehow the words he had prepared could not now be said.

"I hope that when I've explained," continued the chief inspector, "it will help you to make sense of today's events. We've had concerns about this so-called Antonio for a while. We've had calls about the activities taking place at the art studio, but we hadn't so far obtained any evidence; none of the girls would talk. Then, in the last few days, we had a complaint from one of the houses here in the village and this tied in perfectly with your nocturnal visit. You will understand now why our officers visited you so promptly, although I regret their behaviour. Bennett contacted me yesterday and gave me the identity of the prowler, and warned us that it looked like he was planning to do a runner to London, or who knows where."

Leslie glared at Bennett who returned his gaze impassively.

Ridgeway continued, "This enabled us to put some pressure on the, shall we say, key witness. She eventually named the suspect. By the time she'd talked, and we were in a position to arrest him, he was on his way to meet you in Lymeford. I hope you can see that we didn't want to waste time pulling him in.

"There's another thing too, and this is strictly off the record for the moment: until a year ago he was a school teacher, an art master, in a girls' school. He left mid-term; the school made sure of that. There was no evidence; none of the girls there would talk, either. He's a persuasive fellow. The witness in the village is only fourteen, by the way."

"I see," said Leslie reluctantly. "That does change things rather. You could hardly leave a paedophile on the loose. I gather from what I heard in the commotion that he's really called Anthony, not Antonio. I suppose he was trying for a more romantic or glamorous name."

"Anthony was good enough for Shakespeare," observed Bennett.

"I'm terribly sorry that you got caught up in it," said Ridgeway, returning to the subject. "I had the dickens of a phone call from Paul about it, after him giving me orders that you shouldn't be disturbed. But I've some other news for you, too. Your bête noire, Kenny, is in the clear. After you mentioned him, I had him followed up. He was in the betting shop in Temple Ducton for the whole of Saturday evening, with CCTV evidence to prove it. The film even captures him having rather a good win, which he then celebrated in the pub along the street, The Greyhound. He went along to The Greyhound at ten pm when the betting shop closed and was there until he was kicked out at closing time."

"Ten o'clock, you say?" said Bennett.

"Yes," replied Ridgeway. "We double-checked his movements with the managers of the betting shop and the pub. Kenny is quite a regular in both. Neither of them would be in a hurry to cover for him; they both seem to loathe him. He was too legless to drive home so he staggered back to a friend's house in the town. The friend's wife, who was none too pleased about it, confirmed that he was snoring his head off on the sofa until after breakfast time the next day."

"That's that, then," said Leslie glumly. "What about Robin? How are you getting on with him?"

"We're still questioning him. There haven't been any charges made – yet," said Ridgeway.

Thoroughly depressed, Leslie made for the sanctuary of the kitchen. The saucepan was still on the cooker. It contained a burnt residue of soup, with the ladle glued to the base, suggesting that the pan had been replaced, empty, on the hot hob. A trail of congealing puddles on the cooker and work surface told of the ladle being slopped from the pan to the bowl on the far end of the work top. Breadcrumbs were scattered across the table and floor as though Bennett had been feeding the birds. Defeated by fatigue, Leslie made for the bedroom. As he passed to the foot of the stairs he heard Bennett saying, "Leslie's convinced that Robin is innocent and that Kenny is in some way implicated. That's worth taking note of."

"The evidence is rather the other way round at the moment," replied Ridgeway apologetically.

"Bugger your evidence," said Bennett. "I'll go with Leslie's judgement every time."

Those few words had a miraculous effect upon Leslie's spirits and, weary though he still was, he went upstairs in a different mood altogether.

A little while later, when the chief inspector had gone, Bennett came up to the bedroom and sat on the end of the bed. "Martin's supposed to be coming this evening for chess. He rang and invited himself over after you met him in The Woodman the other evening. Would you rather I cancel?"

"No, don't do that," said Leslie. "There's no reason why your chess game need disturb me. You can look after Martin this evening."

As was inevitable though, by the time Martin arrived, Leslie was up and about, taking his coat and providing coffee and slices of cherry cake. "You haven't brought Cromwell with you," commented Leslie, trying to keep the relief from his voice. The last time the dog had visited, he had succeeded in breaking a favourite milk jug from Leslie's collection with his tail.

"I left him snoozing," said Martin, "which is what you should be doing by the look of you. Whatever happened?" He was looking with interest at the wound on Leslie's forehead.

Leslie muttered something about having tripped over in the pub and Martin raised his eyebrows.

"You want to be careful," he said. "I'm being serious. We've had enough bad luck in the village recently."

Leslie gave a hurried reply and disappeared to the kitchen to avoid further questioning. Once there, he suddenly found himself in the mood for tidying up. Bennett had made an effort at cleaning, but it wasn't until Leslie had spent an hour or so pottering about, that he was satisfied. By that time, the chess game was over, and Leslie joined them in the library where Bennett was pouring drinks.

"I had a word with my wife about Jeff's planning permission application, as you asked me to," said Martin to Bennett. "Sylvia says that Jeff is the worst applicant she's ever had to deal with. He's incredibly impatient to get the application considered; it's already been brought forward from the date originally set just to shut him up. He's on the phone nearly every day. He was in there again today, ranting and raving."

"I know, I saw him there when I went into Lymeford for my optician's appointment. I forgot to tell you, Bennett."

Martin was delighted when he heard about the parking ticket. "Who says there's no justice in the world?" he said with satisfaction. "Nothing's too bad for him, as far as I'm concerned. Can you believe it, but a few weeks ago he actually asked what would happen if George died before the planning meeting."

"He told me that, too," said Leslie. "I was shocked."

"What answer did they give him?" Bennett enquired.

"They told him it would hold things up," said Leslie, "and that's why he was in such a hurry to get the case heard. It all seems back to front, to me. You'd think the sensible thing would be to withdraw the application and start again after George had gone, but apparently he has a buyer for the land so I suppose it's worth the risk."

"It's not that much of a risk," said Martin. "Sylvia says there's no reason it won't be successful, given some of the other developments which have recently been granted. As I mentioned before, applications that would never once have been entertained are going through, even when objections are raised."

"Jeff said he'd been optimistic that this planning permission would be granted," said Leslie. "I wonder who told him that. It's rather worrying."

"It certainly is. As I told you the other day, George had taken it up with the council because he thought there were irregularities. He believed there was something fishy going on."

"Did he get any response?" asked Bennett.

"I never got a chance to find out from him. Sylvia's view is that it's partly to do with government pressure for new housing and there are targets that have to be met. Some of the regulations have been relaxed, but Sylvia's still uneasy about the way they're going about it. She has an admin role; she's not involved with the decision making or any of the technical stuff, but she processes some of the applications. That house on the road into Stretton Cross, for instance: Sylvia's convinced that was rushed through and not properly scrutinised. In fact, she even suspects that some major changes were made after the approval process.

There's another dubious one at the moment in Lymeford. Sylvia started dealing with the application but now they've passed it on to someone else. This is what happens – if questions get asked, the application gets passed around."

"Has Sylvia challenged it?" asked Leslie.

"She's tried. But there's a serious bullying culture in the department, with constant threats of redundancy. It's not worth your job to ask too many questions. According to Sylvia, the bosses are on performance-related pay; if they meet their housing targets, they get a big bonus, so they don't want anyone standing in their way. These guys are philistines. The top man lives in Exeter in a huge mansion on a gated estate. He doesn't give a damn about the environment and he probably doesn't know what Dartmoor looks like. He's retiring any day now and has been showing off the pictures of the luxury holiday villa he's bought in Portugal."

"It sounds as though he's reached all his targets, then," said Leslie.

"My thoughts too," agreed Martin. "He's being replaced by someone from outside. Sylvia is desperately hoping things will improve."

"Let's hope so," said Leslie.

"I wouldn't trust that Jeff, though," Martin continued. "You mentioned just now that he wants to rush his planning permission through because he has a buyer; this is what everyone is saying. Sylvia's friend works for Eastons, the estate agents he's registered with, and she says there's not a squeak of interest in his land. Either he's got a private buyer and he's not telling the agent, or he's got more than his handkerchief up his sleeve."

* * *

"There was a lot going on between George and Jeff," observed Leslie to Bennett, after Martin had left, "the row over planning permission and Clarissa carrying on with Jeff. Do you think Jeff was involved somehow in the blackmail or the murder?"

"He can't be ruled out," said Bennett.

"And what about these supposed irregularities at the planning office that Martin was telling us about? Do you think the concerns are really valid, or is it just about a few locals resenting any new properties being built in their villages?"

"Good question," Bennett replied noncommittally.

"It would seem that George was worried enough about it to follow it up with the local council, from what Martin said," Leslie continued. "Mind you, he was hardly a disinterested party; he would have been badly affected if Jeff's planning permission was granted."

Before anything more could be said on the subject, he was interrupted by the ringing of the doorbell. Surprised, for it was late, he went to answer it, thinking that perhaps Martin had left something behind and returned for it. He was astonished to see that it was Annie, looking very worried.

"I'm sorry to call so late, but I could see you were still up. I don't know what to do; Daniel's gone missing."

23

Leslie ushered Annie into the sitting room and they sat down together.

"I had Daniel's aunt on the phone in a terrible state. She came home from her shift at the hospital and was surprised to see that he hadn't been in; he normally goes home and has his tea before going off to college. He usually leaves a bowlful of washing up, but today he obviously hadn't been in at all. When he wasn't home by ten pm she tried calling him, but got no reply, and there's still no sign of him. At the moment there's no way of knowing if he even got to college this evening; she's got no numbers for any of his friends. She's driven round all the lanes looking for him."

Bennett poured three glasses of brandy.

"It's not like him," she continued. "We all know he's no saint, but this is completely out of character. Unfortunately the police weren't very interested when the aunt rang them; a nineteen-year-old late home by a few hours isn't a police case."

Bennett took his glass of brandy and sat by the French windows.

"Do you think he's had an accident on that bike of his?" asked Leslie.

"No, I don't think it's that. Even in these quiet lanes someone would surely have come across him by now. But, more to the point, he was in an odd mood when he left work; you know, nervous and edgy, and he asked to go early. I'm sure something's wrong." Annie took a sip of the brandy. "He wanted to go fifteen minutes early," she continued, "saying that he had some college work that needed to be finished. I've never heard him mention college work before but there was obviously something up, so I let him off. I wish I'd been a bit more sympathetic, or shown a bit more interest. Perhaps then he would have told me what it was all about."

"Don't start blaming yourself," said Leslie. "You've shown more than enough kindness to that young man. Anyway, we don't even know that anything's the matter. Perhaps he's gone back to a friend's and forgotten to ring his aunt, or something like that. He's probably out somewhere enjoying himself, oblivious to the worry he's causing."

"I do hope you're right," said Annie. "I've tried calling him and leaving messages and he hasn't replied. That's not like him; he's practically welded to that phone of his." Annie finished her brandy. "I can't help thinking," she said, standing up to go, "that something has happened to him."

* * *

As soon as The Daffodil opened the following morning, Leslie hurried across, eyes bleary from lack of sleep. "Any news?" he said.

Annie shook her head. "I've asked Laura, my waitress, if Daniel mentioned anything to her, but he didn't. Heaven knows how we're going to manage today."

"I'll tell you how," said Leslie. "I've come to offer my services as kitchen boy. I'm a dab hand at wiping tables and loading a dishwasher. I'll be too distracted with worry to achieve anything at home, and it drives Bennett mad if I keep interrupting him. Just tell me what you want me to do."

"You're an absolute angel, Leslie. I'm going to take you up on that offer before you change your mind."

It was the perfect antidote to anxiety and Leslie threw himself into the work. Annie, Laura and Leslie flew past each other all day in a fever of activity. The first customers were mostly visitors and walkers fuelling themselves for their morning's exertions, and then came the lunchtime rush. The locals came in the afternoon, seeking coffee and conversation, and today they were richly rewarded.

"What hypocrites they are." Annie thumped a tray down next to Leslie as he loaded the dishwasher. "They're hanging on her every word, full of supposed sympathy, but you should hear what they say about her when she's not there." Clarissa had come in at half past two and, almost immediately, all the Irenes, Veras and

Marians of Dartonleigh were round her table, like moths drawn to a lamp. "Not that she doesn't deserve it; she's the biggest hypocrite of them all. I don't know when she ever stepped through this door before George's death. Now here she is, talking about her business at the top of her voice. The woman has no shame."

Leslie had to agree. It had been impossible not to overhear Clarissa while he was clearing the tables. 'I don't know what was worse', she'd been lamenting. 'To have been deceived by George, or betrayed by Antonio'. She had paused to receive the condolences of her audience. Clarissa really was a fine actress and she had that magnetic personality possessed by some people, regardless of their merits or defects. 'I can't remain at the Grange', she'd continued. 'Too many painful reminders and memories. I'm going to stay with my son Gordon in Richmond. He's been begging me to go to him since George's death. I have to tell the police where I'm going; it's outrageous. They've more or less confirmed that I'm in the clear and George's bastard son is to be charged with his murder. They told me it was just a formality that I notify them, but I still think it's disgusting.'

Leslie told Annie what he had overheard Clarissa saying. "It's strange that she's going to stay with her son," he said. "I'm sure she told me he didn't approve of her."

"Good riddance," Annie declared. "The sooner she goes, the better," and she seized a tray laden with scones, cream and jam, and headed back into the fray.

By five o'clock only a few stragglers were sitting over their empty cups, and at five thirty the café closed and Annie let Laura, who looked quite worn out, go home.

"Poor girl," said Annie, pouring Leslie a cup of tea. "She hasn't been herself all day. I'm sure she's been upset by Daniel's disappearance. She doesn't have much time for him, but she's very good-hearted." As she spoke, Laura reappeared through the kitchen and, seeing Annie, burst into a flood of tears. "Whatever's wrong, love?" said Annie, jumping up to comfort the girl.

"I've found it," she sobbed. "I've found it; out the back." She buried her face in her hands, crying uncontrollably.

"What have you found? Tell me," said Annie urgently.

"It's behind the storeroom. Daniel's bike."

As they hurried through the kitchen after the distraught girl, Leslie felt a surge of relief, as from Laura's reaction he had feared it was something much worse. Beyond the kitchen door, out of sight of the pleasant teashop gardens, was a utility area with a small brick shed in the corner. Laura led them onto the track that ran behind the teashop and to the rear of the shed. The bicycle had apparently been lifted over the wall and hidden between the wall and the shed. Concealment could be the only motive for placing it there.

As far as Leslie could see from where he was standing, the bike was in good condition. Had there been a flat tyre, one might imagine Daniel abandoning the unusable machine there, in a safe hiding place, and continuing on his way on foot; had there been any visible damage, one might have imagined a third party perhaps involved. Leslie shuddered at the thought of someone wrestling Daniel off the bike, dumping it over the wall and... Then what? "Does Daniel normally go home this way?" asked Leslie.

"Never," said Laura. "He always goes off from the front, through the village. Anyway, how could you ride a bike along here?" The track was little wider than an alleyway and wasn't intended for vehicles, though the occasional farm machine squeezed its way down to the fields beyond. The surface was rutted and uneven; certainly unsuitable for the lightweight racing bike behind the shed.

"How did you find it here?" Annie asked.

"I cut through this way to the bus stop on the main road," said Laura. "I noticed that the weeds and honeysuckle that grow over the back of the wall had been dragged down, so I had a look. There it was. What do you think has happened to him?" With that, she burst into another flood of tears.

"You take Laura inside, and I'll have a look around," said Leslie to Annie. It seemed to Leslie that the girl was excessively upset by this discovery, but he too felt rather unnerved as he carried on down the path, looking over the wall on both sides. Finding nothing, he retraced his steps, vaguely looking for clues. The track gave up no secrets, but what was he expecting to see? There were no footprints, no items carelessly discarded, no trampled vegetation and blood stains to suggest a struggle.

Leslie made his way round to the front of the shed. Blanking his mind to the anticipation of what may be within, he took out his handkerchief and gingerly turned the door handle. Standing slightly back, he kicked the door open and then, without allowing himself to think, took a step inside. It was Annie's storeroom and the shelves were neatly stacked with cleaning materials, a mop and bucket and several brooms propped tidily in the corner. There was, to Leslie's great relief, no corpse or trussed-up body to be seen, and no possible place to conceal one. He left the shed and spent a few more minutes searching about, before returning inside. Puffy-eyed, but composed now, Laura sat drinking tea with Annie who was looking grave.

"Laura has just been telling me about something that happened yesterday afternoon." Annie indicated to Leslie to sit down.

Laura nodded miserably. "I'm terribly sorry. I should have said straightaway this morning, but I promised not to tell," she said, looking down at the table. "It wasn't much, but I should have said."

"Go on," encouraged Leslie.

"It was yesterday afternoon, about three o'clock, and it was really busy. I came through to the kitchen and Daniel wasn't there. I was annoyed, more than anything, because the kitchen was a mess and the washing-up was all behind. There wasn't even a clean tray for me to take my next order out on. I went to the sink to wipe a tray, and noticed Daniel outside the kitchen door talking to someone. At first, I thought it might be that man he was talking to the other day when Annie called him back in."

"That was Kenny Barr, wasn't it?" said Leslie, and Annie nodded.

"Well, it wasn't him, anyway," Laura continued, "it was Jamie. You know Jamie, that daft boy who worked here last year; Jackie's son."

"Yes, I know Jamie," said Leslie. "He does some odd jobs for me sometimes."

"I was surprised at first to see them together because they don't get on. But then I realised that there was something going on between them; it looked like they were having a row. I didn't hang around to watch, but the next time I went back into the kitchen Daniel was just coming through the door and he looked terrible. I was about to have a go at him about the state of the kitchen when he said, 'Laura, I've got myself into a mess, a right mess'. I was so mad at him I didn't take it seriously. I thought he was trying to avoid a rollicking, and anyway, he's always exaggerating and making things up. I just said, you can't be in as much of a mess as this kitchen, and you'll be in more than a mess if Annie comes out and finds it in this state." She looked apologetically at her boss, who smiled encouragingly and patted her on the arm.

"Next time I went through to the kitchen, I stopped to give him a hand because he'd got so far behind with everything. He said, 'Don't tell anyone you saw me talking to Jamie, will you?' I said of course not. I thought he was asking me not to tell on him for going outside again and getting behind with his work, and he ought to know I wouldn't do that. But then he said, 'Do you promise?' I just said OK, if you want. Like I said, I just thought he was making a drama out of the situation. I feel terrible about it now. Looking back, I remember he was nearly in tears, and that's not like him at all. He must have been properly upset, and he wanted to tell me about it. I should have listened. I hope he hasn't gone and done something stupid. I wish ..." Her words faded out as she buried her face in her hands in another paroxysm of sobbing.

They got little more out of her. She had overheard nothing of the conversation between the two boys and Daniel had never confided any problems before. She'd been annoyed when Daniel had asked to go early; she didn't think he was telling the truth about having college work to do and thought he was skiving. She didn't see him cycle away.

They locked up The Daffodil and Annie drove Laura home. Leslie had reported the whole episode to Bennett by the time Annie arrived back and came across to the cottage. She joined them at the kitchen table and took the glass of wine that was poured ready for her. Leslie was serving up pasta onto three plates, realising as he did so just how hungry and tired he was.

"I suppose we should be calling the police," said Annie.

"Bennett suggested that we might just have a word with young Jamie, first," said Leslie.

"I think that you and Leslie have more chance of getting the lad to talk," said Bennett. "I don't see him confiding in the police."

"You're probably right about that," said Annie. "We don't want another boy doing a disappearing act."

They ate quickly and then Leslie reached for the phone. "Let's find out what young Jamie has to say for himself," he said, but the only response was an answer message. "I'll ring the house phone," Leslie said briskly, dialling the number. This time the phone was answered almost immediately by Jamie's mother, Jackie.

"I'm sorry, but if you're wanting him for any jobs, I don't think that will be possible for a while," she replied, sounding agitated.

"That's not why I'm ringing," Leslie answered. "It's about something else, and it is rather important."

"What's going on? Don't tell me he's in trouble!" Jackie wailed, unexpectedly. "Oh, I do wish you'd come here and speak to him, Mr Mountfield, Leslie, I mean. He might listen to you. He's in his room packing. He says he's leaving and going to stay with his father again. He won't tell me anything else."

It took less than fifteen minutes for Leslie and Annie to make their way to Jamie's house. They waited in the sitting room, surrounded by all the paraphernalia of family life, while Jackie went upstairs to persuade Jamie to come and speak to them. Eventually Jamie appeared and stood framed in the doorway, his face white and his eyes wild. After much encouragement, he came reluctantly into the room and stood with his back to them, rearranging the items on the mantelpiece.

"We need your help, Jamie." Leslie tried to keep his voice neutral. "Daniel has gone missing. You were speaking to him yesterday."

"I don't know where he's gone," said Jamie, without turning.

"That's as maybe," said Leslie firmly, "but I think you know why he's gone."

"I'm not saying anything," Jamie retorted, petulantly. Increasingly agitated, he continued fiddling with the objects above the fireplace.

"It would be much better to tell us than to have to explain it to the police," said Leslie.

"I'm not explaining it to anyone," he said defiantly, swinging round to face them. "I don't have to tell you or the police anything."

Jackie appeared, her face lined with tension. She put mugs of coffee on the table and then withdrew, leaving them alone with her son.

"I'm sorry you're not able to help." Leslie injected disappointment into his voice. "I felt sure you knew why he'd gone, but I was obviously mistaken."

"I know why, all right. He's gone because I made him go." His voice was loud with triumph. "I made him go." After that, everything came tumbling out. As his mother had said previously, the boy really wasn't cut out for keeping secrets. "I said I'd tell everyone what I'd seen if he didn't pack up and leave. He said he wouldn't go, but now he has gone, and I'm glad of it. We don't want people like him in the village, blackmailing and taking other people's jobs."

"Blackmailing?" Leslie exclaimed.

"Yeah, blackmailing. I saw him with the money – Mr H-T's money."

"George's money? Whatever do you mean?"

"Daniel was the blackmailer, of course," said Jamie impatiently. "I saw him take the money."

There was a pause while Leslie and Annie tried to digest this startling indictment.

"Why don't you tell us exactly what happened, Jamie," coaxed Annie. "Start from the beginning."

Calmer now, Jamie sat on the arm of a chair opposite to Leslie and screwed up his eyes, as if recalling the event. After a few seconds, he opened his eyes again and began his story. "It was one evening a few weeks ago, I don't know exactly when, but I was out on one of my walks. I wasn't surprised to see Daniel as he often goes by on his bike, on his way home from college, I suppose. He thinks no one knows he smokes, but I do because I've seen him hiding in the bushes doing it.

"On the night I'm telling you about, I'd been sitting on the stile, that one you climb over onto Stag Lane, just thinking out a new picture in my mind, when Daniel cycled past. He didn't see me. After just a few yards, he got off and propped his bike up. I thought he was getting off to have a smoke. But he didn't do that, he started walking up the lane. I wondered what he was doing so, quiet as anything, I started to follow him, keeping well back so he didn't see me. Almost right away I lost sight of him; he was nowhere to be seen in the lane. It was strange because it was one of those really light nights when you can see nearly as well as in the daytime. I thought he must have gone off into the woods, but when I got near to Compton Grange, there he was, under the big walls just outside the gate. He must have been creeping along the edge of the path, right in the shadows where I couldn't see him.

"I stepped back into the shadows myself, and I watched him. Guess what he did next? Well, you know that big stone thing outside, beside the gates, that thing like a giant vase?"

"The stone urn, do you mean?" asked Leslie.

"That's it, the urn," said Jamie. He seemed to be enjoying the story now. "Well, clear as anything, I saw Daniel reach down behind that urn, and pick up a package. It was like a big folded-up envelope, and he put it inside his jacket. I stayed where I was and he crept back through the bushes towards his bike. He went right by me, but he never saw me.

"I've been wondering all this time what he was up to. I never said anything to anyone – I couldn't, could I? I was supposed to be at home minding my sisters. The other day, when I was at that coffee morning in the village hall, I heard Mrs H-T saying that old Mr H-T had been blackmailed. I realised straightaway what I'd seen. Daniel was picking up the blackmail money from Mr H-T. What else could it have been?"

"If you were so sure that was what he was doing, what made you go to Daniel about it rather than the police?" asked Annie.

"Like I said, I shouldn't have been there, should I? And I'm not getting mixed up with police and getting into trouble. I just want Daniel to go." Jamie's agitation was rising again. "I just want him to leave the village, that's all, to get out."

"Why do you want him to go?" asked Annie

"So I can get my job back at The Daffodil," he said desperately. "He took my job, and I want it back. I have to have it back. I just have to get some money to go to uni and get away from this place. And if I was working, I could give some of the money to my ma so she wouldn't have to work at the pub anymore, or at least not every night. Then everything might be all right again."

Poor Annie was looking quite devastated, so Leslie cut in quickly. "What happened when you spoke to Daniel?"

"I told him I knew he was the blackmailer, and that he had twenty-four hours to leave Dartonleigh or I'd go to the police. He denied it, of course, and got really mad. But I know it's true; I know what I saw."

"But why do you want to leave now and go to your dad's?" asked Annie.

Jamie was on his feet again, and he turned back to the fireplace. "Daniel's seen some of my pictures. When he first came to the village he was OK, he was, like, friendly. One day he saw me drawing and I showed him what I was doing. That was a big mistake. After I told him to leave the village yesterday, he messaged me and said he'd tell the police about my pictures and then they'd think I was the murderer. He said he'd see to it that I was put away for life. He called me a weirdo and a creep. He said that everyone knows I'm not right in the head and no one would believe anything I say. I just have to get away from this place. No one's locking me up!"

"But you know that what Daniel said isn't true," exclaimed Annie. "You must know he only said those silly things to get back at you."

"Oh, it's true all right," said Jamie, his voice raised. "Everyone thinks I'm crazy. My dad's always telling me they'll lock me up one of these days." With one angry gesture, he swept his arm along the mantelpiece and sent everything crashing to the ground.

Jackie appeared in the doorway, and the look of resignation on her face indicated that this was the sort of situation she was accustomed to dealing with. "Jamie, love," she said calmly, ignoring the mess all over the floor, "it's getting late and I'm putting the girls to bed. Lisa asked if you'd go up and give her a goodnight kiss. Then why don't you get some rest yourself, love? You look tired out."

The storm had blown over and, no longer agitated, Jamie skulked out of the room. Before Leslie and Annie were halfway through their apologies for causing such a disturbance, Jamie reappeared with a sketchbook.

"I've just remembered something," he said, quite calm again. "I can tell you the date I saw Daniel with that package. I came home and sketched it straightaway, and I always put a date on my work. I learned to do that at school." He opened the sketchbook and, to their astonishment, revealed a line drawing of an individual, a perfect caricature of Daniel, bending over beside a stone urn, in the act of furtively pocketing a package. It was a very clever sketch, capturing the moment perfectly, and it was quite unlike the gruesome works Leslie had previously been subjected to.

"Have you done any other drawings like this?" asked Leslie, genuinely interested.

"Oh yeah," said Jamie. "This whole pad is full of them. I do them whenever things happen. They don't take me long."

"Is it a sort of journal, or diary?" asked Annie.

"I suppose it is. Only I don't draw something every day, of course, only when something happens. Do you remember this, Mr Mountfield?"

Leslie exclaimed in amazement at the perfect likeness of Bennett leaning out of a patio door and looking into a garden, quite clearly the back of their cottage. There was a broken gnome in the foreground. "It's brilliant," exclaimed Leslie. "Just look at Bennett's expression! Is it for sale? I'd love to buy it."

Jamie looked uncertainly across to his mother.

"Well, love," she said kindly, "it looks like you've got yourself your first art sale. Why don't you make a copy of it tomorrow, and then take it down to Mr Mountfield and you can decide on a price between you. Well done, love."

Bennett was in the sitting room when Leslie and Annie got back to the cottage. He was listening to something that sounded like a Spanish guitar solo with twice as many semi-quavers as any Bach piece, and Leslie was relieved that he switched it off as they went in.

"Whatever Jamie saw, or thought he saw, I can't believe that Daniel is the blackmailer," Leslie said as they reported the evening's events. "It's preposterous. A young lad like that doesn't go in for that sort of blackmail."

"And besides," said Annie, "how could he have come by any information to blackmail poor George with? He's only been in the village a couple of months."

"Remember, Daniel did work in the leisure club at The Imperial previously. I suppose it's just possible that he overheard something about George there, from one of the locals, especially as that's where Clarissa and Antonio used to meet," said Leslie. "But I must admit it does seem highly unlikely."

"I don't know what to think," said Annie. "It seems impossible, but on the other hand I felt that Jamie was telling us the truth about what he saw. Didn't you think so too, Leslie?"

"I certainly don't think he was lying," said Leslie. "I think he saw something; his drawing backs that up. But whether he really saw Daniel taking a package, and whether it contained blackmail money, is quite another matter."

"Yes, that's true," said Annie. "There could be an innocent explanation. Supposing Daniel had dropped something as he was cycling along then jumped off his bike and went back to retrieve it. Jamie's impression that he was picking up something hidden behind the urn might all be in his fevered imagination."

"Quite," agreed Leslie. "If it was his cannabis joints he'd dropped, he might well have looked a bit furtive."

"Oh – perhaps it's a drug drop-off point? They do have such things, I believe. And just a coincidence that it was outside the Grange. For all we know, Daniel could have been on more than cannabis."

"All that may be true," observed Bennett, "but there's one thing to keep in mind."

They both looked at him.

"When Jamie accused Daniel of blackmail, he disappeared."

24

Leslie brought a tray of cheese and biscuits through to the sitting room, and Bennett poured the port.

"So do you think that Daniel really could be the blackmailer, then?" Annie asked doubtfully.

"I didn't say that," said Bennett. "But he's taken himself out the way for some reason."

"You do think he's run off, not—nothing worse?" Annie asked.

"Think about it," Bennett said. "Why would he ask to leave fifteen minutes early on this occasion? Why would he leave his bike behind? My guess is that he shoved his bike behind the shed and cut down the track to the main road in time to catch the bus. Leaving the café early as he did, he would be just in time for the one that goes right through to Horton Bishop."

"That seems plausible," said Annie, sighing. "He could have caught a train from Horton if he went that far; he could be anywhere by now. But what's to say he hasn't gone off somewhere to harm himself?"

"There's the bike," said Bennett. "He hid that bike carefully. He means to be back for it."

"I hope you're right," said Annie. "But I suppose we ought to contact the police. Whatever we might think, Jamie has connected him with the blackmail, and he has disappeared."

"Whatever Jamie saw or thought he saw, I honestly can't bring myself to believe that Daniel was blackmailing George," repeated Leslie. "But I suppose you're right and we ought to report it. You sound reluctant though, Annie."

"I'll tell you what I'm worried about: they'd be sure to contact Daniel's mother. At the moment Linda doesn't even know Daniel's missing. The worry would be terrible for her."

"What do you think, Bennett?"

"Why not sleep on it," said Bennett. "See what his aunt has to say in the morning if nothing's developed."

Annie took the last mouthful of her port and sighed. "But what if he is in danger, or has done something silly?" she said.

"Yes, that's the risk," said Bennett unhelpfully.

Before going home, Annie composed another message to Daniel avoiding, of course, any mention of Jamie's disclosures.

"Let's hope he's got the sense to respond," said Leslie.

"Let's hope he's able to," Annie replied.

* * *

It was early when Leslie woke the next morning. Tired though he was, his mind was racing and it was impossible to get back to sleep. He had agreed to meet Gloria for lunch at her shop in Temple Ducton, in return for his earlier hospitality, and now he was regretting it. He would rather be at home while Daniel was missing, as although there seemed to be nothing he could do at the moment, he wanted to be available in case something cropped up and he was able to help. On the other hand, he hated to cancel arrangements, and the thought of a long day ahead with nothing to distract him was unwelcome.

It was intolerable to lay in bed any longer and, deciding that he would make up his mind about it after breakfast, he went downstairs and drew open the sitting room curtains to the glorious view he never wearied of. Beyond his beloved garden and the fields and hedges behind, the distant moor rose up, wreathed in faint wisps of mist, like cobwebs, and the pink-gold of the sunrise coloured the entire scene. He made a cup of camomile tea and sat by the French windows watching the light change over the unchanging terrain.

It was one of those bittersweet moments when he felt acutely alive to all the joys and miseries of the world. Here they were in this idyllic village, wanting for nothing, with the spring days lengthening and exuding hope and promise. Yet his heart was heavy with regret over George who had faced his last hours in loneliness and with unshared troubles. There was the terrible fact of his murder and the anxiety that an injustice was being committed in the arrest of his son. Leslie thought of Robin, polite and vulnerable, and felt the weight of obligation to clear his name and find the real murderer. But how? Then there were the perplexing events around Jamie and Daniel, culminating in Daniel's alarming disappearance. These were all young men with everything ahead of them, but at that age when everything was so important, so immediate, so overwhelming, and so ungovernable.

While he was lost in thought the doorbell rang. It was Annie.

"Thank the Lord!" she burst out. "Daniel's safe; he just rang me. He's at a friend's house in Monkton Beckett, that's the other side of Tiverley. He can't stay there another night and he's run out of money. I said I'll pick him up this evening; I can't go any sooner because of the teashop. He said he'll be all right at the friend's house until later. I'm just so relieved that he's OK. I've let his aunt know."

"Did he say why he disappeared?"

"He said nothing about it, and I didn't ask. Plenty of time for that later. I wonder if you'd be kind enough to come along with me to pick him up, Leslie. I'd appreciate the company."

There was now no time for melancholy musing as there was dinner to prepare for four, because Leslie was determined to persuade Annie and Daniel to eat with them later. That boy had some explaining to do and Leslie always found that people talked better after a good meal. Moussaka was just the thing; it always went down well. It could be cooked in advance and surely even Bennett could be trusted to heat it up later while they were on their way to Monkton Beckett. He investigated his larder and fridge and then trotted across to the shop, praying that they had some decent aubergines in the rack today.

As he left the shop, his purchases successfully made, a car pulled up on the narrow cobbled road behind him and Leslie heard his name. He turned round to see Edgar leaning out of the open window of the car.

"Wait there a minute, Leslie," he said urgently, "I want to tell you something. I'll find somewhere to pull in."

Leslie sighed. Trust Edgar to pick such a moment to hold him up with no doubt another repetition of his self-inflicted problems.

But Leslie waited patiently until the scurrying figure appeared from the other side of the church.

"A peculiar thing has just happened," said Edgar. "I've just been to our warehouse. I haven't been there for a long time – Kenneth's taken over managing the stock and he gets very funny if I even mention going there. I have to be very careful as he thinks I'm undermining him, that I don't trust him." Edgar looked around shiftily, as if expecting Kenny to appear through the church lychgate. "Well, this morning I was awake rather early and it was on my mind. Kenneth is away on business for a few days so I thought I'd just take a look. I felt rather bad about doing it, being that Kenneth doesn't like me to, but you know, I've been feeling a little uneasy. Worried, you know?" He looked over his shoulder again and lowered his voice. "When I got to the warehouse, I couldn't get in. All the locks have been changed. I'm sure Kenneth didn't mention it. I know I haven't been feeling quite myself lately, but I don't think I could have forgotten something like that. It's very odd. I can't help but feel, you know, concerned."

"Why not just ring him up and ask him about it?" said Leslie. "It is your business as well, after all."

"I couldn't do that!" exclaimed Edgar. "I'm not even going to tell him I've been to the warehouse. Don't mention it to him, Leslie, will you?"

"Of course not," said Leslie, "but it's a shame you can't discuss it with him."

"Kenneth doesn't really discuss things, he's apt to get annoyed." He looked behind him yet again and whispered, "You can't know what it's like."

"When you say Kenneth gets annoyed," said Leslie, cautiously, "do you mean you're nervous of him?"

"Nervous? No, not nervous," Edgar said faintly. He stared past the church to some faraway point and said, with a humourless laugh, "Damned petrified, more like." Without making eye contact with Leslie, he scuttled back to his car, ignoring Leslie's attempts to continue the conversation.

"What the devil do you think Kenny's up to?" said Leslie to Bennett as he unpacked the shopping. "What do you think he's done with all the cheap shoes and handbags, or whatever it is that Edgar's been importing for years?"

"God knows," said Bennett without looking up from the newspaper which was spread untidily across the kitchen table. "The warehouse is probably full of illegal immigrants now, or a cannabis plantation."

Leslie made coffee and brought it to the table. "I must try to have words with Edgar about Kenny. He's actually terrified of him and they're living under the same roof." As Leslie was speaking, his eye was drawn to a picture on the open page in front of Bennett. He turned it towards himself and read the caption above the photograph: *Dartonleigh village murder: man still being questioned.* "They've managed to find a photo that makes him look quite insane," said Leslie angrily, as the face of Robin stared wildly out of the page. The article depressed Leslie's spirits further:

A 25-year-old Surrey man continues to be questioned by the police in connection with the murder of George Harrington-Thomas on 26 April. The man, who is being named locally as Robin Sheraton, the murdered man's son, voluntarily attended a police station close to his home in Guildford last Thursday. He has been taken to Lymeford for further questioning. Police are appealing for any witnesses to come forward. Detectives would particularly like to speak to anyone who may have been in the vicinity of Stag Lane, Dartonleigh, that evening. Meanwhile, the wife of the murdered man paid tribute to her 'much loved and missed husband' and has asked for privacy to grieve.

Leslie pushed the newspaper back to Bennett in silent indignation. He was soon distracted by the preparation of the moussaka and, more than once during the following hour, he regretted deciding on such a time-consuming recipe when he had a bus to catch into Temple to keep the appointment with Gloria. He set about slicing and salting aubergines, chopping onion, garlic and herbs, and peeling and cutting potatoes at record speed. If the preparation of this meal did not have the usual effect of pacifying his nerves, at least it diverted him from the problems that had been preoccupying him. And it was difficult to feel completely without hope when delicious aromas were filling the kitchen and promising a satisfying meal later on.

Bennett sat at the end of the kitchen table watching Leslie wielding knife and spoon and whisk with the speed of a percussionist playing the *Sabre Dance*. Apart from commenting that Leslie gave a new meaning to the term fast food, he sat in silence. At last the final spoonful of béchamel sauce was poured over the layer of steaming, sliced potatoes and Leslie set the dish aside and cleared away. Giving Bennett directions about what to have for lunch, and issuing sinister threats about what would happen to him if he left the kitchen in disarray, Leslie hurried to the bus stop.

Leslie rarely went into Temple Ducton, a picturesque town which was popular with tourists, and had shops and prices suited to that clientele. Although it was only five miles along the main road, the bus route was circuitous, meandering into the villages and hamlets that could accommodate such a vehicle. It was a pretty route and, now that Daniel was located, he could settle down to enjoy the ride.

It was a bright sunny day and the journey took them past all the typical features of the area: quaint thatched cottages, babbling streams, boulder-strewn fields filled with frolicking lambs, and glimpses of the open moorland. It was impossible not to be charmed by it all. Leslie's natural geniality was sufficiently revived so that by the time he alighted the bus in Temple Ducton, his earlier lack of enthusiasm for the visit had vanished. Although Leslie was rather sceptical about Gloria's business, he was also possessed of an innate curiosity and he was genuinely interested to see the shop she was so passionate about. He was perfectly capable of feigning polite interest in her natural cures, unlike Bennett who was likely to mutter 'bunkum' or 'poppycock' under his breath, and Leslie was not sorry on this occasion that Bennett had declined the invitation.

The pavements were quite crowded, as usual for this time of year, but Leslie had no difficulty in spotting Gloria's emporium, as a large sign bearing the legend Healing Temple protruded from above its door. However, his attention was also caught by a property across the road. He had forgotten that Antonio's art gallery was directly opposite Gloria's place, but there it was. Leslie was a few minutes early for his assignation with Gloria so he crossed the road and peered through the window. The shop was shut up and therefore unlit inside, but as far as Leslie could see, it seemed to be a cross between a gallery and an arts and crafts shop. At the back, he could just make out a door which was labelled *Studio*, and Leslie shuddered at the recollection of what Jamie had told him about that room.

A middle-aged man came out of the café next door to clear the outside tables and said, "If you're looking for Picasso, you're out of luck." He fixed Leslie with a suspicious, even hostile, stare.

"Oh no," said Leslie hastily, anxious to distance himself from Antonio. "I'm on my way to visit Gloria, the lady who runs Healing Temple opposite. But I was just having a look in here, first."

"Gloria – what a star!" exclaimed the man, his face breaking into a smile. "You're a friend of our Gloria, are you? We could do with more people like her on the high street, and less like that filthy animal." He nodded towards the art shop. "He's gone, and good riddance to him."

"I heard about the... the trouble," said Leslie, ambiguously, "and I suppose I was just curious to see what sort of a place it was."

"I could tell you what sort of a place it was, all right," the man replied. "If I'd known what he was up to, right next door to my café, I'd have— Well, I'll not say what I'd have done. My daughter nearly signed up for some drawing lessons. Dear God, the thought of it."

Leslie murmured some sympathetic noises and took his leave, pondering that if Antonio was ever allowed his freedom, he would be wise to give Temple Ducton a wide berth.

Healing Temple was a quaint, bow-fronted shop with leaded windows and a low doorway, and Leslie stepped inside to an interior that was equally olde-worlde. On one side, behind a mahogany counter, wooden shelves displayed dozens of old-fashioned jars filled with all kinds of herbs and roots and barks.

Beneath the shelves were rows of little wooden drawers, neatly labelled, and from one of these the shop assistant was taking a small bottle to show to a customer.

Gloria was engrossed with another client, but Leslie was quite happy to take his time exploring the wares. The shop stretched well back and was much larger than it looked from the street, and it seemed to be stocked with every kind of health and natural product. Near the entrance were several racks of herbs and spices, which accounted for the delightful smell that pervaded the air. Leslie picked up a basket and meandered along, browsing the section for herbal remedies, passing by the natural cosmetics and stopping with interest at the aisle devoted to health foods. After feasting his eyes on the selection, he took a paper bag and scooped in some plump dried figs, and filled another with dried pears and apple rings. He was now within earshot of Gloria, and while he was busy filling bags with these irresistible foodstuffs, he could hear her saying, "I'm sure the St John's Wort is exactly what you need. But I wouldn't be happy to let you buy it until you've checked with your doctor, since you're already on medication from him."

Leslie moved towards the counter with his laden basket, feeling reassured that whatever one thought of the efficacy of her practice, Gloria was obviously not unscrupulous. She now caught sight of him and, with a beaming smile, broke off her consultation long enough to call out that she would be with him in just a minute. There was no need for her to rush as there were several other customers ahead of Leslie in the queue. The shop was certainly popular, and there was quite a cluster of people around Gloria wanting her advice. Eventually, however, she extricated herself and joined Leslie at the section for essential oil and flower essences, where he was waiting patiently.

"Do let me show you around," she implored and, pleasantly fending off the customers who were wanting her attention, she took Leslie around the shop.

"My dear husband left me very well provided for, and I've always wanted my own shop," she said. "It was quite a risk, so I started on a small scale, but look at it already. I'm bursting at the seams. I wish I'd opened something much bigger. I feel that I could be doing twice as much good if I had somewhere twice the size. But never mind, we manage."

As they went up and down the aisles she discoursed on the benefits of herbs, the wholesomeness of unrefined foods and the advantages of organic products. She seemed extremely well informed about the items on her shelves and totally convinced of their merits.

"What an Aladdin's cave," said Leslie as they eventually started for the door.

"I'm so glad you like the shop," she replied. "I was worried that you might be sceptical; so many people are. But really, the customers are the ones whose opinions I care about, and they come back time and time again and tell me how much they benefit from my products."

Leslie, feeling rather duplicitous about his views, was about to reply with some platitude or other but they had stepped outside and Gloria was speaking again.

"We'll go to the café opposite; they do lovely food, though nothing would match that superb lunch you gave me, Leslie. I certainly couldn't produce anything like it myself. In fact," she giggled, "I'm quite ashamed of my domestic skills. Everyone talks about your cooking; you put me to shame. Perhaps you could give me some of your recipes, only you'll have to give me all the instructions. You wouldn't believe how silly I am in a kitchen."

Leslie readily agreed, and was just starting to politely rebuff Gloria's self-deprecating comments, when he stopped suddenly and exclaimed. Gloria also stopped and followed his gaze. There, coming out of a footpath which led from the car park was Kenny; Kenny who, according to Edgar only a few hours ago, was away on business.

"I recognise that man," she said. "I've seen him... yes, I've seen him in The Woodman. He doesn't look a nice fellow. I say, I hope he's not a friend of yours. If he is then I'm sure I must be mistaken about him."

"No, he's not a friend," Leslie reassured her.

"You seemed surprised to see him," said Gloria.

"It's just that someone told me he's away at the moment," Leslie said.

Kenny tossed down a stub, paused to light up another cigarette, and then set off again, stomping along towards the top end of the shops.

Gloria scrutinised Leslie with great interest. "I say, is he a suspect?" she asked breathlessly.

"Well, not really," said Leslie, but he was unable to disguise his mistrust of the man.

"He is a suspect!" exclaimed Gloria. "Let's see where he goes." And, with unexpected speed and agility, she sped after him, leaving Leslie no alternative but to follow.

The top of the high street, up which they were now hurrying, had quite a steep incline. It was also possessed of fewer shops and less tourist appeal; an estate agent, a hairdressers, a funeral directors, and a few other utilitarian stores interspersed with residential properties, some advertising themselves as holiday lettings. Leslie could see a small chapel ahead and just beyond that was a side street. He caught Gloria up just in time to see Kenny turning into the street.

"Quickly," said Gloria. "We don't want to lose him."

Leslie obeyed without answering. He could see there was no point arguing and he was also somewhat out of breath after rushing up the hill. He had never had any reason to come into this part of the town before and, as they turned the corner, he was surprised to see a bookmakers, a fried chicken shop and an Indian take-away which looked as though they would have been more at home in one of the seedier London suburbs than on the fringe of Dartmoor.

"I don't usually venture into this part of the town," confided Gloria, as though they had entered the red-light zone.

Leslie was just about to suggest turning back when Kenny crossed the road and entered The Greyhound which Leslie could see, even from this distance, was an insalubrious establishment. Undeterred, Gloria also crossed the road.

"Surely we're not going in?" said Leslie. Conscious that he sounded ridiculously prudish, he added, "I'm sure we would be terribly conspicuous."

"Does it matter?" said Gloria. "No one will say anything, and if they do, I'm sure we'll think of something."

"But there's no point," said Leslie. "Kenny isn't really a suspect. I should have explained, he has an alibi for the time of the murder. He was in this very pub; there's CCTV evidence."

"Never mind that," said Gloria, "they always tell you not to trust a cast-iron alibi. And anyway, he might have had an accomplice."

"I really don't—" began Leslie, who could think of no purpose in tailing Kenny, alibi or not.

"You don't like him, and you think he's involved, don't you?" interrupted Gloria.

"I certainly don't like him," admitted Leslie. "I think he's probably a crook, and if there wasn't such hard and fast evidence..."

"Always trust your instincts," said Gloria with conviction. "Intuition is completely scientific, you know; it's when your feelings and your senses have just got a little ahead of your conscious, reasoning mind. And we're here now, so we might as well go in. There's nothing like a bit of an adventure."

Leslie had a strong preference for peace and predictability, but since Gloria had already made an entrance he had little choice but to follow.

It was no surprise to find that the pub was dark, dingy and in need of decoration, but this was plainly no deterrent to the large crowd of men gathered there. At a glance, Leslie could see no women other than Gloria and the middle-aged lady serving behind the bar. One large screen on the wall was silently showing a horse race, but on the other screen, around which most of the men were assembled, two heavy-weight boxers were squaring up to each other in what was obviously the lead-up to a fight.

Gloria had stopped by a table in the centre of the room, but Leslie steered her towards the side where the tables were flanked by high-backed settles and might provide at least a little cover. It was impossible to hope for more than that. Gloria's personality alone made her conspicuous in any company, but add to that her multi-coloured frock, cerise jacket and turquoise chiffon headband, and she was a bird of paradise among a flock of pigeons.

Gloria pointed to a notice above the bar indicating that food was only served from six until ten pm, exclaiming in great disappointment. Leslie, who had not even considered that they would be lunching there, breathed a silent sigh of relief, and suggested they just have one quick drink and return to the cafe. He went across to the bar to order a shandy for himself and a glass of wine for Gloria.

While he waited at the bar, Leslie kept a watchful eye on Kenny who he did not particularly want to encounter. Fortunately, Kenny was engrossed in the screen, like most of the men. It seemed a strange time of day for a boxing match important enough to draw such interest, until Leslie realised that it was coming from some other part of the world, and snippets of conversation revealed that they were all betting men. Leslie guessed that on another day they might be gathered round to watch Irish greyhound racing, table tennis from China or the Portuguese football league, if such things existed.

Leslie was served his drinks by the taciturn barmaid. If she wondered what he and Gloria were doing there, she gave no sign of it. However, as Leslie turned from the bar, he was disconcerted to see a ruddy-faced man approaching Gloria, and Leslie reached the table in time to hear him say, in a strong West Country accent, "Or' right, my lover? What's a priddy maid like you doing in 'ere?"

"Oh, I say!" said Gloria, her face flushing scarlet.

The man was blocking the table and, from behind him, Leslie gave a couple of coughs and an ineffectual, "Excuse me, please."

Paying Leslie no heed, he repeated his words exactly, and Leslie wondered, rather uncharitably, if this was the only chat-up line in the man's repertoire.

"Well," said Gloria, confidentially, "it's rather a secret. I wouldn't want it to get about."

Leslie tried desperately to edge past the man, but he was large, solid and immovable. Leslie attempted, instead, to lean round him and call off Gloria's attention but, to his consternation, she ignored him. The man made no reply but also showed no signs of moving away and Gloria said, in a secretive whisper, "I'm an author, you see. I'm writing a thriller about a murder set in a pub just like this. I've come in to get what they call 'local colour'. And my friend, who is trying to get past you, has come along to look after me. So if you wouldn't mind stepping aside to let him past. And remember, mum's the word!" She pressed her index finger to her pursed lips.

Looking somewhat baffled, and muttering 'Oh, ar,' a couple of times, the man took himself and his pint back to the throng.

"How about that!" said Gloria, triumphantly. "I knew I'd think of something!"

Leslie was certain that this subterfuge was more likely to excite interest than divert it, and he cast an anxious glance into the room. But Gloria's admirer was already silently transfixed by the boxing match which was now underway, his brief effort at flirtation evidently forgotten.

It was difficult to converse above the noise which now accompanied the fight. The air was peppered with expletives and invectives of the most vulgar kind, but Gloria seemed unperturbed and drank her wine as serenely as if they were in the snug bar of The Woodman after choir practice. Leslie noticed that one or two of the men spoke, or shouted, with a noticeable Devonian accent, not as distinct as Gloria's suitor, but more marked than Leslie was used to hearing in the local area. In normal circumstances it would have been a pleasant novelty to listen to them, but the context was hardly conducive to cultural appreciation.

There was a sudden roar, followed by exclamations of victory and angry shouts of defeat from the crowd of men. On the screen, the camera focussed in on the ring showing one of the pugilists flat on his back and the other dancing about, punching the air.

Kenny was obviously on the victorious side and he congratulated himself heartily, gloating over his comrades who had backed the loser, and even over the other winners. "Yeah, but you don't get it, do you?" he crowed. Kenny's accent surely betrayed South London origins. "I really am quids in. I bet on a KO in round two. Bang on, me. It was fifty to one. What a result!"

"Well, it be your round then, Ken," someone shouted.

"I haven't collected my winnings yet, have I?" he retorted without hesitation.

There was a lot of muttering and then Gloria's admirer called across to Kenny, "They ain't arrested you yet then, Kenny, for that murder?" He gave a great belly laugh.

Leslie sat attentively, wondering if Gloria's fanciful explanation had triggered a train of thought in the man, and hoping that he wouldn't now draw attention to them.

"What you on about, Joe?" Kenny responded, in a mocking tone. "If you mean the old geezer at the Grange, I was in here all evening, wasn't I? So I couldn't have done it, could I?"

"T'was the wife that done it, the old haggage. Stands to reason," someone else called out.

"What do you know about it?" retorted Kenny, and there was something unpleasantly gloating about his manner. "I bet you don't know anything about it."

"His wife's got an alibi," shouted another man in the crowd, and gave a vulgar report of Clarissa's rendezvous with Antonio. Some very uncouth comments were expressed and Leslie dreaded to think what the proprietor of The Imperial would have said if he had heard his revered hotel referred to as a 'knocking shop'.

Everyone was now joining in the banter.

"Are you sure it weren't your old man, Ken? After all, he was the last one to see him, and they always say as it's the last person to see someone alive who did it."

"'ark at 'e," chipped in the red-faced Joe. "Thinks 'e's Sherlock 'olmes." He roared with laughter at his own lightening wit.

"What the hell are you going on about, Andy?" someone shouted.

"I'm telling you, Ken's old man was the last person to see the poor old bloke. He was shouting his mouth off about it in The Woodman. He was telling everyone that he went up to see the old boy that night and he left the place at ten fifteen, or some such time. And he reckons that makes him the last one to see him alive."

"I know all about that," said Kenny, with an air of smugness still about him. "But I can't really see my old gaffer doing anyone

in, can you? The old man couldn't hardly squash a fly these days."
Everyone joined in the laughter and Kenny threw in some further
disparaging comments about his father.

It was horrible to hear Edgar spoken of with such disrespect,
but there was no question of challenging it. The only thing that
would achieve would be to draw attention to himself, and he was
relieved that so far he and Gloria had miraculously remained
unnoticed.

"No, it stands to reason that it was the tart that did it. It's
always the wife, isn't it? After her old man's money, especially
when she's got a bit on the side. Yup, it was the missus all right."

Kenny started to take his departure, crowing again about
collecting his winnings from the betting shop.

"You coming back in to buy us that round, Kenny-boy?"

"Not tonight," he said. "I got business elsewhere." He
winked, made an explicit arm gesture and swaggered out to a
chorus of jeering.

When he had gone one of the men said, "Yeah, he's got a
woman on the go at some place on the way down to the coast, I
dunno where exactly. Poor cow, she must be desperate."

The crowd started to break up, some leaving, some going to
the bar, and Gloria leant forward and hissed, "Time for us to go,
don't you think?"

They slipped out through the front door and as they stepped
onto the pavement, they saw Kenny coming out of the betting
shop halfway down the road. A couple of the men who had gone
out just before them also saw him and one of them gave a shrill
whistle while the other yelled, "Who are you knocking off,
Kenny-boy?"

Kenny, who must have heard them, did not break stride, and
they hollered and taunted him with great enjoyment. Fortunately
the two men went off in the other direction and Leslie and Gloria
crossed the road, following in Kenny's footsteps. As they turned
the corner back onto the main street, Leslie was relieved to see
Kenny ducking down the path towards the car park. Further
pursuit would be futile, which even Gloria admitted. She checked
the time.

"Oh good," she said. "We can still have our lunch in Maurice's café, after all. He knows me and he'll serve us straight away."

They went inside and Leslie thought that a greater contrast between this and The Greyhound would have been hard to find. The café was what could only be described as genteel. The lace-clothed tables, which were decorated with fresh flowers, were occupied by neatly attired customers, sipping tea from dainty china teacups. Like Gloria's shop, it extended well back and, despite being busy, a table was found for them. Maurice, the man who Leslie had spoken to earlier, took their order.

When he had moved away, Gloria leant forward and whispered, "What about all that in the pub, then? Don't you think that Kenny had a strange attitude when they spoke of the murder? He looked very pleased with himself."

"I'm not sure," said Leslie. He did not disagree that Kenny had been smug, but that was hardly surprising given his win on the fight and, perhaps, the prospect of an amorous night ahead. "At least we might have an explanation for why he has told Edgar that he's away on business when he's still in the area."

"The woman!" hissed Gloria. "I wonder if she's his accomplice. Why else would he pretend he was on business if it's just a girlfriend he's with? We're not living in the 1950s, even in these parts."

It was more likely that the woman was married, Leslie thought, but before he could say so Gloria exclaimed, "But, I say, perhaps there is no woman after all, and it's all a blind! He's up to no good, I'm sure."

Luckily at this moment Maurice appeared with their lunch, a bacon and avocado sandwich for Leslie and a brie and cranberry panini for Gloria. There was some friendly chatter with him and, after that, Leslie managed to keep the conversation away from Gloria's fanciful speculations. She was quite right that Kenny was up to no good but she obviously did not know about his nefarious activities with Edgar's business, and Leslie was not going to enlighten her. Who knew what other dodgy dealings Kenny was involved with? But as for murder, much as Leslie would have liked to pin it on Kenny, what possible reason could there be?

Moreover, it was senseless to deny his alibi, and absurd to start inventing an accomplice.

Gloria eyed the dessert counter longingly but Leslie had a bus to catch and, with Gloria sighing that there was always tomorrow, they took their leave. They walked across to Healing Temple to collect Leslie's shopping which he had left behind the counter for safe-keeping.

"You will be careful, won't you?" said Gloria as she handed over his bag. "That Kenny fellow is a nasty piece of work, I'm sure of that. You don't want to tangle with him."

This was rich, considering it was Gloria who had just insisted they pursue him, but naturally Leslie did not say so. He tried to assure her that he had no intention of putting himself in any danger.

"Yes, but don't forget," she said darkly, "if you stir up a hornets' nest, you're likely to get stung."

25

It was just after five thirty when Annie, looking fraught and tired, called for Leslie and they set off for Monkton Beckett.

"That young man had better have a convincing explanation," she said. Her earlier sympathetic sentiments had evidently evaporated. "It's been frantic all day, and I could do without this excursion now."

Leslie also had a strong desire for an armchair in his own sitting room after his lunchtime outing, but as he would not dream of adding to Annie's misery, he kept these thoughts to himself.

The journey took them across Dartmoor, breathtakingly beautiful in the early evening light. They wound their way through the moorland village of Harpin-on-the-Moor, a pretty little place but with rather too many trinket shops and ice cream vans for Leslie's taste. Even at this time of the day they had to squeeze by the tourist coaches parked up on the narrow street and stop and start for the pedestrians, not to mention ponies, wandering about on the road. Leslie was very thankful that Dartonleigh, with its inaccessible lanes, was spared all this. "Fancy having a teashop there," said Leslie nodding towards the café they were creeping past. The waitress was serving some customers who were seated outside, inches from his window. "It's more like a drive-through. If I reached out the window now I could help myself to that man's pasty!"

"But I bet they're not having to manage with staff who steal the tips and then go AWOL," Annie replied bitterly. "I'm sorry, I'm not usually like this. I do feel very sorry for Daniel really, but I can't run a business on sympathy."

At last they reached Monkton Beckett and soon they were turning off the main street into a rather gloomy housing estate. They saw Daniel before he caught sight of them. He was sitting hunched up on a garden wall at the front of a drab house and he looked the picture of woe. Immediately they drew up though, he was on his feet, the cocksure facade restored.

"It's good of you to come out to collect me," he said as they pulled away. The words were right, but Leslie was taken aback by his supercilious attitude. He might have been a lord thanking his chauffeur for working overtime at short notice.

"I suppose you're wondering why I did a runner," he said, affecting a careless manner. "It was college. I had an exam and, well, exams and me have never got on. I guess I just freaked out. Stupid, I know."

Annie and Leslie ignored both his manner and his lies. This was no time for a confrontation.

"I've had a chance to think things through over the last couple of days," he continued. "It's not the right college for me. I know Mum won't like it but when I explain about the exams, I think she'll understand. I've been looking online at other colleges, and there are some which have more coursework. One of those would be better for me. They're all a long way from here, though."

"Try not to do anything hasty," said Annie.

"I must admit, I was never very fond of exams at school," said Leslie, and commenced on a long saga about his school days. Daniel, seated in the back of the car and occupied with his phone, didn't even pretend to listen.

As they pulled up in Dartonleigh, Daniel was anxious to get away as quickly as possible, but his attempts were foiled.

"Your aunt is on a late shift today," said Annie firmly, steering the reluctant boy into Leslie and Bennett's cottage. "I promised her that we would give you a hot meal. She would never forgive me if I let you go without feeding you. You wouldn't want me getting into trouble with your aunt, would you, not after I came all that way to collect you?"

Bennett had managed to switch the oven on according to Leslie's instructions, and the mouthwatering aroma wafting from the kitchen made them all realise how hungry they were. The moussaka was golden brown and bubbling as Leslie brought it to the table.

"I'm starving!" exclaimed Daniel, making perhaps his first honest statement since they had picked him up at Monkton Beckett.

The moussaka, which tasted every bit as good as it looked, was accompanied by a crisp green salad with glasses of red wine. Leslie followed it with Greek yoghurt drizzled with honey which he served with an almond shortbread. It was a meal that would normally conjure up the deepest contentment of the spirit. On this occasion Leslie hoped it would at least weaken the toughest defences.

In the sitting room after the meal, Bennett poured out the port, and Daniel stared with incredulity at the glass offered him.

"I've never had a meal like that before," he said, suddenly guileless. "It's better than any restaurant."

"Well now, Daniel," said Bennett, unexpectedly taking charge of the conversation. "I hope you will repay Leslie and Annie for their kindness by telling us what it was that Jamie saw you doing at Compton Grange. We know about your conversation with him at The Daffodil, so it's no good denying it. It was overheard." Bennett had few scruples about precise honesty.

Daniel turned his head sharply towards Annie. "I didn't see you there. Where were you? I was certain no one could hear me. I made sure Laura was out of the way. I didn't realise you were listening."

Taking advantage of this misunderstanding, Annie simply said, "Why don't you give us your side of the story? Believe me, Daniel, I want to help you, for your mother's sake if nothing else." Seeing his sudden agonised look she added hastily, "Don't worry, your mum knows nothing about this so far, but we'll never be able to keep it from her if it becomes a police case."

Daniel seemed suddenly to repent of his hasty response, and said guardedly, "What did you hear? What do you know? I mean, what do you think you know?"

"No," interrupted Bennett, "just you tell us what you were up to. This is no time to play games. There have been some serious crimes in this village: murder, blackmail. I could have the chief inspector here in twenty minutes." This was a different Bennett from the impassive person that most people were used to, but of course in the years that Bennett had taught at the university, he'd dealt with many errant young men just like this one.

Daniel stared into his glass of port and said sullenly, "OK, what do you want to know?"

"Start by telling us what you were doing when Jamie saw you."

Daniel took a tiny sip of his port. "I was picking up a package, but it was for someone else. I agreed to collect it for them and I passed it on. I can't tell you any more than that."

"Come on, let's have the whole story," said Bennett with authority. "You know that there's no turning back now. We'll help you if we can, I guarantee you that, but we can only do that if we have the truth. All of it. Start at the beginning. Who were you picking the package up for?"

"I don't know his name and if I did I wouldn't tell you. It's more than my life's worth."

"OK, we'll come back to that," said Bennett. "Where did you meet this person?"

Daniel drank some more port. "The Flying Pig," he muttered. "It's the nightclub in Tiverley. I met him not long after I came down to stay with aunty. He was OK then, friendly. He was selling grass really cheap. We all bought it from him. Then I got some Es, you know, party drugs, from him. I couldn't believe how cheap he was; practically giving it away. Then one evening he told me he couldn't get to the club the next week – would I mind taking the Es there for him. I could get mine for free and he'd give me a cut of what I sold. It was just like I was doing him a favour, you know, helping out. Somehow, it started to become a regular thing. I've got to admit it, I needed the money, and it was only party drugs and a bit of weed I was selling; stuff everyone uses all the time. I thought it would be all right.

"It wasn't long before I realised what I'd got myself into. He told me to ask around at the leisure club where I was working to see if there'd be any interest in gym candy, you know, anabolic steroids. That's not my scene at all, but when I refused he got really nasty. He asked me if I knew what happened to drug pushers like me and how long I could get for supplying illegal substances. He scared the sh-, sorry, he really scared me. Then he started on about Mum. I don't know how he found out about her, but he told me to think what it would be like if it got back to her that I'd been selling. Of course I agreed about the steroids then. What choice did I have?

"He told me what to say and what type of people to approach about the drugs. I wasn't any good at it. I only spoke to two of the clients, and the next morning I was called into the manager's office and I got the sack. He said if I left straightaway he wouldn't take it any further – I think he wanted to hush it up for the sake of the hotel.

"I stopped going to the Flying Pig after that and hoped to God that would be the end of it. I got the job at The Daffodil and after a couple of weeks I started to forget about the man. Then one afternoon I was serving some customers at the front of the teashop and when I turned around he was staring in at me through the window. We were face to face. It was awful. He went away but I knew he'd be back.

"He was waiting for me in the lane on my way home a few days later. He said he had a little job for me. He was back to being nice again and he said this was a different sort of a job. All I had to do was collect a package from outside Compton Grange. He told me the man living there was dying and the drugs the doctors prescribed him weren't strong enough. He'd managed to get something powerful for him, drugs you'd get in a hospital. I was to pick up the payment.

"You might not believe me, but it sounded true. I knew that's where the old man lived who everyone in the village was talking about as being so ill. I know that sometimes people don't get enough painkillers and I know as well that some hard drugs, like heroin, are also painkillers used in hospital, only with a different name of course. With Mum being so ill on and off these last five years, you get to know about this kind of thing. It all seemed to add up, and this bloke made it sound like he'd done the man a good turn. I agreed without arguing; I knew I'd have to do it anyway.

191

"It was dead easy. I cycled past the house to make sure no one was there, watching or waiting, then left my bike in the bushes down the lane. I crept back through the trees and then I kept close to the wall surrounding the house – you know how high that wall is. The package was there, an envelope, and I could tell from the feel of it that it was stuffed full of notes.

"I had to cycle out of the village on the Stretton Cross road and drop the package by the post box and cycle on. He was going to be following me in his car to pick it up, and I suppose make sure I did what I'd been told. If anyone stopped me, I was to tell them I'd found the envelope in the lane and I was taking it to hand it in. But no one saw me. No one except Jamie, of course. That was on the second time, about a week or two later.

"The first I knew about blackmail was when Jamie came to The Daffodil the other day. Honestly, believe me, I'm not involved in anything like that; that was nothing to do with me. I know you must think I'm rubbish, a complete loser, but I truly couldn't do a thing like that to anyone, let alone someone who was dying." This long speech over, Daniel slouched back in the chair. His face was the picture of misery and he was quite different to the brash, conceited young man they were used to.

"Thank you," said Bennett. "You seem to have told us nearly everything."

"There's nothing else to tell. Really," said Daniel defensively.

"Apart from the name of this person. Come on, who is he?"

"No," said Daniel shaking his head. "I can't say. He threatened that if I grassed, he'd make sure my Mum was told everything. He meant it all right, too."

"The only way you will be safe from this man is if he is arrested and in the custody of the police."

"You can't make me. I've said all I'm going to say. I want to go home now," Daniel said, standing up.

"Sit down and listen to me." Bennett spoke with authority and the boy sat down. "The news that Mr Harrington-Thomas was blackmailed is now common knowledge. This blackmailer isn't stupid. He won't risk you working out what it was you were picking up from Compton Grange, and telling the police. Think about it."

"You're just trying to scare me into telling you," Daniel retorted angrily. "I can't risk it."

"Do I have to spell it out? You know too much for your own good. He will want you out of the way. For all we know this blackmailer might also be the man who murdered Mr Harrington-Thomas. Another murder may be nothing to him. You are in far greater danger if you don't say who it is."

"But everyone's saying that they've caught the murderer," said Daniel. "It was that guy who was staying at The Woodman, wasn't it?"

"No one has been charged," Bennett replied. "As far as I'm concerned, the murderer is still on the loose."

"Oh God," said Daniel hunching down in the chair as if he was about to be assaulted there and then. "I have to get away from this village."

The room fell silent. Leslie went to the sideboard and poured the boy a small glass of brandy. "Drink this, son," he said kindly.

Daniel only took a couple of small sips but it seemed to break the spell. He looked up, directly at Bennett. "I bet you know who it is already. I bet you've guessed."

"Just tell me," said Bennett.

"It's Kenny. Kenny Barr."

26

"I knew that Kenny was up to no good," said Leslie to Bennett when they were alone, "but blackmail!"

There had been little more conversation after Daniel's revelation. Annie drove Daniel home and Leslie cleared up. Despite his loathing of Kenny, Leslie derived no satisfaction from his accurate assessment of the man's nefarious character. He had convinced himself that the blackmailer and murderer were one and the same person, yet Kenny's alibi for the time of the murder was beyond doubt. So the murderer was still unaccounted for, and in the meantime Robin remained the chief suspect. They seemed no nearer to clearing his name and finding the true culprit, and he was left wrestling with the improbable conclusion that George had become the victim of two separate crimes.

"I suppose we believe Daniel's account, do we?" said Leslie. "He could be inventing the whole story. The boy's not renowned for his honesty."

"What's your feeling?" asked Bennett. "That kind of thing's your department."

Leslie reflected. "I'd say that what he told us was the truth. But, to be honest, I wouldn't be surprised if he's still holding something back."

"Interesting, but he was obviously going to say nothing more tonight. We were lucky he said as much as he did. I'll give Ridgeway a call in the morning. There's nothing to be gained by doing anything sooner."

"What do you think Kenny could have been blackmailing George about?" said Leslie. "It's hard to imagine how Kenny would have got close enough to George to know anything about him; it's not as though he worked for him, or anything like that. It can't have been anything to do with Robin. The blackmail was weeks ago and Robin's only just appeared on the scene. If Kenny won't talk, we may never know."

"That's probably what George would have wanted. He certainly didn't volunteer the reason to me, and no one gets blackmailed for information they want broadcasting."

"True," said Leslie. "I wonder where Kenny is now. The woman he's supposedly favouring with his attentions lives somewhere between here and the coast, if the gossip in The Greyhound is to be believed, but that hardly narrows it down. At least he's not here in the village so Daniel's not likely to run into him."

"If there's a wasp in the room," said Bennett, switching off his bedside light, "it's better if you can see it."

It took Leslie a long time to fall asleep and, as a consequence, he woke late. By the time he got up, Bennett was already downstairs and had phoned the chief inspector. Ridgeway had not been available and Bennett had left a message. Leslie made breakfast, all the while feeling agitated. Bennett was as composed as ever, but Leslie could not be easy until they had disclosed what they had been told about Kenny.

"I'd be reluctant to talk with anyone other than Ridgeway at the moment," said Bennett when Leslie expressed his anxiety. "The last thing we need is a couple of uniformed officers quizzing Edgar on Kenny's whereabouts."

"That's true," agreed Leslie. "Edgar would be bound to contact Kenny and tell him the police were looking for him, even if they ordered him not to. Nothing would stop him from shielding him, he couldn't help himself." This reasoning did nothing, however, to alleviate Leslie's impatience which he exacerbated by thinking up ever greater catastrophes that could occur as a consequence of withholding the information. Bennett, in contrast, munched his toast in inscrutable silence. As Leslie was bringing the cafetiere to the table, he saw Martin hurrying through the front gate, with Cromwell a few paces behind.

"I'm just taking Cromwell for a walk," said Martin bursting into the cottage, "but I had to come and tell you. They've suspended the chief planning officer, Sylvia's boss. They're saying he may get sacked, just a couple of weeks before his lucrative retirement was due. Who says there's no God?"

Happy to share Martin's elation, and glad of the distraction, Leslie buttered fresh toast and poured coffee for his visitor, and found some biscuits for the ever-famished dog. With the jubilation of a citizen describing the overthrow of a dictatorship, Martin related the events that had led to this gratifying outcome. It transpired that an investigation into the management of the planning department had been going on for some time, prompted, so it was said, by George's pressure on the local councillors. Rumour had it that the chief planning officer and a couple of his cronies had been accepting bribes to push through approval for unsuitable plans, or to turn a blind eye to building contraventions. "Sylvia's heard that they're questioning Jeff Clayden. He's one of those suspected of paying backhanders to get his planning application approved."

"So that must have been why Jeff was in such a hurry," said Leslie. "It all had to be completed before the chief planning officer's retirement. Nothing to do with Jeff having a buyer for his land, after all."

That would also explain the sums of money withdrawn from his bank account which Veronika had mentioned to Leslie when he met her in the farm shop. Then he remembered the row that Stan overheard in the garden and the extreme animosity Jeff felt for George. These now made sense if Jeff had found out that George had instigated an investigation into the corruption. Leslie voiced these thoughts to Bennett, while he was wielding a broom across the kitchen floor after Martin had left. "Do you think it was enough of a motive for murder?" asked Leslie, sweeping a few crumbs and wiry grey hairs into the dustpan.

"God knows," said Bennett unhelpfully, and withdrew to the library.

Leslie was determined not to make his usual sortie out into the village; he was party to so much information that he must not share and feared it might show in his face or his manner. He doubted himself equal to the wiles of a Vera or a Marian if they suspected he knew things he wasn't telling. So far he hadn't put a foot wrong but he felt it was only a matter of time, and it could jeopardise everything if the village guessed that Kenny was a wanted man. Leslie explored the fridge, freezer and pantry and discovered that he had everything he needed to make a paella for dinner, and he spun the day out between cooking and pottering about in the seclusion of the back garden.

Bennett was in one of his particularly unforthcoming moods and Leslie could barely get a word out of him all day. He was monosyllabic over lunch and even the very excellent paella did not alter his sphinx-like state at dinnertime. Consequently, Leslie had no expectation of lively conversation over coffee, but as he was filling the cafetiere, the doorbell rang. Bennett went to the door and returned, followed by the detective chief inspector.

"Sorry not to have got back to you until now," said Ridgeway, folding his angular frame into an armchair. "It's been one of those days. I was on my way from Lymeford so I thought I might as well call in. I hope it's not inconvenient."

"You've come at just the right moment for coffee," said Leslie and put another mug on the tray.

"I got your message this morning," said Ridgeway, "and I sent a couple of our officers to interview young Daniel."

"Will he get into trouble?" asked Leslie as he put the tray down on the coffee table. "He seems to have got himself up to his neck in the proverbial."

"We've got bigger fish to fry at the moment," said Ridgeway. "He's more use to us as a witness."

"That's a relief," said Leslie, who genuinely felt sorry for the boy. "What are you going to do about Kenny, or aren't you allowed to say?"

"There isn't much to say that you don't already know," smiled the chief inspector, wryly. "I'm sure I don't need to ask you both to keep everything you know under your hats for the moment, as we don't want news that we're after him leaking out."

"We won't breathe a word," said Leslie earnestly.

"We're keeping an eye out for him but I don't want to scare him off by sending officers poking around his house, or the pub, or any of his other haunts, just yet."

"The balloon would definitely go up if you did that," agreed Leslie. "You can't do anything round here without the whole county hearing about it. But what if he's already done a runner?"

"If that's the case, I expect I'll end up with egg on my face," said Ridgeway grimly. "But I doubt he'd get far, and certainly not out of the country."

"Is there really no way that Kenny could have committed the murder, as well as the blackmail?" said Leslie, passing round the mugs of coffee. "I wish he didn't have that alibi."

"I know you've got it in for him," laughed Ridgeway.

"I have," agreed Leslie, "but it's not really that. Isn't it rather a coincidence that George was the victim of both blackmail and murder, if they weren't connected? To suffer one of those crimes is a misfortune enough, but both!"

"Don't forget that at the moment it's still only an allegation," said Ridgeway. "We only have Daniel's word for it that Kenny was the blackmailer."

"Well, don't try pinning the blackmail on Robin, as well as the murder," said Leslie with a mirthless laugh.

"You still seem very convinced that Robin Sheraton is innocent," said the chief inspector. "There isn't something you're not telling me?"

"Oh no, not at all," said Leslie. "It's nothing concrete. It's just that sometimes I instinctively trust or distrust people and I'm not usually wrong, that's all." He finished the sentence half defiantly and half defensively, certain that he sounded ridiculous.

"Well, you know we'll carry on following up all lines of enquiry," said the chief inspector, in a mollifying tone.

"Do you have any other lines of enquiry?" asked Leslie.

There was a short pause and Ridgeway said, "Put it this way, don't raise your hopes."

Leslie felt rather despondent, and no amount of the pleasant small talk with Ridgeway that followed could restore his mood. He felt certain now that Robin was soon to be charged with George's murder. He could not shake off the conviction that he and Bennett bore responsibility for mentioning him in the first place, and therefore that they must somehow exonerate him.

No less disturbing was the fact that if Robin was innocent, as he believed, there was a murderer still at large who was successfully evading suspicion.

The chief inspector eventually peeled himself away from the armchair and took his leave, full of thanks for his coffee, and undertaking to return for a game of chess just as soon as he could find a free evening.

"Once you locate Kenny," said Bennett, as the chief inspector was on the doorstep, "you might have a look inside his warehouse. Apparently he's had the locks changed and even his father, who owns the business, doesn't have a key."

"Really?" said Ridgeway, raising his eyebrows. "That sounds interesting."

When Ridgeway had left, Leslie sat in gloomy silence and Bennett went to the drinks cabinet. "I don't think we should completely dismiss the link between the blackmail and the murder," he said. "Even if they were done by different people."

"What do you mean?" asked Leslie. "How could they be connected?"

"That I can't tell you," said Bennett. "I'm just making a general point. Just because there's no causal relationship, it doesn't mean there's no relationship at all."

"Save your cryptic clues for your crosswords," said Leslie. Picking up his glass, he went upstairs to bed.

27

It was the faintest of sounds, a mere fluttering, and in normal circumstances it would not have woken Leslie. His senses were on such a state of red alert, however, that the rustling noise woke him as suddenly as if a doorbell had rung. The front door – yes that was where the sound had come from. This time there was no mistaking it for foxes; this sound had been inside the house. Leslie lay tense and alert, but there was nothing but silence now. He tried to forget about it, to tell himself that there was a simple explanation, that he had been mistaken. In the back of his mind was the recollection of the occasion when, creeping about the house in the night, he had come face to face with Antonio at the patio door, and he was not in a hurry to repeat the experience.

However, after wrestling with these thoughts for a few minutes, Leslie was defeated by the compulsion to investigate. He slid silently out of bed, pulled his dressing gown round his shoulders, and crept slowly across the room, his eyes adjusting to the darkness. Reaching the end of the bed, he stopped dead in trepidation. Something was huddled on the floor by the window. It took several heart-stopping moments to realise that it was nothing more than Bennett's clothes carelessly discarded over the back of a chair. He silently cursed Bennett's slovenly habits, but by then his pulse was racing and his nerves were completely on edge.

He stopped at the bedroom door to listen but all he could hear was the sound of his own heartbeat. Tiptoeing across the landing he paused again – still nothing. Slowly and very cautiously, he crept down the stairs, and when he was halfway down he stopped suddenly. In the moonlight he could see an object on the front doormat. A few steps further and he could make out that it was an envelope. It certainly hadn't been there when he went to bed.

Reaching the foot of the stairs, Leslie clicked the light switch on. No masked intruder leapt upon him, so he advanced to the doormat and, anxious and perplexed, he stooped to pick up the crumpled envelope. His name was scrawled on the front in writing that Leslie recognised straightaway. He went cold with a sense of foreboding.

Ripping open the envelope, his dismay and horror increased with every sentence he read. He fled upstairs, switching on the bedroom light, and started dressing as quickly as he could.

"What in God's name are you doing, man?" said Bennett, raising himself onto one elbow, his face puckered against the light. "What time is it?"

"It's ten to three. Read this," said Leslie thrusting the letter at Bennett and neatly folding his pyjamas, out of habit. "If I hurry, I may be in time," he continued. "I heard him put the letter through the door; it woke me only a few minutes ago."

Bennett fumbled for his glasses on the bedside table. It was a short handwritten sheet, and Bennett had finished reading it by the time Leslie had pulled on his socks and buttoned his waistcoat.

Dear Leslie,

I don't want to shock or upset you, but you are the only friend I can trust this letter to. I hope you will forgive me putting you through this.

By the time you read this, I will be gone. I have chosen the best way out, for everyone's sake. I have taken a long time to make this decision, and it's what I want, so please don't try and stop me, even if you can. I wish I could explain it to you, I feel I owe it to you, but I can't.

The fact is this: I killed George. It was me. I confess to it here in this letter, and I don't want to see an innocent boy accused. Please see to it that the police receive this confession – I know I can trust you to.

I've done this tonight because Kenneth is away. I don't want him to find me or this letter. Please look after him. I hope he will be able to forgive me, and I hope you can too, though perhaps that will be hard given your friendship with George.

I want to thank you for everything. I know this is for the best.

201

The letter was signed and dated.

"It can't be true," said Leslie in disbelief. "Edgar of all people. I would never have thought him the type. It's not possible."

Bennett started up from the bed. "I'll come with you," he said quickly.

"I can't wait or it may be too late," said Leslie. "If I go straight away, I may be in time to stop him. Stay here; I'll ring you when I get to his house and you can come if I need you."

"Only if you're sure," said Bennett. "Be careful, Les. The village isn't a safe place at the moment." As he spoke, Bennett reached out and caught Leslie's hand, a gesture so unusual that it momentarily halted Leslie, despite his haste to be gone. There was no time to respond though, and Leslie was away from the bedroom and at the front door in moments.

Even with a torch, it was difficult to hurry. The moon was hidden now behind the clouds and, once he had passed the church and left the village centre, the ground was uneven, and the road into Broomhill Lane, where Edgar lived, was a steep climb. Leslie was gasping for breath by the time he turned into the lane, but relief at seeing a light at Edgar's cottage gave him the impetus he needed for the last few yards.

Hurrying up the front path, he hesitated for the first time, suddenly appreciating what he might have to encounter. He stopped, then screwing up his courage, he crossed the small untidy front garden to the kitchen window where the light was showing. It wasn't easy to get a good view. Leslie had to contend with a bed of overgrown and prickly bushes which prevented him getting close up to the window. The curtains had been drawn, but fortunately they were ill fitting, and there was a gap through which Leslie peered nervously.

The first thing that caught Leslie's eye, amid the general chaos, was an open bottle of pills lying on its side, and a packet of tablets on the kitchen table. Pressing his face through the shrubbery to get a better view, he was alarmed to see a bottle smashed on the kitchen floor. He realised then, with horror, that the shape he could see lying along the floor behind the table was a person's leg.

He could only see the lower part, but the shoe was familiar. It was unmistakably Edgar's.

Hopelessness and futility seized Leslie, but instinctively he banged on the window. "Edgar! Edgar! Can you hear me?" There was no response and he hammered on the window and shouted again, louder this time. To his great surprise, and even greater relief, the leg moved. A moment later Edgar appeared in view, scrambling to his feet with an expression of confusion on his face, but otherwise apparently unharmed. He stood there, gesturing vaguely to various things around him and mouthing something that Leslie couldn't hear.

Leslie's relief suddenly changed to fury. Here he was at three in the morning, soaked with sweat, his good shoes ruined and his face scratched to pieces but now it seemed to be no more than a fool's errand. "Come to the front door and let me in," he shouted.

Edgar disappeared from view and obediently appeared at the front door moments later. He was a picture of desolation. "You weren't meant to come so soon," he said bleakly. "It's hopeless. I can't even do this without making a cock-up of it."

Leslie walked past him into the squalid kitchen. He threw a couple of filthy tea towels onto the floor to soak up some of the spilt alcohol, and then added a grubby towel from the bathroom. "What happened?" he asked, scooping up the towels and broken glass into a couple of old carrier bags, and putting them, dripping, into the bin.

Edgar sounded aggrieved as he told his sorry tale. He had placed on the table the means of his exit from this world: a litre of vodka, a bottle of paracetamol tablets and a box of antidepressants, ironically prescribed by Paul to improve his mental state. In his agitated condition, he had struggled to open the cap on the paracetamol bottle. As it finally came loose it slipped from his hand and the tablets went tumbling onto the floor. In trying to grab the falling container, he sent the vodka crashing to the ground. He was on his hands and knees, retrieving sodden tablets from among the broken glass and grime on the kitchen floor when Leslie had arrived.

"You're coming back with me," said Leslie, though really he felt more like shaking Edgar than offering succour. He went upstairs and helped himself to a couple more towels to finish mopping up, taking the opportunity to phone Bennett and briefly apprise him of the situation.

"Are the police coming?" asked Edgar, as Leslie came back into the kitchen.

"No."

"Are you going to call them? What's going to happen?" asked Edgar, but he followed Leslie to the door obediently as he spoke.

"Bennett will decide what to do," said Leslie, and they left the house.

By the time he and Edgar got home, Bennett had made up the bed in the spare room. Even in these circumstances, Leslie could not help but notice that the duvet cover was buttoned-up into the wrong button holes, the pillowcase did not match the cover, and the bottom sheet fell far short of the perfect envelope corners Leslie always achieved. However, the offense this caused his orderly mind was more than outweighed by the relief that Edgar could be got to bed without delay.

"Are the police coming?" asked Edgar again, speaking to Bennett this time.

"No," said Bennett.

"You got my letter, though?" he said.

"Yes," replied Bennett, "and it's much too late to talk about it now. Go to bed and we'll discuss it in the morning." Bennett turned on his heel and strode off to bed, leaving Edgar no opportunity to protest. Leslie provided Edgar with some washing things and lent him a pair of pyjamas.

"I wouldn't have invited you back here if I thought you were going to try anything silly again," said Leslie, "but please promise me you won't."

"I wouldn't do that to you, Leslie, honestly," said Edgar, wretchedly. "Anyway, what could I do? I've nothing with me."

Edgar sounded sincere, but Leslie studiously avoided glancing at the ceiling light or the window; he did not want to give the miserable man any ideas. While Edgar was in the bathroom he removed the little key from the locked window and decided that the light fitting had no chance of bearing Edgar's weight if he thought of hanging himself with the bedsheet. There was little more he could do, and when Edgar returned to the bedroom he seemed calm and ready to go to sleep, as if he was a houseguest on a weekend's visit.

Banishing the gruesome thoughts lingering in his mind, Leslie made for his own bedroom, eager to find out what Bennett made of Edgar's astonishing conduct. However, Bennett clearly thought that a murder confession, attempted suicide and unexpected night-time visitor should not get in the way of his sleep, for the light was off and he was breathing deeply.

While Bennett slept the sleep of the just, Leslie wrestled with a myriad of troubled thoughts. It was impossible to believe that the bungling Edgar could be a murderer. It was, however, equally incredible that he should go to the extremes of confession and suicide if he wasn't. What could possibly be his motive in either murdering George or making a false confession? Perhaps it was a mental breakdown, and Edgar believed he had committed the act. That didn't ring true, either; he had certainly seemed completely rational when Leslie had found him. And what if the confession was genuine and Edgar really was the murderer? Was he, even now, waiting outside their unlocked bedroom door with a knife in his hands? Leslie lay awake for a long time.

Bennett was already downstairs when Leslie woke the next morning. He peered cautiously into the spare room and waited until he satisfied himself as far as he could that Edgar was in a natural sleep. The kitchen held evidence that Bennett had breakfasted, and Leslie was relieved to see that he had attempted nothing more ambitious than a bowl of cereal. He swept muesli from the floor and mopped a puddle of milk from the table before going into the library, where Bennett was reclining on the leather sofa, staring at the ceiling with a blank face. He moved his feet out of the way so that Leslie could sit down.

"Oklahoma?" said Leslie, as the lyrics to *Pore Jud is Daid* played in the background, and Bennett nodded. It seemed a strange choice of listening but there was never any accounting for Bennett.

"What do we do now, Bennett?" Leslie asked. "Shall I phone the doctor? The police? I suppose we should really have called someone last night. After all, it was a suicide attempt. And a murder confession."

"I tried calling Paul earlier," said Bennett. "He's at a conference in London and won't be back until tomorrow. His wife said she'd ask him to ring us as soon as she can get hold of him. In the meantime, let's wait and see how the day unfolds."

"I can't believe Edgar is capable of murdering anyone, let alone George. But he was up at the Grange that evening, and his mental state isn't good. What if something tipped him over the edge?"

"You don't think that, do you?" said Bennett.

"No," said Leslie, simply. "So what do you think of his confession? I take it that you'd have called the police by now if you believed it." Leslie took Bennett's silence as a tacit agreement. "But what if we're both wrong and he really did do it, for some reason we know nothing about, and we're harbouring a self-confessed murderer in the cottage?"

Bennett got up and shut the library door. "Edgar didn't do it," he said. "He didn't murder George."

"How can you be so sure?"

"Because I know who the murderer is."

28

"You what?" exclaimed Leslie. "You know who did it?"

"I think I do," said Bennett.

"Well, go on, who is it?" demanded Leslie.

There was a pause, then Bennett shook his head slightly and said, "I might be wrong."

Leslie was used to Bennett keeping things to himself, and it was bad enough in normal circumstances, but this was too much. "I don't care if you don't tell me," he said, untruthfully, "but why, for God's sake, haven't you told the police?" He would have shouted if Edgar had not been upstairs. "This isn't a game, Bennett, it isn't one of your puzzles. This is murder."

"There's no evidence," said Bennett with aggravating calm, "not a shred. The police won't be interested in my mere conjectures, especially if they've already got a likely suspect in custody. Not even that very pleasant chief inspector. If we're going to get justice for George and an innocent man acquitted, we'll need to find some evidence."

Although Leslie felt terribly aggrieved at Bennett's secrecy, it was a relief that whoever he suspected, it was obviously not Robin, something that Leslie had not been completely certain of before. And it was also reassuring that Bennett knew who it was, for he felt sure that Bennett would not be mistaken, though he had no idea how they could find evidence to accuse this mystery suspect. It was pointless pressing Bennett further and, leaving him gazing out into the garden, Leslie crept upstairs and peeped into the spare room. Edgar was still asleep but stirred slightly, and Leslie shut the door noiselessly, putting off for as long as possible the moment when he had to deal with him.

It was too late for breakfast but Leslie was suddenly very hungry. Welsh rarebit was exactly what was needed; the perfect brunch. This was no time to worry about cholesterol, and he was generous with the cheese. He was about to take Bennett's plate through to the library, when he appeared in the kitchen.

"Smells good," he said, sitting at the table and helping himself to a piece of toast still bubbling with melted cheese. He dosed it liberally with Worcester sauce and tore the slice into two ragged pieces. Strands of cheese and Worcester sauce trickled onto his plate as he ate in happy oblivion. Leslie carefully spread mustard onto his piece and cut it into neat triangles. He ate with a knife and fork and, sitting opposite Bennett, remembered why he didn't make Welsh rarebit very often.

"Can you cater for Edgar if we can get him to stay until dinner tonight?" said Bennett.

"Any particular reason?" said Leslie, knowing that this uncharacteristic gesture of hospitality must have an ulterior motive.

"We need to get to the bottom of this stupid confession, and there's nothing like one of your dinners for doing that," he replied.

"I'll happily invite him," said Leslie, though the adjective was not strictly truthful. "Goodness knows what frame of mind he'll be in when he wakes up, though. What if he refuses and goes home?"

"We obviously can't force him to stay, but I think he'll come back later. Not many people can resist one of your dinners."

Remembering Edgar's kitchen, Leslie agreed. At the moment, Edgar would probably accept an invitation from the Borgias. "I ought to go and check on him again in a minute. I've been putting off waking him but it is nearly lunch time." Leslie brought the cafetiere to the table and a plate of little Florentine biscuits. "Do you think I'll give the game away if you tell me who you think the murderer is?" said Leslie suddenly. "Or is it just for amusement that you are keeping it to yourself?"

"Is that what you think?" said Bennett.

"Why else could it be? Or aren't you going to tell me that either?"

Bennett ate a Florentine, and then another. "I don't want to influence you," he said at last. "Your judgement of people and their reactions to you are all we've got at the moment. People trust you, they know you're open and honest, and they talk to you. You hate covering up and telling lies. If I tell you who I think the murderer is, it changes everything. That's all."

Leslie pushed down the plunger in the cafetiere and took a couple of biscuits. He believed Bennett's explanation, for Bennett would never say something just to appease or placate, and he felt less wounded. "Certainly plenty of people have talked to me," he said, "but whether they've spoken the truth is another matter."

"The half-truths and the lies are important, too. They might even be more revealing than the truth."

"If you say so," said Leslie, wearily. "As far as I'm concerned, the one thing that's been revealed is that there is a lot more unpleasantness in Dartonleigh than I ever imagined. It's not just the lurid scandalmongers. There's Daniel getting into one lot of trouble after another, and Jamie with his dreadful pictures, and interested only in getting Daniel away from the village. They've got some excuse; they're young and they've both got a lot of problems. But what about Jeff and Veronika, wishing that George had died six months earlier to save them from the inconvenience of having their planning permission challenged? As for Clarissa, she's the worst of them all. Having the nerve to make out she's the poor victim of deception by the man she was having an adulterous affair with, and then by George because he had a son she never knew about." Leslie was getting into his stride now. "And then, to top it all, going as far as to wish that Robin had been aborted before birth. It's shocking."

"When did she say that?" asked Bennett, taking the mug of coffee that Leslie had poured him.

"She told me that night I went up to the Grange to collect the photo. She said it was a shame Robin's mother was a Catholic otherwise she might not have gone ahead with the pregnancy, and it would have saved Clarissa a lot of trouble. I can't remember the exact words but it was something totally disgraceful and self-centred and completely typical of Clarissa."

"You never mentioned it before," said Bennett dabbing up Florentine crumbs with his finger.

"I suppose I didn't," said Leslie. "It's not surprising; it was the day Antonio chased me through the woods and I came home looking like I'd just come back from The Somme."

Bennett took his glasses off and leant back in his chair, staring up at the ceiling.

"All that talking and listening," Leslie continued, sighing with despondency. "But there was one conversation which might have saved everyone a lot of trouble."

Bennett looked at him enquiringly.

"It was that conversation with George which was never finished."

29

Shaking himself into action, Leslie took a tray of tea up to Edgar's room. He was surprised to see that Edgar was awake, but he was laying very still and staring at the ceiling.

"Hello, Edgar," he said, "I've brought you some tea. Have you been awake for long?"

Edgar continued staring into space. "Are the police coming?" he asked.

"No, no police, Edgar," said Leslie. "Drink your tea, then have a shower. I've put a towel and some clean clothes ready for you. You'll feel better after a shower. It's getting on for lunchtime."

Leslie had found some trousers and tops which had fitted him before retirement, and which, in a moment of self-delusion, he had folded away in the hopes that he might one day wear them again. He picked out the smallest sizes for Edgar and added a belt as even these outgrown garments would be hanging off him. Down in the kitchen, Leslie made more cheese on toast, and had just put it on the table when Edgar came into the kitchen.

"You can't keep me here, you know," he said, truculently.

"Whoever said anything about keeping you here?" said Leslie mildly. "But do have some Welsh rarebit before you go."

Edgar looked at the door, then the plate, and sat down at the table without further argument. While Edgar was eating, Leslie busied himself by constructing the evening meal. At first Edgar ate silently, other than protesting that he was going home as soon as he had finished lunch. Leslie started preparing a shepherd's pie and soon Edgar forgot about being silent and commenced on one of the life histories for which he was famous, and which could clear the lounge bar of The Woodman in minutes. His monologue continued, and twenty years of loneliness was unleashed into the kitchen. By the time Leslie had finished spreading mashed potato over the top of the mince, Edgar was recounting the tragedy of his wife's death for the third time.

Bennett sat unobtrusively in the corner of the kitchen reading the paper, and Leslie managed to find a stream of odd jobs to do while Edgar talked without intermission. He talked freely about his wife, her illness and death, its effects on Kenneth as a child, and his business in its heyday. There was, however, little reference to the current state of his affairs and no mention of George's death or the letter of confession he had written. At last Edgar's autobiography petered out. He finished his coffee and stood up, looking self-consciously about him. "I'll be going then," he said awkwardly. "Thank you for lunch, and, of course, a bed for the night. I was just wondering, you know..." His words drifted off.

Leslie looked across at Bennett, who glanced up, looking unconcerned. "I thought you were staying for dinner, Edgar," said Leslie. "I've made enough shepherd's pie for all of us, and I'd hate it to go to waste."

"You're trying to keep me here," said Edgar, suddenly suspicious again. "It's a trick, isn't it? The police are coming to arrest me." Poor Edgar. He had been prepared to make away with himself following his confession to murder, but was obviously far less keen to be questioned about the offence.

"Edgar," said Leslie firmly, "don't start working yourself up. If we were going to call the police they would have been here long ago, or they could find you at your own house. Go home, by all means, but do come back for dinner and then you can go home again for the night."

"Well I don't understand it. I don't understand why you haven't called them."

"I'll tell you all about it over dinner later," said Bennett, standing up. "I've some other things to tell you then, too, things that you'll be sorry to miss if you don't come back."

"What things? What... what things?" stuttered Edgar. "Tell me now. I'm not going until you tell me."

"Later, Edgar," said Bennett decisively. "Do excuse me as I have work to be getting on with." Bennett took himself off into the library and shut the door.

It took Leslie some time to convince Edgar that he didn't know what Bennett wanted to talk to him about, and when Edgar eventually left, Leslie was not convinced that he would return. Kenny was due home that evening, so Leslie told himself that this would prevent Edgar from being tempted to finish the job he failed to complete the night before. Despite this he spent the afternoon preoccupied with misgivings of every kind. He hoped that Bennett knew what he was playing at.

Annie called at the cottage later on, after she had shut up The Daffodil for the evening. Daniel, too nervous to remain in the area, had been allowed by the police to go to stay with his brother in Bristol. The Daffodil, she said, was coping admirably without him as Laura had found a friend to help out. "I hope, for his sake, that he doesn't come back," she said. "If the circumstances were different, I'd ring his mother and tactfully suggest she gives up her own ambitions for him and lets him find something he's suited to. Not everyone's cut out for studying and university. He's not a bad lad really, but I've come to the conclusion that under all that swagger, he's not actually the brightest spark. When he told us he can't cope with exams, I think that was quite true, even if it wasn't the reason he ran away."

"Kenny certainly saw him coming," said Bennett who had joined them.

Annie stirred a sweetener into her coffee and sighed. "Do you know," she continued, "when I drove Daniel home the night before last, after we'd had dinner here, I said to him that it must have been a strain keeping all those secrets and problems to himself. He told me he'd had a lot of practice keeping problems to himself over the last few years. It broke my heart. I know it's silly but, now he's gone, I almost miss him." Annie chatted on and although she was obviously still full of concern, she was much more relaxed now that Daniel was out of harm's way and no longer her responsibility. The conversation came round to the inevitable subject.

"I do hope they get to the bottom of this business with George soon," she said. "It's the only topic of conversation in the teashop and the stories are getting more and more farfetched. Doreen was in with a crowd today and, from the way she was talking, you'd have thought that Stan had spent the evening on surveillance of the Grange, and had been an eyewitness to the crime itself."

"When in fact," said Leslie, "Stan told me he had his curtains closed from seven o'clock and didn't see anything apart from a distant figure running down the road in the pitch dark, later in the evening. And Stan didn't have his glasses on at the time." Immediately the words were out of his mouth, Leslie realised that he was not being as careful as he should. He hoped that Annie didn't ask him anything about this conversation with Stan, as it only took one unguarded moment to accidentally let slip some prohibited fact, like Pete Parkin's presence in the lane. Leslie found all this censored conversation exhausting and for a moment, at least, he was glad that he didn't know who Bennett thought the murderer was.

Before Annie had a chance to say anything at all, Bennett stood up and said, in a perfectly even voice, "I've been a damned fool. It's been staring me in the face all this time." Without further comment, he left them and made for the library, leaving them shaking their heads in bafflement.

It was with great relief, and some surprise, that Leslie saw Edgar returning to the cottage at seven o'clock, looking reasonably tidy, still in the clothes Leslie had loaned him. He was, moreover, clutching a bottle. It proved to be a rather nasty-looking Croatian wine, guaranteed, thought Leslie, to induce heartburn, but he took it gratefully. It would always do for a raffle prize which, judging by the tell-tale remnant of sticky tape on the neck, was how Edgar had come by it.

Leslie showed Edgar through to the sitting room but he immediately followed Leslie back into the kitchen and stood at his shoulder talking incessantly while Leslie finished off the cooking, though with no mention of their conversations earlier in the day. To Leslie's annoyance, Bennett had waited until now to go upstairs to shower and change, and was therefore unable to relieve him of Edgar's company. Then, while Leslie was simultaneously pouring a jug of iced water, attending to vegetables that were boiling over and listening to Edgar's prattling, a phone rang. It was Bennett's, abandoned on the kitchen dresser. The caller was Ridgeway.

"Bennett rang me earlier," said the detective chief inspector.

"Oh yes," replied Leslie. "I'll get him for you."

"Would you mind just passing on a message? I'm right in the middle of things at the moment and I'll call him back a bit later. For now, would you tell him that the answer to both his questions is yes?"

Leslie hurried upstairs to deliver this cryptic message to Bennett who was dressing himself at a leisurely pace. Conscious of the green beans that were in danger of spoiling in the pan downstairs, Leslie didn't waste time in trying to obtain an explanation that he knew would not be forthcoming. He did, however, pause by the bedroom door on his way out. "If you don't get yourself downstairs and entertain Edgar," he said in a voice that was dangerously calm, "it won't just be the vegetables that are boiling over."

Back in the kitchen, to get Edgar from under his feet, he instructed him to take the water jug and then the bread and various other items to the table. Leslie was just straining the vegetables when the phone rang again. This time it was Daniel. What could he be phoning about? Leslie guessed that he must have something important to say, but he was exasperated that the boy had chosen this moment to call. He answered as civilly as he could while trying to deal, one-handed, with a colander full of steaming beans.

"I'm now at my brother's house in Bristol," the boy said. "There was something I didn't tell you the other night. I had to wait until I was at a safe distance before I mentioned it."

"Go on," said Leslie in a low voice. He thrust the cruet set at Edgar to get him out of the way, covered the colander with a lid, and withdrew to the utility room, shutting the door behind him.

"Kenny came to see me again, after I'd picked up that last packet for him," he said. "It was at The Daffodil but I can't remember exactly when; I've lost track of time. It was maybe about a week ago."

"Go on," said Leslie, again.

"He said he had another job for me, just like the other one. He was really threatening. That's why I had to get away and why I couldn't say anything about it the other evening. I've had a couple of messages from him since, really nasty. He obviously doesn't know I've left the village because he's sent a message today threatening all sorts if I don't contact him straightaway."

"Have you any idea what he wants you to do?"

"No, I've no clue."

"Have you told the police?" said Leslie.

"I tried to, but the liaison person I was given is off duty and I couldn't face explaining it to anyone else. That's why I rang you."

As soon as the conversation was over Leslie tipped the now tepid beans into a tureen and thrust it into the oven. He ran upstairs past Edgar who was standing in the middle of the kitchen like a lost soul. Bennett was just emerging from the bedroom and Leslie shoved him back in and shut the door.

"What the devil do you think Kenny's up to?" said Leslie when he had passed on what Daniel had told him.

"I'm not sure," said Bennett. "I'll let Ridgeway know when he calls me back."

"I'm glad Daniel's out of the way," said Leslie.

"Yes," said Bennett. "Kenny could be a very dangerous man."

Five minutes later they were all seated at the dining room table, tucking into Leslie's superb shepherd's pie as though it was a normal dinner party between three friends. Leslie made small talk and Edgar reprised much of the life history they had heard earlier in the day, but no mention was made of any of the issues that had brought Edgar there. Edgar ate like a starving man, and nothing ever spoiled Bennett's appetite. Leslie was beginning to flag and by the time he filled the cafetiere at the end of the meal he was wondering how he could endure another minute of Edgar's company.

When they moved through to the lounge with their coffee, Bennett patted Leslie on the shoulder and said quietly, "We're nearly there.

"Well, Edgar," said Bennett, as he settled himself into his chair. "How about you tell us about that note you put through the letterbox last night." Bennett's tone suggested he was inviting Edgar to share his holiday photographs, but Edgar's manner changed instantly.

"What is there to explain?" he said shortly. "You read the letter. I can't understand why you haven't called the police."

"Because I know you didn't kill George," said Bennett. "Why don't you tell us what did happen that Saturday?"

"You can't know I didn't kill him," said Edgar, petulantly. "Because I did."

Leslie passed Edgar a glass of port, but the poor man's hand was trembling and Leslie did not trust him with the glass. "Come on Edgar, dear," he said, putting the drink down on the table, "be a good man."

"I do know for sure that you didn't go to the Grange that evening and murder George." Bennett's voice was quiet and decisive.

"You can't know. You can't," said Edgar, his voice rising, "because I did."

"Don't lie to me, Edgar," said Bennett, quietly. "There is no way that George would have set up a meeting at that time of night. Everything you said about the meeting may be true, every detail; all except the time. You went much earlier that day, didn't you?"

"No!" said Edgar, urgently. "No!"

Bennett leant forward and, fixing the man with an expressionless gaze, said, "Kenneth has an alibi. He was in the betting shop in Temple the whole evening, until he went to the pub. There is CCTV evidence and the police have seen it. This is what I wanted to tell you. This is why I wanted you to come back this evening." There was a pause while Bennett allowed Edgar to digest this. The blood had run from Edgar's face and he was an unhealthy shade of grey. "Kenneth was nowhere near Compton Grange at ten o'clock on the evening George was murdered," said Bennett.

"Does that jog your memory?" said Leslie, unsure himself of exactly where this conversation was leading. "Perhaps you were confused about the time you went? Maybe you are getting the time mixed up with another evening when you went there?"

There was a very long silence. Eventually Edgar spoke. "Perhaps I was wrong about the time," he said faintly. "I have to think about this. What can I do? What will happen to me?"

"We'll do our best to help you," Leslie replied, though not entirely sure of what was going on, "but you have to tell us the truth."

"Is it true about Kenneth?" said Edgar, appealing this time directly to Leslie. "How do you know? You're not tricking me?"

"It's the absolute truth," said Leslie. "The chief inspector was here, and he told us categorically that Kenneth is not a suspect. He told us about the CCTV evidence."

Edgar looked as though he was going to say something more about this, but he sunk his head into his hands and sat there like it for a long time.

"Why did you think Kenneth had done it?" Bennett asked, quietly.

"I'm too tired," said Edgar without looking up. "It's too long a story."

"OK," said Bennett, casually. "Did you know that Robin was George's son when he arrived in the village?"

"No," said Edgar emphatically, looking up. "I'd no idea. I don't think I even saw him."

"But you did know George had a son," said Bennett.

"That's the worst of it," said Edgar. "I'm responsible for the boy coming here. If it wasn't for me, none of this would have happened. I might just as well have committed the murder."

30

"Whatever do you mean, Edgar?" asked Leslie, utterly astonished. "How on earth were you involved in Robin coming to Dartonleigh?"

"I phoned the boy's grandmother and told her that George was dying," said Edgar. They waited in silence for him to explain this mystifying statement. He shook his head wearily and said, "It all goes back a long way." Once Edgar started, the whole story came tumbling out. With the aid of questions and prompts to keep him on track, they gradually pieced the story together.

As they already knew, Edgar had lived in the same village as George twenty-odd years ago and George was married but with no children from the marriage. George's wife, Edgar told them, tragically developed cancer at a young age; she had a lot of treatment and was in and out of hospital. George ran his own business and while his wife was very ill he had a fling with the young woman who was his secretary and she became pregnant. To make matters worse, the girl was also a member of the same church as George, where he held some respected position. The girl moved out of the village so that it could all be hushed up, and no one knew about George's indiscretion or the outcome of it. However, the girl's mother was Edgar's next door neighbour.

This neighbour was a great friend to Edgar, supporting him as he struggled to raise Kenneth, his own wife having sadly died. Although the fact of George's infidelity was not generally known in the village, this lady confided in Edgar, not unnaturally. Over the course of time Edgar found out from her that George had settled quite a tidy sum on the girl, but would have no contact with her, even after his wife died and even though the baby was his only child. Edgar's neighbour was very bitter about it. George moved away soon after he was widowed and there had been no contact between the men until Edgar had moved into the village about three years ago. George had been completely unaware that Edgar knew anything about him having fathered a child.

"That was when my business was doing really well with my previous business partner," said Edgar. "We were expanding to the West Country and we opened a bigger warehouse down this way. I moved into Dartonleigh with no idea that George lived here. I was very surprised to see him, and even more surprised to see that he'd married Clarissa. She was so different to his first wife.

"I still keep in touch with my old neighbour. She's a lovely lady and rings me from time to time to see how I am, and she always remembers Kenneth's birthday, even now. When I moved here she was amazed to hear that I'd caught up with George again after all that time as she and her daughter had lost contact with him completely and, as I said, the boy had never known his father.

"Earlier this year, when I realised that George didn't have long, I rang her to let her know. It must have been from that phone call that the boy ended up coming to the village; I'm the only link they had. Now I wish I'd left well alone, but I couldn't have known it would end up like this, could I? I keep trying to tell myself it wasn't my fault."

"So where does Kenneth fit into this?" asked Bennett. "Why did you think he was responsible for George's death?"

"Oh," said Edgar rather vaguely, "it was just something he said."

"Go on," urged Leslie.

For a time it seemed that Edgar was going to divulge nothing more, but eventually he spoke. "As you know, my affairs are in bad shape. I'd been trying to get George to buy into the business. In fact, a couple of months ago I'd made a decision that if I couldn't get George to invest I'd have to declare myself bankrupt. It was a terrible thought, after all those years of building the business up, but I made the decision.

"Kenneth was also putting a lot of pressure on me to persuade George to invest, going on and on about it. You remember, Leslie, Kenneth was with me in The Woodman, the day before George passed away? I'd been to see George earlier in the day and he'd insisted he wasn't interested. Kenneth was in a terrible temper with me about it. He saw that George was in the lounge bar on his own and told me I had to go through and have another try. I tried to make him see that there was no point going back twice in one day, but he said that if I didn't go, he would, and if George refused him, 'he'd know about it', or something like that. At the time I thought it was just the sort of silly thing Kenneth says when he's upset. But the next day, in the light of what happened, I started to think that Kenneth must have gone to the Grange and lost his temper, especially when I heard that a young man had been seen nearby."

"You thought that the young man seen in Stag Lane might have been Kenneth?" queried Leslie.

"Yes," Edgar replied.

"Why would you think that, Edgar?" asked Leslie. "Kenneth isn't a young man."

Edgar looked up, puzzled. "Isn't he?" he said. He shook his head vaguely, and continued.

"When I thought it was Kenneth, I panicked. I phoned the pub in Temple where Kenneth drinks and asked the landlord what time Kenneth had got there. I don't know what excuse I made. When I found out that he arrived there sometime not long after ten o'clock it reinforced my fears. I lost my head and told everyone I'd been to see George at that time to give Kenneth an alibi.

"The landlord told Kenneth I'd been asking. Kenneth was furious at first because he got a real ribbing for having his father check up on him. Somehow he put two and two together and realised I'd thought it was him who'd murdered George. He had such a go at me and eventually I sort of admitted it, and let on about giving him an alibi. I've never seen him so wild and I wouldn't repeat what he called me. But then, it was very odd: really suddenly he stopped shouting and he started to laugh. I found that more frightening than when he was angry." Edgar rested his head back in the armchair, seeming to have finished what he had to say, but Bennett spoke again.

"What time did you really go and see George?"

"I'd gone first of all in the morning," said Edgar. "That was just before I met Leslie and we went for a coffee. That was when

George refused point blank to get involved. Then, after lunch I was in the Woodman and Kenneth made me go through to the lounge bar and speak to George. As you know, George was feeling a bit rough, and I offered to take him home in the car. I happened to have the car parked outside as I'd been planning to go on to Lymeford to talk to a chap there who said he could advise me about bankruptcy. I thought that if I gave George a lift home it would give me another chance and I could ask him one more time, and get Kenneth off my back for a bit.

"I started to mention the business again, and as we arrived outside his house, imagine my horror when I broke down. I told him that the business was virtually bankrupt, and that I was going to lose everything I'd ever worked for. I even went so far as to tell him about some of my problems with Kenneth. To my amazement, he said, 'Why didn't you tell me this before? How much does the business need?' and when I told him he invited me in and asked for the paperwork to sign. I still had the folder in the car, from earlier in the day, but I kept back the sheet with the false accounting that Kenneth had prepared and said I'd bring it the following day. He signed the other documents there and then.

"I was over the moon and went home feeling better than I'd felt for weeks. Kenneth wasn't in; he'd told me he had another appointment somewhere, and he'd left while I was still in the pub. I nearly rang him with the good news, but he gets annoyed when I disturb him, so I left it. The next day brought the news of George's death, and dashed my hopes of rescuing the business.

"After that, things started to go from bad to worse. I've told you how I changed the times of my story; I tried to keep most of the details of my meeting with George the same as they really happened, so that I didn't get caught out contradicting myself, but the strain was terrible. I'd got Kenneth off the hook, but I hadn't accounted for the fact that an innocent boy, George's own son, would get blamed. Now that I know Kenneth didn't do it, perhaps the son wasn't innocent after all, but that's what I thought at the time.

"It was hopeless. I felt so guilty and I couldn't see a way out. Then suddenly the solution came to me: I would do away with myself and leave a confession. It solved everything." He announced this as though he still thought it had been a sound idea. "You know the rest," he said, composed enough, at last, to hold the glass and take a mouthful of the port.

"But Edgar," said Leslie, "when you thought Kenneth had really committed the crime, and you gave him a false alibi, didn't you think that was wrong?"

Edgar looked at him, frowning as if with incomprehension. "What else could I do?" he replied. "He's my son. He's the only thing I have."

There wasn't much else to discuss after that. Although it was getting late, Edgar refused to stay another night, despite Leslie's best efforts to persuade him. Kenneth was expected home, and Edgar was insistent that his absence would alarm him.

"You won't try anything silly again, will you?" said Leslie. "I'll be lying awake all night worrying about you if you go home."

"Oh no, I couldn't do that with Kenneth coming home tonight; I couldn't put him through that," Edgar replied emphatically.

As a compromise, Leslie insisted on walking home with him. It was a dreary night and a fine drizzle had just started. Leslie pulled his jacket round himself and tried to suppress a gnawing sense of foreboding. At the house, there was no sign of Kenny and Leslie wondered if he would really show up. Edgar, who was obviously very tired, went straight to his bedroom upstairs, without seeing Leslie out.

As Leslie turned to the front door to leave, he heard the sound of a car and, peering through the window, he saw it pull up in front of the house, and Kenny got out. He was deep in conversation on his phone and, instead of coming to the front door, he walked, rather furtively Leslie thought, to the side of the house as if to come in by the back. Leslie took the opportunity to escape, opening the front door quietly to avoid being heard.

To his surprise, as he stepped outside, shutting the door silently behind him, he could hear Kenny speaking quite clearly. He must have stopped at the side of the house, just out of sight. Instinctively, Leslie stood very still in the porch, and as he heard what Kenny was saying he was horrified.

"You've had twenty-four hours to get the money. If it isn't outside your front gate behind the big stone urn in five minutes, you'll end up the same way as your old man did. I'm warning you." There was a short pause, and Leslie could only imagine the anguished reply. "Save your breath, darling, I carry out my threats. You've got five minutes. I'm on my way."

So it was Kenny after all. Now that Edgar had admitted lying about the timing of his visit to George, everything had changed and all the alibis needed to be reconsidered. Leslie knew he must do something. He had to get to the Grange to help Clarissa, for she was obviously the recipient of Kenny's menacing threats. Hunched against the rain, Kenny stamped down the path and got in his car, slamming the door. The car swung round and headed back down the road.

Leslie had not bothered to take his phone with him and it would waste too much time to go home. He set off in the opposite direction to Kenny, towards the path at the top of the road that cut through the woods into Stag Lane. If Kenny drove straight to the Grange, it would be impossible for Leslie to get there before him, but if he ran all the way, he might still be in time. In time for what? Leslie had no idea of what he intended to do or how he could help, but nonetheless he felt impelled to get to Compton Grange as quickly as he could.

It was raining heavily now and it was very dark. Leslie was gasping for breath by the time he reached the top of Broomhill Lane, and it took him a moment in the darkness to find the path. The yellow light from his torch did little more than pick up the slanting rain as it fell. He pulled his hood further forwards and made his way, slithering and sliding along the short, steep path which cut through the woods.

He emerged into Stag Lane, above Compton Grange, and arrived at the entrance, half walking half running, with his head down into the driving rain. He had no idea what scene he would find, but as far as he could see or hear through the downpour, there was no sign of Kenny yet.

All was in darkness as Leslie turned into the entrance of the house. The gate was open. He took a few steps in and was suddenly dazzled by the headlights of a car which blazed on, pointing directly at him. He threw one arm across his eyes in confusion, and signalled with the other to alert the driver to his presence. A second later he heard the engine roar and panic seized him as the car started towards him. Frozen with shock and overwhelmed by physical exhaustion, he experienced the dreadful sensation of paralysis, only encountered before in nightmares. He tried to shout, to signal again to the driver, but he knew it was futile; the car was obviously driving at him on purpose.

The blinding lights of the car were feet away now; it was accelerating. He heard himself shout, "No!" and he threw himself sideways, landing heavily and rolling over. The car missed him by inches and he lay on the wet gravel, winded, unable to move himself, but still alive. Relief had no time to surface, for a moment later he realised that the car had screamed into reverse and was about to come at him a second time.

He couldn't do it again; he couldn't move from this position on the ground. He had no breath left, there was something terribly wrong with his chest, and his arms and legs wouldn't move for him. An appalling sense of inevitable death overcame him. This was it. This was how the end was going to be. The two headlights merged into a dazzling, rain-streaked blur, speeding towards him.

31

So it was true, your life does flash before you. In a split second he saw all the things he cared about: the village, their cottage, and Bennett. By now the speeding car was starting its course towards his prone body, and suddenly he was thinking of being parted from Bennett for ever and leaving him alone.

Some primitive power got him onto his feet, and in two strange unsteady steps he threw himself out of the way a second time. There was a screeching of brakes, the sound of skidding on the puddled ground and then a sickening crash. He was propelled forward and then a chunk of metal came crashing down on his head, and he blacked out.

It was a disorientating awakening. First he was aware of being cold; he had never, ever been so cold. Then he was aware of a horrible noise and flashing lights. The noise stopped and the lights, bright blue, gradually started to look familiar – on, off, on, off, on, off.

Leslie still could not move but he squinted painfully through his left eye. The right one did not seem to be working. A dreadfully smashed car was about ten yards away and leaning against it, freakishly lit by the neon lights of a police car, was Clarissa, her rain-soaked face running with blood.

A uniformed policeman strode round the back of the car and, ignoring her injuries, said,

"Clarissa Harrington-Thomas, I am arresting you for the murder of George Harrington-Thomas." As he gave the caution, Leslie wanted to shout out that he was wrong, they had the wrong person, that someone was getting away, but he couldn't remember who it was, and he couldn't move or talk anyway. He felt himself drifting and shut his eye again, but a light, a white one this time, shone straight at his face and he heard a sharp expletive.

"Hey, Sarge, here, quick. We've got a casualty – Christ, I think he might have gone. No, he's still breathing."

There was a lot of sudden activity around him. Some part of him was excruciatingly painful but fortunately he did not stay conscious long enough to identify which bit of his body it was. Each time he woke there seemed to be more people about and then, at last, there was Bennett. Bennett fell to his knees on the wet ground beside him.

"I thought I'd lost you, you silly bugger," Bennett said, and Leslie drifted off into blessed oblivion again.

32

It was three days later and an unusual sight could be seen: Bennett wearing an apron and collecting up the empty cafetiere for refilling. From his recumbent position on the settee, supported all round by pillows and cushions, Leslie tried hard to be grateful and not to think about the probable state of the kitchen.

"How are you enjoying your new role, Bennett?" asked Paul. He was sitting on the armchair opposite Leslie. The doctor had called in to check up on his patient, although it was officially his day off. In another chair sat Detective Chief Inspector Charles Ridgeway, who had dropped by on the way back from one of his ubiquitous meetings in Lymeford. Paul and Ridgeway had been discussing golf handicaps for the last half an hour as though they were in the club room after the 18th hole.

Leslie was still overwhelmed by the perplexing events of the last few days, and by the constant stream of well-wishers with their gifts and enquiries. The sitting room was filled with a rather overpowering fragrance; every surface was covered with flowers and there were dozens of cards balanced between. Bennett had, of course, used all the wrong vases, and Leslie was particularly vexed by a bunch of tulips leaning unsteadily in one of his vintage milk jugs.

They had kept him in hospital for only forty-eight hours; that was long enough to ensure that the head injury had resulted in nothing more than mild concussion. The dislocated shoulder had been put back into place. Luckily Leslie could remember nothing about that procedure, and his arm was now supported in a collar and cuff sling. The broken ribs would mend themselves, and various sutured wounds and grazes would all heal better in the tranquillity of his own home.

Leslie was slowly piecing together the confusing events surrounding his misadventure, but there was still much he couldn't understand. He was aware that his haste to help Clarissa had been his undoing. Clarissa was no pushover, and her response to a blackmail threat was to wait in her car until the blackmailer appeared to collect his money and stage an accident. Unfortunately, Leslie had got there ahead of Kenny, and Clarissa had mistaken the figure hurrying to her aid through the rain for the blackmailer. Bennett had compared the incident to the legend of Gelert, which sounded gallant until Leslie discovered he was being likened to a dog.

The police had found Clarissa's bags packed, not for a sojourn in London with her son, but with a passport in her previous name, but still valid, and a one-way ticket to Spain booked for the following day. The arrest had come not a moment too soon. It had been a tip-off by Bennett to Ridgeway that had sent the police car to the Grange.

Bennett had long suspected Clarissa, and was only waiting until Edgar admitted the truth about the time he had visited George, to show that George could have been murdered much earlier, when Clarissa had no alibi. He rang Ridgeway while Leslie was walking Edgar home, and a police car was dispatched to bring Clarissa in for further questioning. It had come quite unexpectedly on the scene of Leslie's accident. There had been no sign of Kenny. It was supposed that he had seen the police presence when he subsequently arrived at the Grange, and he had bolted.

According to Gloria, who had called in during the morning bearing a basket of alternative remedies from her shop, Compton Grange was once again a crime scene, the house crawling with police, and Stag Lane obstructed by reporters. "I knew you'd solve it all you clever thing, Leslie," said Gloria. "But I did warn you to be careful."

Leslie's attempt to rebuff Gloria's praise was futile as she foraged in her basket for the remedies which were to be the panacea for all his ailments. As she bent over, tubes and packets spilled out of the basket and tumbled onto the floor. She looked about her in mock helplessness, but to no avail; Leslie was incapable of helping and Bennett sat in passive observation. Gloria was reduced to the indignity of grovelling about on the floor to rescue her goods, but she seemed to bear the men no ill-will. She heaved herself to her feet and, to his shame, Leslie was put in mind of a hippopotamus rising from the swamp.

"What you really need is a little holiday, the two of you," she gasped. "Bennett, you must take Leslie away somewhere to convalesce."

"Are you two in league with each other?" asked Bennett.

"I don't know what you mean," said Gloria. "Are you teasing me again?"

"By no means, dear lady," said Bennett. "Leslie has been trying to persuade me to have a rest cure since my heart attack. He was unsuccessful, so he has staged this little drama, just to get his own way. We mustn't give in to him or he might make a habit of it."

"I'm taking no notice of you," Gloria scolded. "My cousin, well she's a sort of cousin, has a hotel on the coast near Alemouth. I've told her all about you and it's all arranged. You're to go there as soon as Leslie is able to travel. It's a lovely quiet spot; no chance of getting caught up in any dramas there." Before there could be any further discussion of this, Gloria launched into a detailed explanation of each of the products in her basket. She prescribed a strict treatment regimen for Leslie and promised to return the following day to assess the efficacy of her remedies.

Annie called in briefly a little while later, bringing a shepherd's pie and two casseroles, and was full of concern for Leslie. She stopped long enough to tell them that Daniel was planning to stay with his brother in Bristol for a while and had found himself a job in a sports shop. "I'm just glad no one asked me to write a reference for him," she said as she left to return to her duties in The Daffodil.

Martin had been the next to arrive, minus Cromwell, but bearing a bottle of champagne and more interesting news from the planning office. The corruption scandal was now a police matter and several senior members of staff had been suspended while investigations were going on. "This is from my wife," he said, handing over the bottle. "She's in celebratory mood. She said she owes the champagne to George, who she believes was responsible for the fraud being uncovered, but as he can't be thanked she said she'd like you to have it, after your ordeal. Jeff's house plans have been taken away for evidence and that's about all that they'll ever be used for now."

"George got the result he wanted," said Leslie. "That house will never be built on Jeff's land."

"Such a bloody shame he's not here to celebrate," said Martin glumly.

It was after lunch that Paul had dropped in, with Ridgeway arriving a few minutes later. "Still no sign of Kenny?" asked the doctor, when they had exhausted conversation about handicaps, slow play and Paul's new clubs.

Ridgeway shook his head. "We'll catch up with him before long, don't you worry," he said. "We've got too much on him: description, car registration, contacts. He didn't have time to collect his passport either so he can't have gone far."

"Would someone mind explaining to me what has been going on?" said Leslie, who had been wondering when he could get a word in. "All I know is that Clarissa has been charged with George's murder and Robin has been released without a stain on his character. I'm totally confused. The last thing I remember was that Clarissa had an alibi."

"Are you sure you don't want to wait for explanations, Leslie?" said Paul. "You've not long come out of hospital after a bad knock on the head. You should be resting."

"As if I can rest without understanding how all this came about!" Leslie replied rather more acerbically than he normally would to the doctor.

"Fair point," said Paul and he looked across at Ridgeway.

"I'd better be careful about what I say now that charges have been made," said the chief inspector, unfurling himself from the chair. "I need to be on my way now, in any case, and since Bennett still probably knows more about it than I do, I'll leave you to it." He looked across at Bennett and gave a wry smile. "Just off the record, though," he said, pausing by the door, "what was it that particularly put you onto Clarissa? I get the impression now that you knew it was her from the start."

"It's probably too strong to say that I knew it was her all along, but she was always the obvious suspect for the murder," said Bennett. "To start with, Leslie said that she was one of only two people in the village capable of doing something so wicked, the other person being Kenny, of course."

"It's true. She's completely – I'd even say pathologically – self-centred," explained Leslie. "It's easy to imagine her dispensing with poor George and justifying it to herself as simply bringing forward the inevitable."

"Clarissa obviously had free access to her own home and could simply walk into the bedroom and commit the deed," Bennett went on. "And I guessed straightaway that it was nonsense about her finding George dead in bed in the morning; she rang the doctor at six forty-five. Can you imagine Clarissa getting up before seven o'clock on a Sunday morning in normal circumstances?"

"So all you had to do was to set about finding a motive, disproving her cast-iron alibi and supplying the proof," the chief inspector said, with the same ironic smile. "I'd heard about your reputation with puzzles, Bennett, and it's certainly been justified. But, fascinating as this is, I'd better be on my way so I'll say cheerio for now."

"I must admit I'm curious to hear all the details," said the doctor as he returned from the front door where he had shown Ridgeway out.

"Bennett never tells me anything," said Leslie peevishly.

"No more of this silence, Bennett!" Paul called out to Bennett who had returned to the kitchen. "The chief inspector has gone, so you can tell all."

Bennett was not, at that particular moment, silent, for exclamations and curses could be heard emanating from the other room. He was trying, without success, to open a packet of biscuits. He eventually reappeared with an untidy heap of digestives on a plate.

"Come on, Bennett," said Paul, "spill the beans."

It looked more likely that Bennett would spill the coffee as he adjusted the tray awkwardly on the coffee table between cards and flowers, and balanced the plate of biscuits on a bowl of fruit.

Averting his gaze from this potential disaster, Leslie said, "You can start by explaining why Clarissa murdered George, when the poor man was already so close to death."

Bennett pushed the plunger down slowly in the cafetiere. "Why would anyone murder a dying man?" he mused. "That was the question you asked at the outset, Les. It was the perfect starting point: what was so urgent that his death couldn't wait? It turned out to be money, a lot of it. Clarissa thought she was about to be disinherited."

"By Robin? So Clarissa did know about him after all?" said Leslie.

"Of course she did. We only ever had her word for it that she didn't."

"I suppose so," said Leslie, frowning as he cast his mind back, "but she had an alibi at the time so I suppose it seemed plausible."

Paul said, "Why doesn't Bennett tell us the whole story from the beginning? Come on, Bennett, let's hear it. And don't forget that I don't know much of the background to this."

There was a short pause while coffee mugs were replenished and the plate of biscuits was rescued from its precarious perch and passed around. Then Bennett seated himself in his favourite chair and leant back with the expressionless gaze he always adopted when he was marshalling his thoughts. After a moment he said, "The murder and the blackmail both started with one phone call: the phone call that Edgar made to his old next door neighbour, who was the grandmother to Robin, George's secret son. Edgar told her about George's prognosis and, a few months later, Robin appeared in Dartonleigh to see his dying father for the first time. They met initially in The Woodman. I don't know how that came about, but Gloria and her daughter witnessed it." Bennett paused briefly to take a few mouthfuls of coffee.

"We know from what Gloria's daughter overheard that an arrangement was made for Robin to meet George at seven at Compton Grange. Robin kept that appointment. At seven o'clock, Clarissa was also at the Grange, unbeknown to George. When Robin arrived, she overheard the conversation between him and his father and learned that George was about to change his will in favour of his son. She waited, unseen, in the house until George went to bed and then carried out the crime, hoping no doubt that given George's prognosis no one would question his death. It was as simple as that." Bennett sat forwards and reached for his coffee.

"How did you work that out?" Paul asked. "Or was it just guesswork?"

Bennett gave the doctor a withering look.

"Come on, Bennett," said the doctor, undaunted. "How could you know that Clarissa was at Compton Grange at seven, when you never bestir yourself from this cottage?"

"Stan, the chap who lives at Moor View Cottage, overlooking Compton Grange, made a throwaway remark to Les that both the cars were down at the Grange when he shut the curtains at seven o'clock that evening," said Bennett.

"So he did," said Leslie, the significance dawning on him. "Clarissa said she was with Antonio then, but she couldn't have been if her car was at the Grange. That didn't register with me at the time."

"Nor me," admitted Bennett, taking a digestive from the plate. "It wasn't until you mentioned it again later that the penny dropped."

"OK, but what made you say that George didn't know Clarissa was there, and that she overheard George talking to Robin?" the doctor asked. "How could you possibly know that?"

"Ridgeway has since confirmed that Robin spoke to his father in the study and that neither of them was aware that Clarissa was in the house. But I'd already made that assumption," responded Bennett. "It was a fair deduction that George wouldn't have invited his secret son to the house if he thought Clarissa was going to be there. I think George expected her to be out all evening as usual but, unexpectedly, she came back for something. The house is huge, George was deaf and if she'd driven round the back and come in by the kitchen, as she usually did, there was no reason why he would have seen or heard her come in. And Robin, arriving to meet his father at seven o'clock, wouldn't have had any reason to know she was in the house either, unless she'd chosen to make herself known."

"That's true," said Leslie, "her car wouldn't have been easy to see if she'd parked it in her usual spot round the back." Leslie was becoming engrossed by the story, and all thoughts of his injured shoulder and bad nerves were forgotten. He continued. "Clarissa could easily have listened in on their conversation without them knowing she was there. Think how loudly George usually spoke, and if they were in George's study, Clarissa could have simply sat in the kitchen next door and eavesdropped from there. Remember, Jamie clearly overheard Clarissa and George talking about him when he was in the kitchen."

"Quite," said Bennett. "George would hardly have admitted his son to the house and carried on a conversation with him, talking about changing the will, if he thought Clarissa was there, listening in."

"But what makes you think that was the substance of the conversation?" asked Paul.

"Again, Ridgeway has confirmed that George and Robin did discuss the will; Robin told him. But it wasn't difficult to deduce it, before that. From the outset I knew it could only have been something sudden and urgent that would make Clarissa act so precipitately. Even the amoral Clarissa must have had a strong reason for murdering her husband and it was obviously a risk, however confident she was that no one would question his death. The arrival on the scene of a new boyfriend may have made her impatient for George's departure but it seems certain that something unforeseen had occurred to make her act without a day's delay. After all, she didn't even give herself an alibi. The alibi she acquired from Edgar's lie about visiting George late evening, when she was at The Imperial, was pure chance which she couldn't have predicted. No, something unexpected and serious had happened to make her act there and then. Something to do with money was by far the most likely reason. She almost certainly married George for his fortune and it's easy to imagine that she would have stopped at nothing if she thought she might lose it.

"The sudden and serious event had to be the arrival in Dartonleigh of the young man I recognised as George's son. When we found out that he had been to see George on the evening of his death, it seemed a reasonable conclusion that George was going to bequeath his son all, or most, of his substantial fortune, and that Clarissa knew about it."

"But surely the evidence at the time pointed more towards the son," interrupted Paul. "There seemed to be so much against him. Those things you've just said: his arrival in Dartonleigh, his meeting with his father the very night he died, his odd behaviour, his abrupt departure."

"I dare say it was compelling, but you're forgetting the vital thing," said Bennett.

The doctor looked at him enquiringly.

"In the face of the full weight of evidence against Robin," said Bennett, "Leslie would not have it. He was adamant that Robin would not have committed such a crime. Leslie might have been wrong, but he never is."

They sat in silence for a moment or two while the doctor pondered on Bennett's reasoning, and Leslie realised that he was starting to feel better.

Bennett took up his mug of coffee and dunked a biscuit. As he lifted it out a lump broke off and fell into the mug with a splash. There was a pause while he concentrated on scooping it out with a teaspoon. He scowled at the offending biscuit pulp and, defeated, placed the blighted drink on the tray.

The doctor, shaking his head in mock despair at the mishap, said, "And you think that having overheard that conversation, Clarissa simply hid in the house until George went to bed and then... then did what she did?"

"As simple as that," said Bennett. "And then she went off to The Imperial for the night."

"It seems that everyone would have been saved a lot of trouble if Edgar hadn't come up with that cock and bull story of his about a meeting with George at ten o'clock which gave Clarissa that alibi," said Paul.

"That man has been a perfect pest the whole way along," said Bennett.

"We knew Edgar's account was peculiar from the start," Leslie replied. "George wouldn't have arranged a meeting with Edgar at that time in the evening. Even before he was ill he was always an early-to-bed, early-to-rise sort of person."

"Indeed," agreed Bennett, "but it wasn't just that. I also remembered the description Leslie gave when he first came back from the Grange the morning after George died. He described it as a lonely sight; a single glass, the brandy bottle, George's rug which would have been over his knees. That didn't square with Edgar's story of sitting by the fire with George drinking coffee.

"It was obvious that Edgar was up to something. Why would he tell a lie that could put himself in such a compromising position? I was certain that he wasn't willingly colluding with Clarissa, though I did wonder briefly if Clarissa had some hold over him. There was, of course, only one person Edgar would perjure himself for, and that was Kenny.

"Once we convinced Edgar that Kenny wasn't a suspect, we got it out of him that he was lying about the time he last saw George alive. Of course, that meant that the time of George's death could easily have been earlier, and Clarissa had no proper alibi for the time before she arrived at the hotel."

"Why on earth did Clarissa go off to The Imperial after she'd committed the crime?" Leslie asked. "If she was going to pretend she woke and found George dead in bed, why go to the hotel? It only increased suspicion against her when it was discovered she'd been lying."

"It was a stupid thing to do," agreed Bennett. "Maybe she couldn't bear to be alone in the house all night with George's dead body, or perhaps the lure of Antonio was too much."

"She did say to me that she hated being in the house," said Leslie. "Whatever the reason, by sheer chance it gave her that alibi for a while."

"I take my hat off to you, Bennett," said the doctor. "You had it all worked out."

"Working out what happened wasn't the main problem," said Bennett. "But getting some kind of proof or evidence was a different matter. It's a shame that it took so long for me to register the significance of Stan's comment about seeing Clarissa's car." He did not look unduly contrite at this oversight; it was not in his nature to be overburdened with remorse. "And, at about the same time," he continued, "Leslie told me that Clarissa had mentioned that Robin's mother was a Catholic, like George."

"She did," said Leslie, grimacing at the memory. "That was when I went to get the photo from her. She said that awful thing: that it was a shame Robin's mother was a Catholic otherwise she might have ended the pregnancy which would have saved Clarissa a lot of bother."

"What's the significance of that?" said Paul, "other than further proof of Clarissa's character."

"I see it!" exclaimed Leslie. "How could Clarissa have known about that? She said she knew nothing about Robin's existence until the police told her, so how could she possibly have known his mother was Catholic?"

"Precisely," said Bennett. "I guessed that she'd obtained this information from the conversation between George and Robin. Remember that phone message from the chief inspector, Les, when he said that the answer to the two questions was yes?"

"I do," said Leslie. "I wondered what that was about."

"After you'd mentioned that reference to Robin's mother, I rang Ridgeway and asked him to find out from Robin if the subject of his mother being a Catholic had been discussed. When he confirmed it had, I knew for sure that Clarissa had been eavesdropping."

"What was the other question?" asked Leslie.

"I asked him to find out if George told Robin that he was leaving him an inheritance. When the answer came back in the affirmative, I knew that my deductions had been right."

"I hope the evidence is good enough for the courts," said Leslie. "Clarissa is a cunning actress and I can just imagine her in the witness box before a jury, fluttering her eyelashes at the men."

"The evidence was good enough for Ridgeway," said Bennett. "Let's hope he can put together a good case against her."

"She would have got away with it completely if you two hadn't raised the alarm," said Paul. "Even if it had come to light that Clarissa had been at The Imperial and not at home like she said, no one would have treated George's death as murder. There might have been gossip in the village, but I very much doubt if it would have gone beyond that."

"We would probably have greeted his death with nothing more than surprise, just like everyone else in the village," said Bennett, "had we not been aware of other suspicious information: the blackmail threat, the shock that George reported to Les, and the recent arrival of the young imposter in the village who was the very spit of the photo of George as a young man "

The three men fell into silence. The doctor finished his coffee, Leslie nibbled a biscuit and Bennett gazed into the middle distance.

"Hmm," grunted Bennett, at last. "Never be worth more dead than alive, that's what I say."

The doctor smiled and Leslie muttered something about them both being quite safe on that score. "But how does the blackmail fit in to it?" said Leslie, suddenly. "You haven't explained that."

"Ah yes," said Bennett. "All along there was that blackmail story in the background. It was another complication, working out where it fitted in. As Leslie had pointed out, it was hardly credible that the two crimes were unrelated."

"I knew it," said Leslie, "it couldn't be a coincidence."

"As we know, Kenny was the blackmailer," said Bennett, and he briefly explained to the doctor what Daniel had told them.

"Do you know what he was blackmailing George about?" asked Paul. "Or had I better not ask?"

"George only had one skeleton rattling in his cupboard," said Bennett. "Kenny was threatening to reveal that George had an illegitimate son."

"How did he know about him?" asked Leslie. "George told you he was being blackmailed long before Robin appeared in the village."

"It goes back to that first phone call that Edgar made to his old neighbour, Robin's grandmother, breaking the news about

George's deteriorating health," said Bennett. "Unfortunately Kenny overheard the phone call. Kenny quizzed Edgar about it, and Edgar foolishly gave in and told him everything about George's past.

"While you were in hospital, Les, Edgar broke down and confessed everything. The real reason that Edgar really thought that Kenny had murdered George was because he'd overheard Kenny making the blackmail threats to George on the phone. When he heard about the murder he leapt to the conclusion that the blackmail had gone wrong and resulted in George's death. Naturally he didn't want to reveal to us that Kenny was a blackmailer so he told us that other nonsense."

"What a lot of tangled webs Edgar was weaving," said Leslie.

"Unfortunately he wasn't the only one who got snared in them," said Bennett.

"When you think about it," said Leslie, "it's strange that George should have been so very concerned about anyone finding out that he had a son. Why should he be so worried in this day and age, and after all this time? He was about to die; you wouldn't have thought he'd have cared much about what anyone would think."

"In my experience," observed the doctor, "dignity often increases in importance when someone is dying, and they cling on to it to the last. It's all they've got left. It must have been a terrible time for poor George, with his wife's adultery the talk of the village. The thought of having his own past adventures dragged up would have been terribly humiliating. Don't forget he had his reputation in the church to keep up, as well as in the village."

"I suppose so," said Leslie. "But Kenny was blackmailing Clarissa, too. How did that come about?"

"Edgar let it out to Kenny that he had lied about the time of his visit to George, to give him an alibi," said Bennett. "Kenny, though thoroughly uncouth, isn't stupid. It didn't take him long to work out that if his father hadn't been at the Grange at ten o'clock, that then left Clarissa with no alibi. He took a gamble that Clarissa had murdered her husband and he tried his hand at a spot more extortion."

"I suppose that's what he wanted Daniel's services for again: collecting the money from Clarissa," said Leslie. "I knew all along that Kenny was a crook."

"Kenny needed the money to feed his gambling habit which appears to have been out of control. Apparently he'd siphoned off and gambled away the company's entire assets," said Bennett.

"That reminds me, I must show you this," said Paul, taking out his phone and scrolling through. "Here it is. Let me read you this piece from the local news.

"*'Warehouse raid in Lymeford Trading Estate,'*" he began. "*'A huge haul of counterfeit designer goods has been seized from a warehouse on the Oak Vale Estate. Acting on a tip-off, police entered the property yesterday and discovered over 500 fake Mulberry and Saint Laurent handbags, purses and pairs of women's shoes. A quantity of ecstasy tablets and cannabis resin was also seized. No arrests have been made.'*"

"It seems like Kenny was diversifying," said Bennett. "The budget handbags and shoes that Edgar had built the business up on obviously didn't bring in enough money. He moved on to fake designer goods and soft drugs, with a bit of extortion thrown in to supplement the income."

"He enjoyed it, too," said Leslie. "I heard him threatening Clarissa. It gave him pleasure. It was horrible."

"Let's hope that Charles Ridgeway is as good as his word and Kenny's soon behind bars," said Paul.

"Where is Edgar now?" Leslie asked. "The man's been worse than a nuisance but I can't help but feel sorry for him."

"Edgar's tucked up in a clinic in Exeter," said the doctor. "He's going to be there for a while."

"What a horrible mess," said Leslie. "That poor boy came down here in search of his father and ended up being the cause of his death. But for that, George would still be alive, and Clarissa would have been a cheating wife but not a murderer."

"That's not entirely true," said Paul. "I'm not sure if I'm supposed to let on about this just yet, but I know you'll keep it to yourselves, and Bennett put us onto it in the first place. At Bennett's suggestion, we had a closer look at George's Ramipril bottle. We'd already established that the tablets in the bottle really were Ramipril, but when you alerted us, we had another look at the bottle itself. There were unaccountable traces of vitamin C.

"The Ramipril tablets were supplied by the chemist in Temple Ducton. Clarissa had been collecting George's prescriptions for him and it looks like she had been substituting the heart tablets with vitamin C. She took care to replace the correct tablets again after his death. The toxicology reports support that theory: there were no traces of Ramipril in George's blood. No wonder he was so breathless. Even before Robin came on the scene, it would seem Clarissa was getting impatient for George to die."

"That's disgusting, but whatever made you think of it, Bennett?" Leslie asked.

"It was another remark that you passed on," said Bennett. "You told me that George had commented that his life was full of little white tablets, including a white heart tablet. I'm on the same medication and it's yellow. George could have been on a different brand, of course, but I had a hunch."

"It was smart work, Bennett," said the doctor as he took his leave from them.

"Very smart: the murderer almost got away, the blackmailer's still on the run and I very nearly got Leslie killed," replied Bennett, but it was in his usual phlegmatic tone of voice. Having seen Paul off the premises, Bennett came back in and, reverting to a more familiar role, went to the drinks cabinet. From the top of the cabinet the photograph of George as a young man looked down on them.

"That photo," said Leslie, taking a glass of brandy from Bennett and swilling it round. "I suppose George spotted the likeness to Robin, and wanted to make sure no one else did, especially Clarissa."

33

While Bennett was replacing the bottle in the cabinet, the doorbell rang. He went to answer it and moments later, there was Robin in the doorway, bearing a bottle, a card and the self-conscious expression that Leslie had seen before.

"Come in, please do, and sit down," said Leslie warmly, gesturing to a vacant seat with his functioning arm, "I'm so pleased you called. How are you? We've been worried about you; you must have had a terrible time."

Robin stepped tentatively into the room and then seemed to notice Leslie's state. "Whatever happened?" he said. "Are you all right?"

"I'm quite all right," said Leslie, though this clearly wasn't completely accurate. "I had a bit of an accident but it looks worse than it really is."

"Sit yourself down," said Bennett. "There's nothing that would do Leslie more good than having someone else to think about. Don't worry about him; he's just playing the sympathy card."

It took a moment to convince Robin that he really was welcome, but eventually he sat down. He declined anything from the drinks cabinet but accepted the offer of a cup of coffee.

"I wanted to come back and see you," he said, looking at Leslie. "I feel I owe you an explanation."

"You owe us nothing," said Leslie. "There's no need to explain anything."

In reality Leslie was itching to hear the background to the whole sorry saga from Robin's side, but he could hardly say so. He was, therefore, highly gratified when Robin said, "I'd like to tell you about it, if you don't mind, if only so that you can understand why I was so peculiar. I've been carrying on like some kind of lunatic; I don't normally behave like that."

Leslie uttered some protests at this description, although it was of course true that Robin had behaved quite bizarrely. Coffee was brought in and Robin began the story. "To make sense of it, I'll have to start at the beginning," he said, settling back in the chair. Much of the background, the two men had already heard from Edgar, but they did not interrupt, and Robin's account was riveting. Robin went on to tell them how his mother had tried to talk to him about his father over the years but he had refused to listen. Eventually though, when she told him that his father was dying, he gave in.

"My mother knew the affair with my father was a terrible thing, since his wife was terminally ill, but she was very young at the time. When she found out she was pregnant, she moved away and it was hushed up because of the poor woman.

"I'm not sure how she found out about my father's illness, but she tried to persuade me to see him, and offered to arrange it. I refused to have anything to do with him, and in the end she gave up. Unfortunately though, I couldn't give up thinking about it; it really got to me, more than I could have imagined. It affected my sleep and I couldn't eat. I split up with my girlfriend; she was pretty upset, we both were. Deep down I knew that there was only one thing for it: I would have to come and see my father.

"Mum had given me my father's name and address when she first tried to persuade me to see him. I told no one I was coming here. I was living on my own once Ellie had moved out, and I often work away from home, so I didn't have to explain my absence to anyone. I wanted to be as discreet as possible, so I came, as I thought, incognito. I even left my car behind and came by train and bus. God, that journey was awful. Dartonleigh was much smaller than I'd expected and I didn't appreciate quite how conspicuous I would be here. Several times I nearly bottled out and went home.

"I didn't really have much of a plan in mind. I don't know if I thought I could just walk up to the front door and knock, but when I went up to look at the house I realised it would be impossible. I don't know what I'd been thinking."

Leslie made some sympathetic noises, but Robin continued, "In the end the meeting happened unexpectedly. I was walking through the pub when my father's name leapt out at me from a photograph on the wall. He was holding a trophy. That was the first time I'd even seen a picture of him and I stared at it for what must have been minutes. I can't tell you what I was feeling. Up until that moment, part of me didn't really believe he existed. Imagine my utter astonishment when I turned from the picture to see the same face just yards from me. My father was sitting at a table on his own in that room at the back of the pub. I didn't give myself the chance to hesitate, I walked straight up to him and introduced myself.

"He reacted pretty much how you'd expect. He was obviously very shocked and more or less speechless for a minute or two. Then he told me to come and see him at his house at seven that evening. I was no less shocked, and when I came out of the pub I knocked into that boy carrying all those boxes. After an agonising few hours, I went up to the house. The first thing he said was, 'Well, you're punctual, I suppose that's something'." Robin took a few mouthfuls of coffee. "It's stupid, I know, but I was pleased," he continued. "In fact, I suddenly realised that I was desperate for any little bit of approval from him. I wanted him to be pleased with me. It doesn't make sense, I know; he never bothered about me so why should I have cared?"

"It would be nice if our feelings were always rational," said Leslie, "but it hardly ever works that way."

"Absolutely," agreed Robin. "I only mention it because it sort of explains my reactions. After my father's comment about punctuality, it was downhill all the way. He led me into his study and he didn't even ask me to sit down. He started to speak really angrily, and I couldn't understand what he was talking about. Eventually I realised that he thought I had been trying to blackmail him. It was awful. It took ages to convince him I hadn't, and eventually he could see that I was telling the truth. After that he did ask me to sit down, but he still got his cheque book out and asked me how much I wanted. He couldn't get past the idea that I had come to get something from him. I lost my cool at that point and said I hadn't come for his money and wouldn't accept it if he gave it to me. Then I calmed down. After all, he wasn't expecting me to walk back into his life out of the blue, and I remembered how ill he was. He calmed down a bit too, but it was very uncomfortable. We talked for a little while and I think he tried to change his tune and find something positive to say. But other than saying something awkward about being pleased that Mum was a Catholic and hadn't done anything stupid, and wanting me to know that he'd provided for her, there wasn't much else. He didn't ask what I was doing with my life, if I was happy, nothing like that.

"To my surprise, as I was about to leave, he said that he already had an appointment with his solicitor on the following day, but while he was with him he would change his will in my favour. I was his son and he had no one else he wanted to leave his estate to. I protested, and repeated that I hadn't come for his money, but he said his mind was made up; if I didn't want it, I could give it to charity.

"I came away in a daze. In my mind I'd prepared myself that it was going to be difficult, and I thought I'd prepared myself for possible rejection. But deep down I'd hoped he might show some sort of pleasure at meeting me. I hadn't even thought of his money, it honestly hadn't crossed my mind, and it hurt that he thought I was that type of a person." There was a longer pause this time while Robin drank some more of his coffee and seemed to be lost in thought. At length he said, "As I ran down the lane, I thought I was losing my mind. I suppose it was a kind of panic attack. I nearly came here." Robin looked at Leslie and gave a cheerless smile. "You'd been so kind to me earlier, I walked past this cottage twice and nearly knocked on the door."

"I wish you had," said Leslie emphatically. Aside from his natural sympathy he was thinking of all the trouble it might have saved.

"I walked for what felt like hours and in the end I plucked up the courage to go back. I told myself that there were things I still had to say to him; I'd been completely ungracious when he offered to leave me his money. But really it was because I just wanted to see him again. He was my father, for God's sake. I'd come all this way and he was dying. I had to see him again. I'd no idea what the time was though I believe now that it was about ten o'clock, as I was obviously the person seen by that dog walker.

"I hammered on the front door, and then went round to the back door, and knocked there. I couldn't have cared less how late it was; I was determined to see my father. I feel stupid saying it, but I knew that I loved him."

There was a long pause and the three men sat without speaking. Robin seemed to be lost in his recollections, Leslie could think of nothing to say that did not sound like a trite platitude and Bennett was never afraid of silence. After a while, Robin took up the story where he had left off.

"Not knowing, of course, that he was lying dead in bed, I believed that he was refusing to open the door to me. I was distraught. I ran from the house, and walked and ran until I was physically exhausted. I've no idea what time I got back to the pub. I was determined to meet my father somehow in the morning, and spent all night planning how I could arrange it, and what I would say. It was the longest night I've ever known.

"The blow I felt when I found out that he was dead can only be imagined. I was convinced that the shock of meeting me had killed him. The irony is that at that moment I really felt like a murderer. I left immediately and went straight to my mother's house and told her everything. She's been great, but the strain of the last couple of weeks has been terrible. When we read that his death was murder, we were shocked beyond belief. I knew I would have to contact the police, but to be honest I wasn't fit to do anything immediately. A couple of days later we read the report of a young man seen near the house, and I knew it was me. I had to come forward, and Mum rang the local police station. They came to her house and took me away. You can see why I've been out of my mind."

Bennett walked across to the bureau and picked up the picture of George as a young man. "I think you should have this," he said handing it to Robin.

Robin took it without comment and sat contemplating it silently.

"I think the envelope is still in the cupboard, Bennett," said Leslie. "It's a good thick one and will keep the picture safe."

Bennett went through to the utility room and when he returned he held the envelope out to Leslie. "Was this it?"

"Yes, that's the one," said Leslie. "Clarissa took it from George's box, where she found the photo."

"It had a letter tucked inside." Bennett held out a folded sheet of paper. "It must have been in with the photograph, and you didn't see it." He held the sheet of paper out to Robin and said, "It's yours. It's addressed to you."

Robin looked at Bennett in confusion.

"You may want to take this away and look at it later," Bennett said. "It seems that your father had written a letter to you. It may not be something you want to read in company."

Before Bennett reached the end of the sentence, Robin sprang from his seat, and snatched the letter from Bennett. Without moving any further, he opened the letter and began reading intently. To Leslie's dismay, tears coursed down his cheeks and he thrust the sheet back at Bennett. "Read it out to me, will you?" he sniffed. "I want to hear it spoken; I want to hear my father's words said to me."

"I can go through to the library," said Leslie with great self-sacrifice as he was agog with curiosity. He started to rise stiffly from the settee.

"No, please don't go," said Robin, wiping his eyes and returning to his seat. "I'd like you to hear it too."

"If you're sure," said Bennett. "Just say if you want me to stop." Bennett began reading:

> "*My dear son,*
>
> *I beg that you will read this letter, even though I don't deserve that you do so after my shocking behaviour to you this evening. I know I cannot excuse my shameful conduct, but if you can think of it as the behaviour of a sick, weary and foolish old man, this may partly help to explain it.*
>
> *I don't know if you can bring yourself to visit me again before you leave; it is far more than I deserve. If you possibly can it would mean a great deal to me and you can be assured of a very*

248

different reception. However, I will understand if you do not wish to come and it will not change my regard for you.

You may find this hard to believe, but I have thought about you and wondered about you many, many times over the years, and now, having seen the fine man that you are, I deeply regret not having made contact with you. I often considered it, but there were always too many obstacles. I am devastated that having been given a chance this evening, I threw it away so ungraciously.

As you know, I do not have long left, but even if we could meet once more it would mean a lot to me. I know that you have said that you don't want my inheritance, but I have made up my mind that it shall come to you, whatever happens. I know that I cannot make amends for neglecting you all these years, but it comforts me to know that I can pass on all that is mine, even if we never meet again.

I hope you are able to give my apologies and best wishes to your mother, also.

You are a fine young man that any father would be proud of, and I wish you health, happiness and prosperity in the years to come.

I will try to get this letter to you at The Woodman in the morning and hope that we may meet soon.

Your loving father'"

Robin's face was buried in his hands and he continued to sob long after Bennett finished speaking.

* * *

I'm not usually like this," said Robin eventually. He was calmer now, half a glass of brandy having had its effect. "I'm quite normal really."

"We know you are," said Leslie, "but the circumstances have been anything but normal. What are you going to do now? Have you come down on your own?"

"No, I've been very lucky," said Robin, "Ellie's with me. She's been brilliant. All the time I was down here she kept trying to contact me, and she's stuck by me since. We're back together again. She's coming to pick me up when I'm ready to go. We've booked into a bed and breakfast in Temple Ducton. I don't know what I would have done without her." Having finished his story and his drink, Robin messaged his girlfriend and the men chatted companionably while they waited for her to arrive.

"There's a lot to do," said Robin. "There's Father's funeral to arrange and the inquest, and then there will be the trial, of course."

"Well if there is anything we can do, you only have to ask," said Leslie. "And perhaps we can meet in happier circumstances in the future."

"Oh, I nearly forgot," said Robin. He reached into his pocket and brought out a new pair of socks and gave them to Leslie. "I'll never forget your kindness." He was not even halfway through his expressions of gratitude when there was a ring at the doorbell and a pretty young woman appeared to take him away.

Exhausted by the events of the afternoon, Leslie shut his eyes and dozed off peacefully.

Epilogue

"It's fair only for the coldest."

The two men were sitting at the kitchen table, and Bennett had his pen and paper out. "Seven letters," he said.

Leslie had finished his dinner. He'd woken from his nap to find that his appetite had returned and the shepherd's pie was delicious. How thoughtful of Annie to provide a meal which even Bennett could heat up without disaster and Leslie could manage to eat one-handed. Leslie did his best to ignore the devastation all around him in the kitchen. Jackie was booked to clean the cottage while he was out of action and would be in tomorrow morning.

"You don't really expect me to try working that out, do you?" said Leslie. "I can hardly think what day of the week it is."

"It's fair only for the coldest," repeated Bennett. "Seven letters and the fourth is T."

Despite himself, Leslie, frowning, tried to make sense of the clue. He reached across with his good arm and took the pen and a piece of paper. "You'll have to tell me," he said at last, "I'm not going to get it."

"Justice. Just-ice."

"Very clever," said Leslie, pushing the pen and paper away. "Let's hope that's what George gets."

"We've done our best for him," said Bennett. "It's down to others now."

"There's a kind of poetic justice in Clarissa having inadvertently put George's photo in the envelope containing his message to Robin, don't you think?" Leslie said, taking the cup of camomile tea which Bennett had made for him.

"'Poetic justice, with her lifted scale, where, in nice balance, truth with gold she weighs, and solid pudding against empty praise'," quoted Bennett. He had collected up the dinner plates and was trying, without success, to balance them in the cup rack of the dishwasher. Defeated by Bennett's impossible obscurity and his domestic incompetence, Leslie got up stiffly from the table and carried his tea into the sitting room. He put the cup on the little side table and wandered across to the French windows to stretch his legs. Dusk was falling, but it was a clear evening and he looked out on his beloved garden. He started with astonishment.

"Whatever's that?" he exclaimed. Bennett came through from the kitchen and he strolled across to the window and stood beside him.

"Ah, yes," he said. "That's Albert." By the garden pond sat a new gnome, fishing rod in hand. It was a huge object and, even among garden gnomes, uniquely grotesque. Leslie adored it.

"He's wonderful," he said. "Whatever is he made of?"

"Stone," replied Bennett, resting his hand lightly on Leslie's good shoulder. "I couldn't find an endearing one, but I thought this one would at least be enduring."

"I don't know what to say," said Leslie. "Thank you. It means a lot to me. I know you've never been keen on my gnomes. You always think them so ugly."

"Luckily for me," Bennett replied, "you seem to have a taste for ugly old men, and I thought perhaps I had better do nothing to discourage it." And he ambled off towards the library.

Postscript

RE: Leslie's recipes

Tue 14/05 11:57
From: gloria@gjfairweather.co.uk
To: lm@LesandBennett.co.uk

Dear Leslie,

Thank you SO much for the recipes. I am SO excited and can't wait to try them out. Gina is coming at the weekend and I said to her that there will be NO takeaways this time – we're trying out Leslie's wonderful recipes.

I will call in again on Thursday and see how you're getting on with the arnica.

See you then!

Gloria

PS I've been in touch with my cousin Valerie again, and she can't wait to have you at her little boutique hotel on the coast. It's a wonderfully peaceful spot, perfect for recuperating, and I know you'll love it!

From: lm@LesandBennett.co.uk
Sent: Monday, 13 May 3.17pm
To: gloria@gjfairweather.co.uk
Subject: Leslie's recipes

Hello Gloria,

It was good to see you again yesterday – thank you for calling in and for the beautiful flowers, and the arnica salve – it was very kind of you.

As promised, I have attached the recipes for:

- Mushroom risotto
- Shepherd's pie
- Pear and ginger pudding cake

I have included some notes, or 'tips', as you requested, which I hope are helpful. If anything doesn't make sense, just ask!

I can't wait to hear how you get on.

Kind regards,

Leslie

<u>Mushroom Risotto</u>

<u>Ingredients</u> (for 2 portions)

1 pint of hot stock (I use a vegetable stock pot or cubes, made up to the instructions on the packet. Since Bennett's heart attack I've changed to a low salt one and haven't noticed any difference.)

A few strands of saffron (dissolved in the stock).

A 6 fluid oz glass of dry white wine (I read somewhere that you should never cook with a wine you wouldn't drink, but I sometimes use a bottle that won't pass Bennett's test!)

200 grams of Arborio or Carnaroli rice (If these aren't available you can use Italian pudding rice, which is also sometimes cheaper. If you substitute it you MUST use a short grain rice as it's starchier - not basmati or other long grain.)

A chopped onion

A crushed garlic clove

Mushrooms – any kind and as many as you like.

A tablespoon of olive oil and a dollop of butter

Fresh herbs, such as oregano, marjoram and parsley (The amount is a matter of taste but start with a sprinkling of each.)

Extra parsley and a grating of nutmeg to garnish

Finely grated Parmesan cheese (or Pecorino is fine, usually much cheaper).

Using a decent pan (something that won't stick):

1. Heat the butter and oil then add the onion and garlic and cook for about five minutes until soft.
2. Add the rice and coat it with the buttery mixture and stir until it starts to go clear.
3. Add the sliced mushrooms. If they are the big flat ones it's better to cook them separately and add them at the end otherwise they will turn the risotto black (which I'm not so keen on the look of).
4. Add the wine and boil briskly until absorbed, then add about a quarter of the stock and stir until that's absorbed. Then add a ladle at a time <u>stirring constantly</u> until it's all absorbed.
    a. Don't take your eye off it or it will stick.
    b. It's likely to take about 30 minutes.
    c. The rice should be al dente and not a gluey blob.
5. Add some Parmesan and put the lid on and let it rest for 5 minutes.
6. Stir in some fresh herbs e.g. oregano, marjoram, parsley.
7. Serve with extra Parmesan and chopped fresh parsley or scattered herbs and a generous grinding of salt and black pepper (I'm trying to keep the salt to a minimum these days!)

Serve with a crunchy green salad for contrasting texture if you like.

Easy Shepherd's Pie

<u>Ingredients</u> (for 2 portions)

Potatoes – 2 large or 3 small

Butter for mashing the potatoes (since the heart attack I use an olive oil spread - it's nearly as good.)

250g minced lamb (you could use minced beef, and call it a cottage pie!)

Carrot, onion, stick of celery (one or two of each depending on size and your preference).

Baked beans (I use a small tin for 2 of us, but it could be padded out by using more.)

Stock or left-over gravy (no more than about 150ml or it could get too sloppy).

A crushed garlic clove <u>or</u> a tablespoon of Worcester sauce <u>or</u> a few chilli flakes (all optional).

1. Put the oven on to heat up 170°C (fan oven) / 190°C / gas mark 5.
2. Put the potatoes on to boil until well-cooked but not watery. Then drain and mash with plenty of salt and pepper and butter/spread. (I've cut down on the salt a bit lately.) Set aside if finished before the meat.
3. Meanwhile, finely chop the carrot, onion and celery, or blitz in machine.
4. In a non-stick frying pan, gently dry fry the chopped veg (and garlic if using) for about 5 minutes until soft and moisture reduces – stir every now and then.
5. Add the mince, stir until it's all coated with the veg and cook until lightly browned (if there is a lot of fat from the mince you can spoon it off carefully, but the fat does add to the flavour.)
6. Mix in the baked beans.
7. Add the stock/gravy – set aside excess once the mixture is at the right consistency (more can be added later if required).
8. Add the Worcester sauce <u>or</u> chilli flakes, if using.
9. Mix well and simmer, stirring from time to time to prevent sticking, for about 15 minutes (mince should be browned through).
   NB – a tablespoon of tomato puree can be added if the mixture needs thickening.
10. Put the meat mixture in an oven-proof dish and pile on the mashed potato, forking it smoothly and evenly to cover the meat.
11. Put it in the oven for about half an hour – make sure it's piping hot in the middle.
    NB – you can make the whole thing ahead of time and just put it in the oven when you are ready to eat later. (May need a little longer in the oven if cooking it from cold.)

Pear and Ginger Pudding Cake

Ingredients

3 or 4 ripe pears (any variety)

6 or 8 pieces of crystalised ginger

4oz self-raising flour

3oz butter or margarine (I tend to use an olive margarine since Bennett's heart attack.)

2 oz caster sugar

1 egg

Sprinkle of ground ginger

3 tablespoons (approx.) milk

1. Put the oven on to heat up 170°C (fan oven) / 190°C / gas mark 5.
2. Bring the butter/marg to room temperature so it is soft enough to beat.
3. Line a fluted flan dish with baking paper.
4. Peel the pears (you need a good, sharp peeler for ripe pears), cut them in half and take out the cores.
5. Put the pears, cut side down and fat end facing the outer side of the dish.
6. Hide one or two lovely chunks of crystalised ginger under each pear half, where the core was.

Make the batter:

7. Beat the butter/marg with the sugar until light and fluffy (can be done by hand but very much easier with an electric mixer.)
8. Beat in the egg until fully mixed in.
9. Beat in 1/3 of the flour followed by 1 tablespoon of milk.
10. Repeat the step above.
11. Beat in the rest of the flour. Only add the rest of the milk if the mixture is very stiff.
12. Don't over beat the mixture – stop as soon as it's all smoothly combined.
13. Spread the mixture over the fruit.
14. Bake in the oven for 30 minutes.

Delicious served warm or cold with whipped cream.

Preview

Missing, But Not Missed
The second novel in J Wilcox's *Leslie and Bennett series*....

"You do think there's something fishy about her death, don't you?" said Leslie.

After all these years, Leslie still found Bennett as impossible to fathom as his crossword clues.

Bennett opened one eye. "Positively piscine," he said.

It should be the perfect holiday: the boutique hotel, the picturesque Devon coastline and the uncharacteristically beautiful weather. But away from his cooking and his garden and the minutiae of village life, Leslie is bored. That is until a body is seen in the sea; one of the delegates on a writing course taking place at their hotel.

Everything points to death by natural causes, but Leslie has his doubts, and he's troubled by the lack of friends or family coming forward even though the woman's body has not been found. Does no one care what has become of her?

Despite himself, Leslie finds he is drawn into investigating. No one seems to know anything. That is until he unleashes his secret weapon – his exquisite cooking – and over his sumptuous meals, people talk.

Leslie and Bennett soon discover that she is not the only one who is missing but not missed.

Milton Keynes UK
Ingram Content Group UK Ltd.
UKHW011940100524
442491UK00006B/332